Too Many Cooks

◆ ◆ ◆

Joanne Pence

HarperPaperbacks
A Division of HarperCollinsPublishers

HarperPaperbacks

A Division of HarperCollins*Publishers*
10 East 53rd Street, New York, N.Y. 10022-5299

This is a work of fiction. The characters, incidents, and
dialogues are products of the author's imagination and are not to
be construed as real. Any resemblance to actual events or
persons, living or dead, is entirely coincidental.

ISBN 0-06-108199-X

HarperCollins®, ®, and HarperPaperbacks™
are trademarks of HarperCollins*Publishers*, Inc.

Cover illustration © 1998 by Moline Kramer

First printing: September 1994

Printed in the United States of America

Visit HarperPaperbacks on the World Wide Web at
http://www.harpercollins.com

With thanks to two very special people:
Barbara Truax, and my agent, Sue Yuen

1

Angelina Amalfi sat on the edge of her chair at radio station KYME, scarcely breathing for fear the sound might be picked up and carried over the airwaves. She watched Henry LaTour hit the button that opened up the telephone line.

"Hello," Henry said into his microphone. "Welcome to *Lunch with Henri*. What may I do for you today?"

"Good afternoon, Chef Henri. I'm Bonnie from San Francisco."

An exuberant female voice pierced through the headphones Angie wore. Wincing with pain, she lifted them off her ears and looked for the volume control. But which knob to turn, button to push, or switch to flick was a mystery. Luckily, as Bonnie continued talking, her decibels dipped a bit.

"Thank you so much for taking my call. I'm a first-time caller, and I'm a little nervous."

She's nervous, Angie thought. She reached for a glass of water, then pulled back her hand. What if she spilled it? Or the ice rattled? Or she gulped too loudly? Never before had she thought about how noisy drinking a little water could be. As she tried to ignore the sudden dryness of her throat, Henry LaTour, called "Chef Ahnree" by his devoted followers, rocked his corpulent body forward in his chair, closer to the microphone, and half closed his eyelids. "No need to be nervous, my dear." His tone was too sweet, too oily—much like his cooking, Angie thought.

"I love your program so much," Bonnie gushed.

Henry's jowls jiggled as he nodded appreciatively. "Why, thank you, Bonnie." His headphones, Angie noticed, pressed grooves into his snowy white pompadour.

She breathed a little easier now that Henry and Bonnie had begun to converse. She knew Chef Henri could waste more valuable airtime listening to a woman sing his praises than any other human being ever. The man was devoted to his own wonderfulness.

This was Angie's second day at the station and her first day performing her new job. Last Friday, she'd sat in the studio and observed the program, then met the station manager, his assistant, his secretary, and the radio engineer.

Henry had introduced Angie to them as his personal assistant, announcing that she would take the names and addresses of callers who requested helpful hints, recipes, or other information about cooking from Chef Henri; write down any particularly prescient statements he made about food and its preparation so he could put them into his next cookbook; and answer his many pieces of fan mail.

None of it was true.

Chef Henri couldn't admit to anyone that he was going to get help from Angie. Their little secret, to Chef Henri, was as hush-hush as the recipe for Classic Coke.

That they ever found each other was a miracle. KYME was a little-listened-to station in the nether regions of the AM dial that blended together a blur of talk shows, sermons, and popular music. A couple of weeks ago, after hitting the "SEEK" button on her car radio, Angie mistakenly stopped it on KYME. On the air, a pompous sounding man bumbled his way through a simple question about pickling green tomatoes. The germ of an idea took hold. She listened to Chef Henri for the rest of the hour and every day for a week thereafter with a mixture of amusement and slack-jawed horror at his assault on the Bay Area's collective palate.

He needs me, she'd concluded. And since she was currently out of work, she had the perfect solution for his predicament.

KYME's small broadcasting studio was located in an old building in San Francisco's South-of-Market area, a rough low-rent district recently showing signs of revitalization into what was being called "SoMa"— a poor man's Greenwich Village. Angie drove there, then paced the hallway until Chef Henri, his show completed for the day, stepped out of the station's executive offices.

"I'm exactly what you need, Mr. LaTour." Angie hurried up to him, her hand extended in greeting. As soon as he got over looking startled, his expression turned skeptical. In fact, he looked at her as if she were crazy and, ignoring her outstretched hand, walked past her, head held high, almost strutting.

"My name's Angelina Amalfi." She chased along beside him and stuck her card in his hand. "I've had my own newspaper food column, where I discussed food preparation and presented recipes. The paper, unfortunately, went out of business. Also, I've written reviews of restaurants for a number of local magazines and newspapers."

He stopped walking and gazed down a long ski-slope-shaped nose at her. "So what?"

"I've got a terrific idea," she said. "I'll sit quietly in the studio with a bunch of specialty cookbooks in front of me. As soon as a caller mentions a topic, I'll find the right book and look it up. Then, if you get stuck—"

"Chef Henri never gets stuck, Miss Amalfi!" He proceeded toward the elevators.

Didn't the man ever listen to himself? No, a man who refers to himself in the third person rarely did. She followed. "Well, what I meant was, if the question was a really bizarre one, I'd hand you the book so you could see what the answer was."

"Oh."

At last he was paying attention to her. "And then," she continued, her enthusiasm growing with each word, "we could discuss some special menus or rare foods, which would be really interesting for your listeners."

"We?" She got his peering-down-the-ski-slope-nose routine again. "As in *you and I?*"

"That's right."

The elevator doors opened and he got on, blocking her entry. "I hardly think so."

Her mouth snapped shut and her smile faded as she watched the doors shut in her face.

Three days later, a caller asked Chef Henri about making walnut catsup. His answer ran true to form. That night, he phoned Angie and told her to come see him at KYME the next day, with the proviso that no one—listeners or station—should know that she was "assisting" him with callers' questions. Couldn't compromise the image of Chef Henri, he'd stated, making Angie shudder.

And so she'd found herself a job in radio. It wasn't exactly what she wanted, but at least it was a start. Now here she was, seated at a desk across from Henry, partitions blocking her from the engineer's view.

"What can I do for you today, Bonnie?" Henry finally asked.

Angie perked up. Her fingers twitched as they hovered over the row of cookbooks propped up between bookends in front of her on the desk.

"I have a general question about making sweet breads."

"Ah, sweetbreads, one of my favorite delicacies . . ."

Henry glanced knowingly at Angie as he kept talking. She flipped to the index of Henry's recently released cookbook, *Luscious Licks from LaTour's,* named after his restaurant. Henry liked to quote himself and plug his restaurant as often as possible on his talk show, given the restaurant's lack of repeat customers.

". . . a dry wine, light," Henry was droning, "with a delicate bouquet so as not to overwhelm the subtle flavors . . ."

Angie madly scanned the index, looking under sweetbreads, organ meats, glands, even innards. Nothing.

What kind of a cookbook was this? She nearly tossed it aside, but then caught herself in mid-toss. No noise! Gently setting it down, she checked the other books, laying them on the desktop as she dismissed them in turn. A promising one was named *Organ Meats Can Be Fun*. She doubted it—probably more like "can be awful," not to mention "offal"—but she flipped to the index anyway. Success! Page 127 began a whole series of examples of how to cook the little devils.

Smiling broadly, she quietly handed Henry the cookbook. This wasn't so bad. It was fun, in fact.

He beamed at her. "Now, Bonnie. What's your question?"

"Well, the dough doesn't want to rise properly. I'm wondering if it has anything to do with the sugar?"

"Sugar?" Henry glanced helplessly at the cookbook, then at Angie, then the cookbook again. "Ah, sweet *bread*. Of course. Bread, the fruit of all life. 'A jug of wine, a loaf of bread, and thou.'"

He was waving his arm frantically, waiting for a cookbook to magically materialize. Angie was too; she had no idea what the question was. Bread . . . the possibilities were endless. She reached for his book, but it had gotten buried in her rush to find one on the gourmet glands. A book named *Simply Breads* jumped out at her and she opened it, ready to research the question—whatever it was.

Bonnie kept talking. "I used a half cup of honey instead of a whole cup of sugar, because it's more natural and all. Do you think it matters? After all, the ancient Egyptians used honey in everything. Pharaohs had it buried in their pyramids, and we all know about the marvels of the Great Pyramid."

"Oh," Henry said, his eyes a little wild. He stood, gesturing for Angie to hurry up. Not knowing what else to do, Angie stood too. But the cord on her headphones caught on the edge of the desk, yanking the phones nearly off her head. She jerked at the cord. The connector pulled free of its socket and flew into the air. With her left hand she managed to catch it before it hit anything. She felt like Willie Mays fighting the winds at Candlestick.

"Honey, yes," Henry blathered. "Nectar of the gods. I love it myself, so smooth, tasty. . . . Uh, Egyptians are nice too." Angie hoped he didn't sound as bumbling to his radio audience as he did to her. Poring over her materials, her heart pounding, she found a pamphlet called *Politically Correct Eatery*. Putting her finger on the section labeled "Substitutes for Refined Sugar," she leaned over the table. Henry's eagerly awaiting hand snatched it from her, making her lose her balance. Waving her arms like a windmill, she somehow managed to right herself just inches above her now freestanding library.

Straightening herself, she caught Henry's eye to find him glaring like a foul-tempered librarian, his forefinger pressed against protruding lips and pointed upward toward his nose. His caller chattered on, now asking him about the evils of corn syrup. He should tell her the ancient Egyptians poured corn syrup on the Sphinx. Maybe that'd stop her.

Angie collapsed into her chair again . . . quietly. Where the hell was the commercial break?

*   *   *

The visitor reached out a gloved hand and rang the doorbell. One would have thought that Karl Wielund, owner of the most popular new restaurant in San Francisco, would live in a more prepossessing place than a middle-class Sunset District bungalow. But Wielund was too busy harassing people and beefing up his restaurant to take the time to move.

Wielund pulled the door opened. His eyes narrowed. "This is a surprise."

"Is that any way to greet me?" The visitor held up a cardboard grocery box holding a wine bottle and a platter with a red-checkered napkin over it. "I want to talk."

"There's nothing more to say."

"Can't I come in?"

A muscle on the left side of Wielund's face began to jump. He didn't answer.

"You can frisk me," his guest said. "If you want. I assure you, I'm unarmed. But you're right to be cautious. This is a violent country. Much more so than Germany. Right, Karl?"

Grimacing with disgust, Wielund stepped aside. The visitor walked straight into the kitchen and placed the box on the counter.

Wielund sat beside his small butcher-block table. Of medium height and weight, Wielund worked out in the gym often enough that his build was solid, with no flab. Blond hair, without a trace of gray, made him look younger than his forty-eight years, and his ever-mocking eyes were a bright clear blue.

The visitor turned on the oven and then, gloves removed, returned to the grocery box, tossed aside the napkin, and lifted out a small quiche.

"What's that for?" Wielund asked, leaning closer to inspect the quiche.

"A peace offering."

"Truffles?"

"Exactly—fresh, from Périgord, the finest in the world."

Wielund's lips turned down. "I don't know that I should eat anything you've cooked."

The visitor placed the quiche in the oven to reheat. "It's your choice. As I said, this is a peace offering. I think we can arrive at an agreement."

"We've already discussed it."

"Not completely." The visitor took out a bottle of Château-Lafite Rothschild, and picked up a corkscrew.

Henry was rattled. The station manager looked anguished, no doubt thinking of the radio dials being spun throughout northern California. Angie suddenly understood station KYME's call letters: Why Me?

As the hour crawled by, with one faux pas after the other, Henry's face turned red and sweaty. Instead of his infamously smooth way with words even if they were wrong, he'd become a man whose mind and mouth were divorced—irreconcilable differences. In a business where elocution meant everything, this was a recipe for disaster.

"And now, friends," Henry said, taking a deep breath, "to my surprise, our hour together is almost up. But it brings the moment I know all of you eagerly await. It's time for our helpful hint of the day. Yes, Helpful Hints from Henri are brought to you each day by Bellwether Automotive Oil, the oil that will keep your engine running smooth as clarified batter . . . butter!"

Angie cringed. This was, for sure, her first and last day on the job.

His sweaty fingers clutched the note Angie passed him. "My hint for today is this." He adjusted his reading glasses and cleared his throat. "A good way to sicken thoup and add a nice nutty flavor to it at the same time is to add two tablespoons of peanut butter per—"

Angie lunged across the desk and stabbed at the words.

"Peanut *flour*, that is," Henry said, mopping his brow. "Two tablespoons of peanut flour per one cup of water of the th—uh, soup."

He cleared his throat, an angry flush creeping up his neck. "I hope you enjoyed our little tête-à-tête today as much as I did. And remember, tomorrow, same time, same place." He took a deep breath and bellowed into the microphone, "Let's *do* lunch!"

Angie draped herself over the top of her desk and tugged off the headphones. Two formerly long, formerly silk-wrapped fuchsia-colored fingernails had broken off, her hair felt as if she'd attacked it with an eggbeater, and she was about to be fired. Some days it just wasn't worth getting out of bed.

The visitor watched Karl Wielund sip the wine. Wielund had switched glasses with his guest and made sure his visitor drank first. No fool, he.

"You must understand, Karl," the visitor said, "how hard I've worked, how important this is to me."

"I don't need a sob story. I've heard them all. *Mein Gott,* I've lived half of them myself!" He leaned across the small dinette, his fist clenched. "This restaurant, this town, is my big chance. And I'm taking it."

The visitor took a forkful of quiche and washed it down with more of the expensive wine. Wielund's gaze followed each movement, his tongue flicking out to wet his lips as he glanced at the slice on the plate in front of him. The lightly pungent scent of the truffles, like nothing else in the world, together with that of mushroom, leek, Gruyère cheese, heavy cream, and the flaky, buttery crust of the quiche, wafted over the kitchen.

The visitor's eyebrows rose. "What's wrong? Are you afraid I poisoned it? Take a different piece, if you're worried. Take what's left of *mine.* I didn't know you were so afraid of me."

Wielund stood and dumped his quiche in the garbage disposal. "How do I know you don't have the blood of the Borgias in you?"

The visitor laughed and continued eating. "Well, at least enjoy the wine."

Wielund gazed again at the quiche, then cut himself another wedge. "On second thought, it looks too good to waste."

He sat, sliced an enormous forkful, and crammed it into his mouth, chewing with his mouth open, then he slugged down some of the wine. "A little runny. Too heavy with the cream. But leek instead of shallots was inspired."

"You think you could do better?"

"Of course, but I won't bother. Quiche has become gauche. Hmmm, not bad: 'quiche is gauche.' Clever."

"Karl, you've got to be fair—"

"Stop! Please, not while I'm eating." Wielund finished his entire piece in four big bites.

"You must see reason."

"I'm always reasonable."

The visitor took a deep breath. "Please, I'm . . . I'm begging you."

Wielund laughed. "So melodramatic. Maybe you should go into acting. Or have you already done that?"

"I'm sorry you said that, Karl."

"Don't be. I'm not."

"But now I'm going to have to let you die."

"What? You think *you* can threaten me? You should know me better than that by now."

"It's more than a threat, though. Monkshood—a most intriguing name for a deadly little poison."

Wielund jumped up. "What? The wine?"

Now it was the visitor's turn to laugh. "No. Not the wine. Guess again."

"But I was careful first to watch you eat everything I did."

"Almost everything. You're such a greedy bastard. The quiche had a little extra rim along the top of its crust, with a special ingredient added to that portion only. My addition."

Wielund stared at the visitor's plate. The part of the crust that extended over the edge of the quiche—baked brown and crispy—hadn't been eaten. "No!" His fingers began to rake his cheeks and neck. "My throat . . . my face . . . they're burning up. What have you done to me?"

"Oh, look at the time. It's after one o'clock. Such a shame, Karl." The visitor's low chuckle quickly developed into a nasty laugh. "You just missed your last chance to ever hear *Lunch with Henri*."

2

The scowl on Homicide Inspector Paavo Smith's face as he sat at his desk with two dozen long-stemmed red roses on one front corner, purple hyacinths on the other, and pink camellias on the bookshelf behind him should have been enough to keep the other inspectors on the far side of the squad room. But it wasn't. He could see them circling around now, not sure of just what to say yet scarcely able to control their mirth. His frown deepened.

Paavo was a tall, rangy man with short brown hair, icy blue eyes, and an expression that could make a panhandler give back change. He would have felt more at home in the middle of a stakeout than at a desk surrounded by flowers. The flowers were compliments of Angelina Amalfi, sent to welcome him on his first day back at work. He'd been out for ten weeks recovering from a nearly lethal bullet wound high on the left side of his chest. He knew Angie meant well, and he knew she'd be mortified to realize her flowers had made the others in the squad room snicker, but he sure would have liked to throw them out. He couldn't do it, though. It'd be like rejecting her, and he couldn't do that either, despite himself and his private demons.

They'd met during his last case. She was wealthy, pampered, and bossy, a pint-sized whirlwind who was far out of his league and whom he would have steered clear of except for one thing—someone had been trying to kill her. As the case proceeded, he discovered that under her rich-kid facade, Angie had a heart that was bigger than her father's fortune. Although she could have used a bundle of her daddy's money to hide somewhere until the danger passed, when things got tough she stuck with Paavo, giving him all her trust. After he was wounded, Angie, the delicate debutante, taught him, the hard-nosed cop, about other kinds of brave.

He'd fallen for her like a loser in cement shoes going off a pier and had spent the last two months recuperating and living a fantasy life that Angie was the main part of. She'd stayed near him day and night while he'd been in the hospital. When he was able to leave, he decided to go to the tiny apartment of Aulis Kokkonen, the elderly Finnish man who had raised Paavo and his older sister from the time they were young children. Angie would bring big pots and platters of minestrone, cacciatore, lasagna—anything she thought might be interesting, healthy, and filling. She always brought plenty because Aulis was a little too thin, and his cupboard a little too bare, to suit her. In time, Paavo was able to go back to his own house. She practically moved in.

But then, Christmas and New Year's arrived and Angie had to go to her parents' large winter estate in Scottsdale to spend the holidays with her family. As Paavo faced those days alone and realized he'd soon be going back to work, cold reality set in.

It was time to get on with his life. His real life. Would Angie fit into it? Given their backgrounds, their differences, one part of him had to admit she probably wouldn't, but another part of him couldn't say good-bye. Angie was the only thing in his life he couldn't be coldly practical about, much to his dismay but also much to his joy.

The flowers had arrived shortly after he did this morning. It felt strange to be back in the Hall of Justice squad room without his old partner, Matt Kowalski—without seeing Matt's slightly balding head down on his desk, taking yet another nap. That was the other thing that happened during his last case. Matt had been killed . . . and a part of Paavo was emptier, colder.

The showy, heavily scented flowers made Paavo's head feel stuffy, made the air thick, the way it had been at Matt's funeral. But now, within the barely controlled chaos of homicide's squad room, voices around him spoke of sudden death on the street and within shabby rooms where there were no flowers, often no light. That their world was without flowers and sentiment was something Paavo's colleagues would miss no opportunity to remind him of.

"Mm, sure smells good around here, man." Inspector Luis Calderon, an eighteen-year veteran, stopped in his tracks and lifted his nose in the air. "Am I still at work?" he asked Inspector Bo Benson, "or is this the perfume counter at Nordstrom's?"

"What d'you know about Nordstrom's, Luis?" Benson jabbed Calderon in the shoulder. "The only perfume you ever smelled was a hooker's."

Calderon widened his eyes in horror. "Don't go using those low-class words around him." He pointed his thumb toward Paavo. "He's gone high society on us."

Paavo folded his arms. "You two'll never make it as comedians. Go solve a murder—maybe your own, if you keep up that talk."

"Oooooh, I'm like scared, man," Calderon said, looking at Benson. "How about you?"

"Leave him alone." The one and only woman in Homicide, Rebecca Mayfield, who'd just recently been promoted from patrol officer to the assistant inspector position, sauntered up. She was a tall woman, with fluffy blond hair and a knockout body, who looked more like she should be wearing floral leotards and teaching Jazzercise classes than chasing hardened killers. She gave Paavo a pleasant smile; but then, she always gave Paavo a pleasant smile. "I think it's sweet his little girlfriend sent him flowers on his first day back. Just because you guys couldn't come up with anything fancier than two dozen Dunkin' Donuts doesn't mean you should put her down."

"Doughnuts are a cop's best friend, Rebecca." Benson took her arm.

"Touch me, you die," she said.

He raised his hands as if he were being held up. "How else is Paavo going to know he's really back with us?"

"Right." Paavo rocked on the back legs of his chair. He began to raise his arms to clasp his hands behind his neck like he used to do, when he felt a twinge in his left shoulder and quickly lowered his arms again. If anyone suspected he was less than one-hundred-percent recovered from his gunshot wound, he might be sent home. He was tired of resting, tired of too much time to think. He wanted to get down to business and do what he did best.

He picked up the top memo in his in-basket and skimmed through it. The memos, he knew, were supposed to help ease him back into his job. He tossed one aside and picked up the next. Snatches of conversation whirled around him, giving a patchwork of the side of urban life Homicide dealt with every day.

"Whaddaya mean he doesn't know why he shot him?"

"It's always the bystanders who buy it."

"He blew him away for drugs. So what else is new?"

Rather than easing him back like the memos, the words knocked him into his job with more force than a Holyfield left hook.

The ring of his telephone jarred him. He picked it up. "Smith here."

"Come into my office." It was Lieutenant Ralph Hollins, head of the Homicide Section.

As Paavo hung up the phone and stood, the other inspectors watched with unmasked curiosity. They'd spent the last couple of weeks, since they'd learned the date Paavo would be back at work, speculating on who his new partner would be. The chief hadn't asked any of them to make a switch, although Rebecca had volunteered. Her partner, Bill Sutter, was six months away from retirement and acted as if he were six days away. Never-Take-a-Chance Bill, they called him, the kind of cop who could get a partner killed.

Paavo walked into the chief's office. Hollins and a large man Paavo had never seen before stood as he entered.

"Smith, I'd like you to meet Inspector Toshiro Yoshiwara. He's just transferred down here from Seattle. We're going to try him out for a while. See how he likes us and how we like him."

"Hey there," Yoshiwara said, his voice filled with friendliness and good cheer as they shook hands. "Good to meet you."

In response, Paavo gave a quick nod of his head. The man was tall, with broad shoulders, a massive chest, and a head that seemed a little small for all that body. His hair was clipped in a short buzz. He looked like someone who could split a house in two and not raise a sweat.

"Sit down, both of you," the chief said. He glanced at Yoshiwara. "Smith is one of my best men. If anyone can show you what homicide work is like in this town, it's him." Hollins returned to his chair. "I'd like you two to work together for a while. As a team . . . partners."

Although Paavo knew the words would come one day, the finality they gave to Matt's death shook him. None of this showed as he said firmly, "Fine."

Yoshiwara jumped to his feet, a big grin on his face. "Hey, that's great. Paavo Smith, huh? I want you to know I heard of you up in Seattle. This is a real honor for me." He held out his hand to Hollins, and when a surprised Hollins took it, Yoshiwara gave it a boisterous shake. "Thank you, Lieutenant Hollins. I appreciate it, I really do."

Hollins stood. Paavo, too, slowly rose to his feet.

"He'll have Matt's old desk," Hollins said. "Show him the ropes, Smith. And do a good job. He got high marks from Seattle."

Paavo opened the door and held it as Yoshiwara passed through. The two of them walked side by side into the middle of the squad room. Calderon, Benson, and Mayfield swooped down on them.

"This is Inspector Yoshiwara," Paavo began. "He's—"

"You can call me Yosh," Yoshiwara said. "It's Japanese for 'Okay, let's go for it.' Like if I said, 'Are you ready?' you'd say, 'Yosh!' How's that for a simple language?"

"You from Japan?" Benson asked.

"Hell, no. I'm from Seattle. My parents were from the old country. You from around here?"

"Mississippi."

"Yeah? Got a family? Kids?"

Benson, in his late twenties, black, streetwise, and handsome, grinned. "No. I got an old lady, though. She wants to get married. I been able to put her off."

Yosh laughed. "It's a tap dance, huh?" He glanced at Rebecca. "A woman detective. Good for you!"

Paavo watched Yosh flatter Rebecca, tease Benson, and buddy up with Calderon. He'd never seen anyone work a room the way this guy did. And the other inspectors ate it up like a Hershey bar. Yosh shook hands, shot the bull, and in less than five minutes he knew almost as much about the three detectives as Paavo had learned in years.

Paavo's old partner, Matt, had been outgoing and friendly; Paavo had always been the quiet, serious one. They'd worked well as a team for that reason. But having to work with Mr. Congeniality here was another matter altogether. You don't stop bullets with charm.

"Well"—Rebecca Mayfield hooked her arms with Calderon and Benson—"we've got to get going. Nice to meet you, Yosh." She all but dragged the two men toward the door.

"Good to meet you, too. I'll bring that ikebana book for your daughter, Luis. And you be careful you don't strain your back again, Rebecca. See you guys later."

"Right, Yosh. So long."

The room was strangely quiet. Paavo couldn't remember the last time it had felt so empty. He glanced at his new partner and walked toward the back where their desks were. Yosh followed.

"This is your desk." When Paavo's hand lightly touched the desktop, he pulled it back as if burned.

He could feel Yosh's eyes following him to the FTD display that was his desk.

"You were pretty close to your old partner, I guess."

"Yeah," he answered. He and Matt had started out as rookies at the same time. "We were close."

"It's tough."

"Right." Paavo sat behind his desk and looked at Yoshiwara. It'd be Paavo's job to work with him, protect him, and inevitably to rely on him the way he had relied on Matt Kowalski. "So," he said, knowing he had to ease up; it wasn't Yoshiwara's fault he had to take Matt's place. "What made you decide to move to San Francisco?"

"It's because of my wife, actually. She was a student at the University of Washington when we met. But all her family is down here. She missed them. I offered to give it a try, and here I am."

Paavo nodded. "Where's your family?"

"They're all up in Seattle—without me." Yoshiwara grinned.

Paavo understood perfectly. Since meeting Angelina Amalfi, he understood a lot that wouldn't have made sense to him before. Like how a little woman could keep a big man firmly under her thumb, especially one that had lilac fingernail polish on it.

The silence in the room grew. Paavo could all but feel Yoshiwara wanting to grill him as he had the other detectives, wanting to ask him if he was fully recovered from the gunshot wound or if he still had any physical limitations or the mental traumas that all cops knew went along with a brush with death. Things like nightmares, like those times he'd wake up in a cold sweat from dreaming he'd walked into a trap and dreaming of his own violent death. Or nightmares about Angie, of trying to find her, to save her. But no matter how hard he tried, he couldn't do it, couldn't reach her in time. . . .

He had no interest in spilling his guts to some stranger, or to anyone, and Yoshiwara had enough intuition—or just plain good sense—to know it.

The phone rang.

Paavo picked it up, listened, and made a few quick notes. An occasional "Uh-huh" was the sum of his conversation. As soon as he hung up, he stood, a surge of adrenaline going through him. "We're sprung from desk work. Let's go."

Yoshiwara grabbed the jacket he'd draped over his chair and put it on as he hurried after Paavo out the door of the squad room.

"What's up?"

"Gunshots at a house in the Mission. A black-and-white called in the report. They found a body, a man with a bullet right between the eyes. They're holding the wife."

Yoshiwara fell into step beside Paavo as they headed for the elevator. "Good. She probably did it."

Paavo stopped and stared at the man. "Oh?"

"Well, hell, you said he got it right between the eyes."

"So?"

"Haven't you noticed?" Yoshiwara deadpanned. "Get a woman mad enough to pick up a gun and she's a dead shot, every time."

For the first time that day, Paavo smiled. It felt good, he discovered, damn good. It felt good to be back at work, to have a partner, to be going out on a case.

3

Angelina Amalfi set up the ironing board and plugged the iron into the socket in the kitchen. Normally, she never ironed. That's what dry cleaners were for. But the silk dress she planned to wear had gotten crushed in her closet, and she wanted to look perfect for Paavo tonight.

Not only had this been her first day on a new job, it was also Paavo's first day back at work after a long recovery. They had lots to celebrate. Or sort of celebrate. It'd be more of a party if her job were a better one and if his were less dangerous. Or if he'd let himself recuperate just a little longer. She didn't believe he was as well as he'd insisted he was.

If she could have wrapped him up in a cocoon and kept him safe, she would have done it. But he wouldn't be happy. And then neither would she. She felt as if they waltzed around their future while their hearts and minds played a fugue; it might be the same song, but it sure wasn't in sync.

Paavo once told Angie that the old saying, "It's better to have loved and lost," was hogwash, and he preferred to live with indifference rather than loneliness. Yet the way he looked at her, the way his eyes followed her as she walked around a room, or turned her way even if he was supposed to be conversing with someone else, told her more about how he felt than words ever could. Once, he even told her he loved her. Of course, it was after he'd been shot and nearly died, and he *was* in the hospital, all doped up with painkillers. Nevertheless, he'd said it.

Someday, she'd get past his reserve and caution. Someday he'd open his heart and truly let her in. That kind of love was worth waiting for.

Now, if she could only learn a little patience.

Loud and lusty, she sang an old Ethel Merman song about having rhythm, music, and her man. She was every bit as off key as Ethel at her worst, but Angie didn't care, shimmying and singing her way into the bedroom to pick up the clothes hanger holding her wrinkled silk dress.

There was a knock at the door.

Now what? she thought. Still holding the dress, she crossed her living room to the door of her Russian Hill apartment and peered through the peephole. Making sure her short pink-satin robe hadn't fallen loose, she pulled open the door.

"Hi, Stan."

"Hi, Angie." Without waiting for an invitation, Stanfield Bonnette, her neighbor from across the hall, walked in. Stan considered himself an up-and-coming bank executive. The more she got to know him, the more Angie considered him lucky to have any job at all.

She headed for the kitchen and he followed. "You busy tonight?" he asked.

She put the dress on the ironing board. "No. I'm ironing a silk dress to sit around and watch *Married with Children.*'"

"Guess you got a date?"

She licked her finger and touched the soleplate of the iron. No sizzle. "Good guess."

"You're not still seeing that cop, are you?"

She glared at the iron. Now what was she supposed to do? "He's a homicide detective. There's a difference."

"Not much of a one if you ask me."

"I didn't," she muttered. "Damn iron."

"Time for a change, Angie."

"The iron?"

"The cop. Drop him."

She touched the soleplate again. It was cold. "I've had it! No more!"

Stan glanced at her with surprise and approval. "Well, it's about time! Good for you! I knew I could convince you that he was all wrong for you—"

"Not *him,* Stan." She yanked the cord from the wall. "This stupid iron. It only works when it wants to." She opened the garbage chute and dropped the offending appliance in. "*Arrivederci,* baby."

"You know, you really should think about recycling—"

A disembodied "Oh!"—almost a yelp yet distinctly human—echoed from the chute.

Stan threw his arms around Angie, more to seek than to give protection, she was sure. "Oh, my God!" he cried. "What's that?"

"I think I know." Angie wrested herself free, opened the chute, and stuck her head in. "Mrs. Calamatti!" she shouted, then listened as her voice echoed down the chute. "Is that you down there?"

"Who's that?" The thin, reedy voice sounded like something coming from the center of the earth.

"It's Angie."

"Oh, Angie! Someone just tried to kill me!"

"Are you hurt?"

"I don't think so."

Angie glanced back at Stan and shook her head. "Are you *inside* the dumpster?"

"Of course, child." The voice was old and quivery. "The Depression. Got to be ready."

Angie put her hand against her forehead. "If there's a Depression," she said quietly to Stan, "she could sell her diamonds and keep living well for forty years!" Angie stuck her head back in the chute. "You could get hurt. Now climb out of there and go back upstairs!"

"Be prepared, Angie!"

"Will you broads shut up?" A man's voice from somewhere along the length of the building bellowed out at them.

Angie jerked her head out of the chute, her face on fire. "Good night, Mrs. Calamatti," she cried, using the chute one last time.

"Good night, dear."

Angie shut the chute door. Stan was still hovering over her shoulder. "I didn't know sound could do that."

"Didn't you ever see the old Don Ameche movie? The one where he invented the telephone?"

"No. I don't do black-and-white."

Angie tried not to think about it. "Why don't you go check to be sure Mrs. Calamatti gets back to her apartment in one piece?"

"Sure thing. I'll just give her some time to get there on her own, first."

Angie took the dress off the ironing board. "I'd better change. I'm going to have to figure out what else to wear." She stepped out of the kitchen, glancing from Stan to her front door by way of a hint.

"Don't worry about me. I'll go see to Mrs. Calamatti soon." He opened the door of her refrigerator. "Ah! Leftover lasagna. I love your lasagna, Angie."

"Take it." She waved her free arm in the air as she went off to the bedroom. As she passed the bathroom, she got an idea. She went in, spun the shower faucet to the highest setting for hot, turned it on full, then hung the dress nearby, where it'd catch a lot of the steam.

As she stepped out of the bathroom, she looked down the hall to see Stan seated at her mahogany dining room table, a plate of lasagna and a glass of cabernet in front of him. She walked to the doorway and stood there silently, watching him.

He turned, as if feeling her stare. "Oh. I forgot to tell you. My microwave is on the fritz."

She glanced at the digital clock on the VCR. "Oh, no!" she cried.

"It's not that bad, Angie. I'm sure there are plenty of good microwave repairmen around."

"No, Stan. The time."

"Oh. How much longer until Dick Tracy arrives?"

"That's just it! He should have been here fifteen minutes ago." She began to pace.

"Fifteen minutes is nothing."

"He's always been punctual before."

"Isn't he back at work now, though?"

"Yes. That's just the problem. It's dangerous. Maybe he got hurt and that's why he's late."

"Don't worry."

"I've got to worry."

"Got to?"

"It keeps people safe. I learned that from my grandmother. We had a big family, and it was her duty to worry about all of us. She scarcely had time to sleep, poor woman. It worked, though."

"Angie, that's just superstition."

She glanced at the clock again, then bit her bottom lip as she clutched her elbows and walked back and forth across the room. "My God, Stan, don't you think I know that? I wasn't born in the Dark Ages."

"Then relax."

"I can't. Don't you see? I know it's superstition, but if I stopped worrying and he got hurt, I'd never forgive myself."

Stan looked blankly at her and poured himself another glass of wine.

A half hour later, Angie sat on the yellow silk Hepplewhite armchair, her feet up on the Queen Anne coffee table. Worrying was exhausting. Maybe she'd have to rethink this new relationship.

A loud knock sounded at the door. She knew that knock. Cops, she thought, hurrying across the room. Sounded as if he'd come to make a drug bust.

She swung open the door. It was Paavo. Soft blue eyes took her breath away and made her heart beat faster. Her gaze raced over his gray sports jacket, black slacks, and pale blue shirt, the same shade as his eyes, then zeroed in closer for any signs of fatigue after his first day at work.

His face was thin, but then it was always thin: his nose highly arched, his brows straight, his eyes intense. Relief, coupled with a pulsating excitement at simply being with him, hammered through her. "You're late!" she cried.

He cocked an eyebrow as he strolled in, the room seeming to shrink in his presence. His gaze pointedly took in her mid-thigh-length robe, then traveled to shapely bare legs and little pink-polished toenails peeking out of the open toes of her fluffy slippers. He shifted his eyes to Stan, who was holding a glass of wine, then back to Angie. "I see you had help keeping your vigil," he said to her. "Am I interrupting something?"

Her whole world seemed to tilt at the smooth, graceful way he glided into the room, at the cool, arch look he gave her now. God, but she was crazy about him! "He's jealous, Stan," she said, and smiled. "Isn't he cute?"

Stan blanched.

So did Paavo.

"He's a regular little *fuzz* ball," Stan replied.

"Did you like the flowers I sent?" Angie asked Paavo, ignoring Stan.

"They were . . . thoughtful," Paavo replied.

"I loved the hyacinth—deep, mysterious, intense." She grinned. "Like you."

"Go on, Angie," Stan said. "Everyone knows he's the petunia type."

Paavo turned toward Stan and gave him a sharp glare. "Stan Bonnet, as charming as ever."

Stan took a quick step backward, nearly stumbling over his own feet. "Bonnette," he squawked. "And I know when I'm not wanted." He lifted his chin and, still holding on to his wineglass, left the apartment.

Paavo looked at Angie as if she were crazy. "Whatever do you see in that guy?"

She walked up to him and put her arms around his neck. "He asks the same thing about you."

Paavo spanned her waist with his hands, then drew her closer to him, feeling the soft warm curves of her body press against him in all the right places. "And what do you tell him?" he murmured as his hands slid over her robe's smooth fabric. She eased herself closer.

"I say I'd never tell."

The delicate scent of roses that touched the air whenever Angie was near enveloped him now, and the unrelenting need that kept him coming back to her again and again, even though every bit of logic and rationality he could muster told him he was crazy, filled his senses. It was one thing to tell himself, while in that cold gray crisis center otherwise known as the Hall of Justice, that she shouldn't be a part of his life, but quite another when he held her so close.

His hands slipped under the neckline of her robe, feeling the silken creamy skin beneath it, and he knew that once again he was lost. He reached for the knot of her kimono's sash.

"Wait." Despite the tremble of anticipation that rocked her, she knew they were already running late. "I made reservations for dinner, and we should leave soon. Wielund's is an incredibly popular restaurant, all but impossible to get into, unless you know the owner like I do."

He said nothing, but everywhere his eyes touched, her skin tingled, and they touched everywhere. Even as her words still rang in the air, her fingers found his tie, loosened it, then slowly pulled the shorter length of it through the Windsor knot.

He looped the sash of her robe around his hands and pulled her toward him, then bent his head to hers. "Wielund's," he murmured, his voice low and husky, his lips nearly brushing hers as the thin edge of his restraint dissolved, "can wait."

4

Yosh had been right about the guy popped between the eyes: the old lady was a crack shot when pushed. That had been an easy call, open-and-shut. But as the week rolled on, so did the count of sudden demises: two stabbings, a cabby snuffed during a botched robbery, and a suspicious suicide—or at least suspicious to Paavo, who just didn't believe in suicidal drug dealers. Big-city life in all its glory.

"Does it feel as if you've never been away, Paav?" Rebecca leaned against the edge of his desk.

"Almost. Some things'll never be the same, though."

Rebecca glanced at Matt's desk, where Yosh chewed a pencil and puzzled over writing out a report; then she gazed back at Paavo. "We missed you around here, you know. Now we should be able to get on with solving some of these trickier cases."

Calderon slammed his desk drawer shut and stood, his lips forming a bitter curve. "Nothing tricky about these cases, Rebecca. Just look for the dumbest and meanest guy around the corpse. If that one isn't the murderer, then it's the dead man's nearest and dearest. Always works that way."

"Sometimes you can't find a friend of the corpse. And you can't find anyone dumb or mean, either."

"Nobody's that empty."

"I had one that was. Sheila Danning. I'll never forget her."

"What case was that?" Paavo asked.

"Me and Never-Take-a-Chance Bill were investigating it while you were in the hospital."

"I remember that case." Calderon slid his gun into the holster he wore at his back. "She bought it in Golden Gate Park, right? Strangled, raped, the usual stuff."

"Real usual," Paavo sneered.

"What was strange was we couldn't come up with a line on her," Rebecca said. "No one really seemed to know her. She lived in a studio apartment out on Ingleside and worked as a cocktail waitress at a fancy bar and restaurant called La Maison Rouge. We found her parents in Tacoma, but she'd walked out on them and they hadn't heard from her in over a year. That was it. We figured she was just an innocent victim. A random thing—she was in the wrong place at the wrong time. Still, it bothers me that we couldn't come up with more."

"That must have been your first or second case, right?" Paavo asked, remembering she'd been promoted shortly after he'd been shot.

Rebecca nodded. "The first."

Paavo rubbed his chin. "How old was this Sheila Danning?"

"Twenty."

"New in the city, no friends?"

"Fairly new."

"How long had she worked at La Maison Rouge?"

"About three months."

Paavo gave her a sharp glance. "Three months and none of them could tell you a thing about her?"

Rebecca shrugged. "We came up empty."

That didn't make sense. Women with enough looks and personality to be hired as cocktail waitresses were usually outgoing and friendly, unless there was something very strange going on.

"Don't file it away as unsolved yet." Paavo said. "Something still might fall into your lap and tie it all together."

"And if it doesn't," Calderon said, his arms folded and his legs wide and rigid, "nobody'll remember for long that you screwed up on your first case. Look at Paavo. He's screwing his *last* case."

Paavo's eyes met Calderon's as he slowly lifted himself from his chair. His voice was brittle as chipped ice, and the temperature in the room seemed to drop. "You want to make something of it, Luis?"

"Back off, Paav." Rebecca placed her hand against Paavo's arm. "He thinks he's being funny. Let's go across the street for coffee."

"Don't waste your time with him, Rebecca," Calderon said as he put on his jacket and tugged at the cuffs of his shirtsleeves. "He don't know a good woman when she's . . . right in front of him."

Angie double-checked the address. Eleven-ninety-nine Pacific Street was the upper story of an old San Francisco "flat"—one long narrow apartment, taking up an entire floor and pancaked on top of another apartment of the same size. Both flats sat atop a garage and entryway. The street was located about midway down the southern slope of Russian Hill. That part of the hill didn't have the view of the upper-most area where Angie lived, but neither was it down near the bottom where the noise, crowds, and tourist traps of Chinatown lay. It was a sunny, pleasant neighborhood of narrow streets and alleyways, two- and three-story flats, corner grocery stores, and two cable car lines that meandered up and down the hills.

Angie rang the bell to Henry LaTour's place, and in a moment the door opened by itself. She stuck her head in the doorway. The small square entry led to a long uncarpeted stairway that seemed to go straight up to heaven. "Hello?" she called.

"Angie!" Henry bent low so she could see him at the top of the stairs, his hand still on the lever that opened and shut the door. "Come on up. We're wait-ing for you."

Her high heels clanged as she hurried up the stairs. Halfway, she slowed down, looked behind her, and nearly lost her balance. It was two stories, nearly straight up, except for a few right-angled steps at the very top.

"I guess you don't have to worry about exercise, do you?" She was gasping for breath.

"Everyone says that. Keeps me young." He ges-tured for her to follow him down the hall to a small living room in the front of the flat. "Here's something else that keeps me young. I still call her my bride, even though we've been married almost five years. This is my wife, Lacy."

Angie stopped in the doorway. Seated on the sofa in front of the window, Lacy seemed to shimmer in a beam of sunlight like the stained glass of the young Virgin Mary being visited by the Angel Gabriel at Our Lady of Guadalupe church. Angie stepped into the room to see Lacy better, and immediately the image shattered. Her bouffant hair, about thirty years out of date, dyed bright auburn, was all swept toward the right ear, where it culminated in a wild upward-pointing fringe that must have been shellacked to stay in place. She wore a surprisingly tasteful (considering her hair), royal blue wool dress that must have cost plenty, and sported a diamond wedding ring that gave Liz Taylor's a run for the money. Her cheekbones were high and silicon-implant round, her nose small and straight, with arching nostrils, and her eyes sported a wide space between her eyelids and her highly arched brows. In short, she had the kind of face usually associated with a plastic surgeon's scalpel.

She stood and walked around the coffee table, her hands outstretched in greeting. "Hello, Angie. So nice of you to come to our home." Her face scarcely moved, although she probably thought she was smiling. Her voice was modulated and accentless—as if she'd gone to a speech coach. Angie wondered if she shouldn't be on the radio program instead of Henry.

Their hands clasped. Covering Lacy's fingernails were three-inch-long acrylics with orange-red polish, so sharply curved she could have used them to climb a tree. Angie decided to rethink her own long nails. "Thank you, Mrs. LaTour. I'm happy to meet you."

"Won't you sit down? We were just drinking some Aljuice. It's a scrumptious algae mix, one of my little things to keep my Henry healthy. Would you like a glass?"

"No, thank you. I'm fine."

"Herb tea?"

"Nothing, really."

They all sat, Henry beside Lacy on the sofa, Angie in a chair facing them. Lacy folded her hands on her lap and primly crossed her ankles. "I'm very glad you were willing to come *here* to talk about the show, Angie," she said. "It's so convenient for us."

Henry reached over and patted his wife's hand. "I told you she was special."

Angie wondered if they planned to give her a halo. "Well, the radio station doesn't have much room for meetings anyway."

"Lacy and I were discussing the structure of the show," Henry said. "We thought it could use some improvement."

"Oh, really?" Angie could think of about five hundred ways to improve it, the first being to let her say a few words on the air.

"Not *too* many changes," Lacy added, cocking her head toward Henry and batting her eyes at him. "Everything Henry does is nearly perfect."

Angie hoped this meeting would be short. She didn't think her stomach could take much more. Besides, watching people drink green frothy stuff with black flecks in it reminded her of old monster movies—the ones where a mad scientist would drink a potion, sprout hair on his face and hands, and go on a rampage. Henry did sort of remind her of a mad scientist. And Lacy was a ringer for the Bride of Frankenstein.

"I'd be happy to do anything I can to help," she said.

"The problem is," Lacy began, "that Henry doesn't know what the calls are going to be about before he hears them. In such situations, he can easily misunderstand, or he has to just say any old thing until you're able to find an answer for him."

"It really doesn't take that long," Angie said. "And with the commercial breaks and all—"

"It doesn't sound good,"—Lacy took Henry's hand—"for my Henry not to have the answer right on the tip of his cute little tongue."

His cute little *green* tongue.

Henry cleared his throat. "I agree. Chef Henri must be able to respond *tout de suite.*"

Lacy glanced at him. "Henry, dear, you don't need to speak French around us. Right, Angie? My big Pooh Bear is such a show off!"

He harrumphed and leaned back against the sofa, his lips pursed indignantly.

"Pooh Bear?" Angie regretted it the moment the words passed her lips. Some explanations were better left unspoken.

"That's what I call him. And it'll explain the new theme music we just picked out. Every show should have something distinctive."

Angie refused the temptation of asking any more about it. "So, about finding the answers for Chef Henri, what does this mean?" she asked.

"What it means is, we want you to screen the calls before Henry takes them. You can find out what the callers' names are and what they want to ask about; then you find the answer and give it to Henry before he ever even says hello to them."

Angie stared at her. Some shows, on bigger radio

stations, went to the expense of paying screeners to answer every call off the air—to make sure it wasn't a wrong number or a crank or whatever. But not KYME. The radio hosts took their own calls, for better or worse. "I really don't understand why I would need to—"

"It's just not right that poor Henry has to take these questions cold, with nothing but that silly time delay to bleep them off if anyone starts to say obscenities. I mean, really, how many people swear at cooks?" Lacy formed her mouth into a pout, her eyes darting from Angie to Henry and back again.

"Well . . ." Angie decided it'd be best not to reply, but from all she'd heard about the cook at Henry's restaurant, she suspected plenty of people wanted to swear at him just about every day, especially after being presented with the bill. "The problem is," she said, "I've got to listen carefully to Henry's calls while they're happening. Many people start out with one question, but before you know it they've asked about something altogether different."

Lacy jumped to her feet. "But that's not what's important!"

Her voice was shrill yet quivering.

Angie leaned back in her chair, looking up at the woman in surprise. "Not important? It seems to me that's the main part of what I do."

"Now, dear." Henry jerked on Lacy's arm, trying to get her to sit back down. "Let's not upset Angelina about this. Good help is so hard to find these days."

Good help! He made her sound like a cleaning lady. Angie was ready to fly out of there, but she forced herself to be patient with them. She wanted this job, she could be good at this job, and if Henry would ever let her say even one word on the radio she could prove it. It was more than a little ironic, she thought, that any Tom, Dick, or Harry from the greater Bay Area could call and be on the radio, but if she said anything and ruined the illusion that Henry's answers were popping full-blown from his head like Athena, she'd be canned. She bit her tongue and did her best to stay calm.

"Angie," Henry said soothingly, "won't you at least give it a try?"

"But Henry, what happens when I'm busily talking to a future caller and the one who's on the air with you asks a follow-up question?"

"I'll just have to answer it."

"Isn't that what got you in trouble the first time?"

Henry's face flushed red. "Trouble? What trouble?"

"God help us," Angie whispered under her breath.

"Henry can do whatever he wants," Lacy said, twisting her fingers. "And if he doesn't know the answer, he can simply take a station break. Right, dear heart?"

"Of course."

Just then the telephone began to ring and Henry went into the hallway to answer it.

"So." Lacy watched Henry leave the room, then stood and began to pace back and forth in front of Angie's chair. "It's all settled."

"It's not going to work, you know."

Lacy spun on her. "It'll work. Whatever Henry does works."

"But—"

"Look, sweetie." Lacy smiled and stepped closer, "I've been around a long time. Girls like you are a dime a dozen here, all looking for their big break in radio. You come and go, thinking you know best. But I care about Henry and what's best for *him*."

"But every day—"

"I know, I know. Every day he gets one or two tough follow-ups. What's that? Two hundred sixty a year. But each day he takes ten to fifteen calls. You screen them, and he looks good twenty-six to thirty-nine *hundred* times a year! I'd take odds like that any time. Wouldn't you?"

Angie's mouth dropped open. She felt she'd just heard from Mr. Wizard. One of the few times she could ever remember, she was speechless.

"Lacy!" Henry stood in the doorway.

Lacy jumped at his voice and turned to face him. "Henry, what's wrong?"

"That was our chef. Karl Wielund's dead. His car went off a cliff up in the Sierras."

"No!" Lacy stared at him, raised her hand to her forehead, and dropped to the floor in a faint.

Henry stood immobile, looking down at her.

"Henry?" Angie said.

He ran to Lacy. Kneeling at her side, he slipped his arm under her head. "Angie, do something!"

She was already hurrying into the bathroom, where she turned on the cold-water tap and held a washcloth under it for a moment. When she ran back into the living room, Henry had Lacy lying on the sofa. She was already awake. Henry took the cloth and placed it on her forehead.

Angie looked long at the woman, trying to figure out why she had such an extreme reaction. "I didn't know she was so close to Karl," she said.

Henry looked at her with astonishment. "Close?

They weren't close. Our restaurants are across the street from each other. We'd see him every day. He's been missing for a few days, and we were all so worried, and now to hear . . ." Henry shuddered.

Lacy stared at the ceiling, her fingers over her mouth.

"There, there," Henry murmured, stroking her hand.

Angie didn't buy it. One rarely fainted over the death of a business acquaintance, even if you did see him every day. Did this mean Lacy and Karl meant more to each other than neighbors? But Karl's taste veered toward much younger women, as Angie well knew. If younger women always turned him down, though—

"Look at her." Henry addressed Angie while staring adoringly at his wife. "How good-hearted she is! I mean Wielund's was killing our business, yet look at how sorry she is that Karl died. I'm sure there are those who expect us to dance a jig at this news. But we're better people than that."

"I'll get her a glass of water," Angie said.

As she went toward the kitchen, she noticed the bedroom at the end of the hall. The door was open. On the far wall, facing the hall, were large framed photographs. Angie walked down to the doorway and looked in. Covering the whole wall were black-and-white photos of a young Lacy. She had been a beautiful woman, one who easily could have been a model. In bathing suits and ball gowns, Lacy looked like someone ready to step into a Miss America pageant— with a good chance of winning. With her light, lustrous, probably red hair, amply curved figure, and surprisingly innocent face, she was an all-American dream. Angie stopped gawking, and rushed to the kitchen to get the water.

"I couldn't help but notice those photos of you. They're beautiful," she said. She handed the glass to Lacy, who was sitting up now.

Haunted eyes lifted to Angie. "I think Henry's the only person in the world who still sees me that way."

"But you look just the same." Henry patted her knee.

"Were you a model?" Angie asked.

"No. I was just a secretary, that's all, until I met Henry. Now I'm on top of the world."

On that note, Angie left.

5

Paavo parked on the street, blocking the driveway of the house next door to Angie's apartment building. He knew he wouldn't be towed or ticketed for the illegal parking because the garage had long before been converted into an illegal "in-law" apartment. Two wrongs might not make a right, but at least they added up to one more parking space in a city where parking was harder to find than public restrooms, and sometimes more badly needed.

He walked into the lobby and waved at Mr. Belzer, a man of about seventy-five years and retired. Angie's father, who owned the building, had decided it might be wise to have a sort of caretaker in the lobby, watching the people who came and went. Mr. Belzer received his first-floor apartment free of charge in return for spending afternoons and evenings watching television in the lobby. At 10 P.M., Belzer locked the lobby door and would only let in those people the residents had previously designated.

Paavo stepped onto the elevator and rode up to the twelfth floor. Getting out, he moved toward the light beige door with gold-plated letters that read 1201. Angie's place.

She opened the door, a small woman with short brown wavy hair that had lots of golden strands—which tended to disappear and reappear according to her visits to the beauty parlor—big brown sparkling eyes, and a wide mouth that often curled up in a broad smile—just like now—for no reason except that she was happy to see him. He was so used to people looking either afraid or angry when he rapped on their door, he was still taken aback by Angie's reaction, even after three months of knowing her.

"You're here!" she said.

"Shouldn't I be?"

"I just tried to call you. The rudest man took the call. Calderon, was it? Just because I asked if he'd hurry up and find you was no reason to bite my head off."

Paavo couldn't help but chuckle inwardly, thinking about Calderon's reaction to her request. "Sorry."

"It's all right. You're here, and I can help you with your case. That's all that matters."

"You can what?"

As he took off his jacket and draped it over the back of a dining chair, Angie went into the kitchen and in a moment came back out, pouring a bottle of Anchor Steam Beer into a pilsner glass for him. "You must be surprised I already know. But he was a cook, so you know how that is. Poor guy." She handed Paavo the glass, put the bottle on the coffee table, and clasped her hands. "Has the department already decided to investigate, or are you here for a little insider information, so to speak? Frankly, for the newest and hottest San Francisco restaurateur to suddenly go sailing off a cliff in the mountains for no good reason is more than a little suspicious, if you ask me. Which I hope you do."

He walked to the sofa and sat, took a sip of the beer, and placed the glass on a coaster before looking up at her. "Now, how about starting at the beginning?"

She couldn't believe how calmly and casually he sat there while she was head-to-toe nerves over all this. "Wait a minute," she said. "You do know he's dead, right?"

"Who's dead?"

She threw up her hands. "Karl Wielund! Who do you think I've been talking about?"

"Until you said he was successful, I thought you were talking about Henry."

"Henry! It's just his *show* that's dead, not Henry. He's alive and well and probably in his restaurant giving customers ptomaine right as we speak. I'm talking about Karl. We ate at his restaurant the other night."

"The owner of Wielund's is dead? The owner of the place that's so popular you said other restaurant owners would love to skewer him like a shish kebab if they ever got him in a dark alley?"

She frowned. "I did say that, didn't I?"

"What happened to him?"

"They say it was an accident in the mountains. But I was talking to his assistant manager, Eileen Powell, who flew back from Paris when she heard the news, and I told her I used to be a good friend of Karl—or not such a good friend, but you know what I mean—and she said nobody believes Karl went to the mountains. It just wasn't like him."

"I see."

He saw, all right, and he'd known this same thing to happen many times in the past. People get involved in a murder, like Angie did last October, and next thing you know they're seeing murders under every corpse. He gazed at her, at the excitement in her face—the thrill of the chase, so similar to the look he'd seen on the faces of rookies when the dispatcher gave them their first big call.

"I'm sorry to hear he was in an accident, Angie. But he was up in the mountains, and it's winter, even though you might not know it looking out at the blue skies of San Francisco. The Sierras are treacherous this time of year."

"I know. I grew up hearing gory tales of the Donner Party. But that's not what happened. Something more did. I can feel it."

"The Sierras aren't my jurisdiction."

She folded her arms. "But he lived in your jurisdiction. What if he was forced there from his house?"

He shook his head.

She said in a hushed voice, "What if he was kidnapped?"

"I doubt that."

She paused. "Are you hungry? How about some dinner? You can relax; then maybe we can talk about it more later."

"Actually, I came by to ask you how you'd feel about a pizza and a movie."

She looked at him with surprise. "Why, that sounds great. We've never gone to the movies together. And I

love films. In fact, there's a new Czech film playing
at the Bridge that I've wanted to see. Do you mind
subtitles?"

"No. But instead, how about German, like the new
Schwarzenegger movie at the North Point?"

She wrinkled her nose. "How do you feel about
Tom Cruise?"

He winced. "Chuck Norris?"

She rolled her eyes. "Sean Connery?"

He grinned. "Sold."

"Let's go." She grabbed her purse. "But first, are
you busy Sunday night?"

"That depends on what you had in mind."

"You are so full of yourself sometimes, Inspector.
Anyway, Eileen said—"

"By Eileen, you mean the manager of Wielund's,
right?"

"Assistant manager. Eileen said she and the chef,
Mark Dustman, will hold a memorial service at Karl's
restaurant late Sunday, after most of the other restaurants are closed. All his friends will be there and
probably all his enemies. So I managed to get an invitation for us."

"Oh, you did?"

"Right. Since everyone is asking why he was in the
Sierras, and since Henry's wife fainted dead away
when she heard Karl was dead, I just knew you'd
want to go to the party—I mean, the service."

He sighed. "Angie, I'm sure the talk means nothing.
It's just gossip."

"But aren't you curious? After all, the top restaurant
owners and cooks in North Beach will be there, all in
one place, all secretly thankful their prayers to get rid

of Wielund's have been answered. You don't want to miss that."

Paavo's talk with Rebecca about the murdered waitress, Sheila Danning, came back to him. The place where she'd worked was one of the fancy North Beach restaurants, a French one. Something here made him suddenly uneasy. "You're pretty sure the other restaurant owners will be there?"

"I know it. After all, Wielund's was *the* place for everyone who was anybody to be seen, so I'm sure his memorial will be the same. I'll point the other owners out to you."

It was too much of a reach to imagine that the death of a ritzy restaurant owner had anything to do with the murder of a waitress who'd just been in town a few months. But then, if Angie's friends were right in speculating about Karl Wielund's death, and if there was a connection with Danning . . .

"What time should I be here Sunday night to pick you up?" he asked.

She grinned. "Come by for dinner. That'll give us plenty of time." She shut the lights and walked toward the door. "Before we leave, I'd like to check on one of our tenants, an older woman named Calamatti. She's been acting awfully strange lately."

"Alzheimer's?"

"No. She worries constantly about the economy."

"So do politicians."

"See what I mean?"

They got on the elevator and she pushed the button for the basement, where the parking garage was. "I thought you wanted to check on Mrs. Calamatti," Paavo said.

"I do."

As they stepped off the elevator, a noise in the corner of the dark garage stopped him. He took hold of Angie's arm, ready to pull her out of harm's way, but she placed her hand on his, stopping him.

"Mrs. Calamatti?" she called.

"Yes. Is that you, Angie? My goodness, you sound so close. It's amazing."

Angie glanced at Paavo and chuckled softly at his puzzled expression. "Not really. I'm right here."

Paavo followed her around the corner of the basement to the area where a dumpster stood at the bottom of the garbage chute. Beside it, a thin white-haired woman wearing a floral housecoat held her hands out in front of her, gnarled string running from one hand to the other.

"What are you doing?" Angie asked, stepping up to the old woman.

"I was thinking about the baby. She died, you know."

Paavo saw Angie shudder and felt a chill go up his own back. "What baby?" Angie whispered.

"Mine. She got sick. A high temperature. We couldn't help her. It was a long time ago. But I thought I had left her baby pictures here. Would you like to see her pictures, Angie? Such a pretty baby."

"Come on." Angie put her arm around the woman and gently led her away from the garbage. Paavo followed. "Let's go upstairs."

"I can't imagine where I put them."

"We'll look for them tomorrow."

"Thank you, Angie. You're a good girl." Mrs. Calamatti glanced back at Paavo and raised one finger, string dangling from it. "Prepare for the Depression!"

Paavo held the doors as Angie led Mrs. Calamatti into the elevator. "Don't worry about him," Angie said. "He thinks he's Franklin D. Roosevelt."

Mrs. Calamatti glanced at Angie and frowned. "Hmph. If he's FDR, *I'm* Jimmy Carter."

Paavo did a double take. He couldn't figure out if the woman was kidding or not.

Angie extended her kitchen table to its full width, then spread a clean sheet over it. Her oldest sister, Bianca, slapped half of the mound of dough they'd mixed onto the cloth. She beat it down flat, and Angie took their grandmother's three-foot-long wooden rolling pin and started rolling out the dough. Bianca was an older version of Angie by fourteen years, her dark brown hair straight instead of wavy, worn in a chin-length blunt cut instead of short, and the only color she put in it was to hide the gray, not to add blond highlights.

"Henry LaTour's pompous with nothing to be pompous about," Angie said, pulling and stretching the dough to make it thinner. Then she picked up the rolling pin again. Using her forearm, she pushed her bangs away from the perspiration that was already forming on her forehead. "His nose is so high in the air I'm surprised he doesn't get frostbite."

"All those radio types think they're such hot stuff. I don't know why you bother with them." Bianca whacked some cloves of garlic with the side of a cleaver and then peeled and minced them. "You need to take charge of your life. Stop frittering it away."

"I don't think I'm frittering anything away."

Bianca reached for an onion. "Teaching adult ed classes on San Francisco history is more a way for you to keep senior citizens off the streets than to build a career."

"I also do Henry's radio show and tutor Hispanic kids in English at the Youth Center, I just sold a magazine article on San Francisco Victorians, and I've got an editor interested in my interview with the retired chef of the St. Francis Hotel—the one who worked back when presidents stayed there."

"Well, lah-di-dah! I still think you need to settle down."

"Give me a break, Bianca! You sound like Mamma."

"So? She's right. What about Chick Marcuccio's son, Joey? You adore Chick, Joey's sister's one of your best friends, and he's always liked you."

"That's why he used to steal my dessert out of my lunch box. I can't stand Joey Marcuccio. Anyway, I *am* seeing someone, you might recall."

Bianca didn't answer. Angie knew all four of her sisters and all four of their husbands didn't approve of her interest in a homicide detective: too dangerous a job and not enough money in it. Her mother, on the other hand, was very fond of Paavo. Her father hadn't met him yet.

She rolled the dough harder, and in no time it reached about three feet around. Spreading a layer of flour over the top so it wouldn't stick, she rolled it up and pushed it aside. While she did this, Bianca sautéed the garlic and onion in olive oil and added a pound each of ground beef and veal.

"Is Henry LaTour young?" Bianca asked.

Angie spread more flour on the sheet, slapped the last half of the dough on it and attacked it with renewed vengeance with the rolling pin. "No, and he's married."

"Too bad."

"Too bad? Give me a break! That man should be selling snake oil instead of dinners. He's so slick he's lucky he wasn't sucked up along with the Exxon Valdez oil."

Bianca was opening and closing all the drawers.

"What are you looking for?" Angie asked, tugging at a particularly thick hard-to-roll portion of the dough.

"Don't you have a Ginsu knife? Like on TV? I've got to chop three bunches of spinach."

"Sorry. You're going to have to make do with one of my professional-quality German ones."

"No need to get snippy." Bianca continued to cook, not speaking as she allowed herself to sulk over Angie's not listening to her big-sisterly advice.

"You ought to spend more time with Mrs. Calamatti," Bianca announced, after the chopped spinach had cooked, her ill temper now gone. She added three eggs and a cup of ricotta to the spinach and mixed it in with the meat.

Angie stopped pushing the rolling pin and stared at her sister. "That's just what I want to do! She's a dear lady, but I'd hate to follow her into dumpsters looking for things to scavenge." Deciding the dough had been rolled thin enough, Angie began adding pinches of thyme, marjoram, and rosemary to the meat dish. "God, this is a lot of work. I hope the Knights of Columbus appreciate it."

"It's only *because* they'll appreciate it that I

offered to cook it—or offered that *we* cook it. Anyway, Mrs. Calamatti's lonely. Did you add salt?"

"Not yet. Here's the pepper. She's got lots of family, but she prefers to live alone. And now her house looks like a garage sale about to happen. Where's the Romano?"

"Uh-oh, I forgot to grate it. Poor lady."

Angie took the mixture off the stove and put it in a bowl. She grated cup of cheese and added it. "Ready?" she asked. Bianca nodded.

They dumped the meat filling onto the flattened dough that covered Angie's table top, spread it evenly, and then slowly and carefully unfolded the other piece of rolled dough on top. Angie picked up their grandmother's ravioli marking pin—a long wooden roller, hollow, with wooden strips that formed squares. Pressing down firmly and evenly, she rolled the pin over the dough to seal the dough layers together and enclose the filling. Then she stepped back to admire her handiwork. The tabletop looked like a computer grid.

Bianca poured them each a cup of coffee. Sitting on opposite sides of the table, the coffee at their sides, they picked up fluted-edged pastry wheels and began to cut the ravioli apart following the lines Angie had made with the marking pin.

"Maybe you'd be better off working in Henry's restaurant instead of on the radio," Bianca offered, carefully separating the ravioli squares she'd cut.

"I'd never do that." Angie made a face. "Henry's restaurant is no better than McDonald's. LaTour's wouldn't have any customers at all if it weren't for radio listeners taken in by Henry's schmooze."

"He can't be that bad."

"Yes, he can. Radio's better. Someday, I might even be able to say a word or two on the air."

"Angie, did you ever think of trying to find yourself a nice dentist to settle down with? Someone like my Dominic? Remember, Joey Marcuccio's *always* had his eye on you."

Angie had her eye on the masterful arrangement of canapés and finger foods on the buffet table. It would have been a meal to fit any posh party, if not for the photograph of Karl Wielund with a black cloth draped over its silver frame.

Karl's chef and his assistant manager, Mark Dustman and Eileen Powell, had thought of everything, including valet parking. Wielund's was on upper Grant Avenue, on the once-Italian, northern side of Broadway. The purely Italian flavor of the area took its first hit in the 1950s when it became a center for beatniks like Jack Kerouac, Lawrence Ferlinghetti, and Allen Ginsberg. They'd come and gone, but the restaurants and coffee shops lingered still, in all their high-priced funky splendor. Wielund's, right on Grant, fit like a fish in water.

Angie and Paavo had been among the first to arrive, but soon about thirty people filled the open area, drinking white wine and eating. Their conversation was loud and often punctuated by laughter. Angie took in the boisterous crowd with amazement. These so-called mourners might next pull out party hats and favors.

What was it about Karl, she wondered, that caused

this reaction in so many people? Arrogance, always acting as if he were doing you a favor just by acknowledging your existence, gloating over his success and other people's failures—yes, that might do it.

Angie stood with Paavo at the edge of the crowd, where they could see everyone who entered the room. In the past, Angie had always been in the middle of crowds, taking in everything around her. Since going out with Paavo, though, she'd learned that cops liked to stand on the fringe, where they can observe and be ready to defend or escape as necessary. It reminded her of old cowboy movies where the gunslingers always sat with their backs to the wall so no ornery polecat could sneak up and get the drop on 'em.

"There's Chick Marcuccio," she said.

"Who's he?"

"He's a close friend of my father. His daughter, Terry, and I were best friends until she got married last year. I can't stand her husband. Chick's also got a son, Joey."

"Another close friend?"

"Hardly. Joey's the sort who thinks a pie in the face is the height of humor. His dad owns Italian Seasons."

Paavo did a double take to see if Angie was kidding. Italian Seasons was the biggest and most expensive of the many Italian restaurants in the city. Her offhand comment was like being in a room full of jewelers and saying, "By the way, that one's the owner of Tiffany's."

Just then, Chick Marcuccio looked in Angie's direction. She waved.

"Angelina! *Come sta?* Good to see you!" He

crossed the room toward her, his arms open wide the whole way. When he reached her, they clasped shoulders and he kissed her on both cheeks.

"Chick, I'd like you to meet my friend, Paavo Smith. Paavo, this is a dear family friend, Chick Marcuccio."

Chick was short and heavyset, with slicked-back steel-gray hair. As he reached out to shake Paavo's hand, a huge diamond in his pinky ring caught the light. "Any friend of Angie is a friend of mine," Chick said earnestly. "And this is *my* very dear friend, Janet Knight. I've wanted you two to meet for a long time."

The woman by his side was tall and slender and flirting with middle age. She wore a sophisticated gray suit, and her blond hair was pulled back in an elegant chignon.

Angie and Paavo shook hands with her. "Janet Knight," Angie repeated, taking in every detail of the woman before her. "I've seen your picture many times. Paavo, this is the food editor at *Haute Cuisine* magazine."

Paavo's attempt to express excitement at this news was about as successful as Angie should have expected from a man whose idea of gourmet cooking was adding onion powder to Stove Top Stuffing Mix.

"I've always wanted to do an article for you," Angie said.

Janet smiled. "Really? You should submit one."

"I have," Angie said, her heart sinking as she realized her submittals never even made it past the first readers and onto the editor's desk. "Several times."

"Ah. I see." A hint of red showed on Janet's porcelain cheeks. "I used to enjoy your food column. I'm sorry it ended."

"Well, those things happen, I guess," Angie replied, her dismay that Janet had never seen her submittals subsiding a bit with the compliment.

Chick jumped in. "Sure they do, Angie. Don't mean nothing. Right, Paolo?"

Paavo winced at this latest mangling of his name, but he saw that Chick was aware of Angie's discomfort and was trying to help. "Right. Sometimes it's for the best."

"Good advice," Chick said.

Angie looked at Paavo as if he'd taken leave of his senses.

"I'm so glad I finally met you," Janet said, addressing Angie. "Chick's told me about you and your family for years."

"Oh?" Angie knew she couldn't hide her shock as she glanced at Chick. Terry hadn't mentioned anything about her father's having a long-time lady friend. In fact, the way Chick hung around Flo, his ex-wife, they had assumed Chick was still carrying a torch for her. "I didn't know that," Angie said.

"Well." Chick looked uncomfortable. "Time to go say hello to the competition. Looks like most of them turned out tonight, the snakes."

"I think everyone's curious about what happened to Karl," Angie said.

"I'd love to get my hands on his recipes. They're a food editor's dream: the menu that made Wielund's famous," Janet added.

"Funny, ain't it?" Chick said. "The way Wielund's was packing in the customers, most of the people here probably wished old Karl was dead when he was alive. Now they're all pretending to cry over his death, when all they want to know is what's going to happen to his restaurant and his notes about cooking."

"Do you think that's all it is?" Angie asked.

Chick stared at Angie as if she were crazy. "The guy was a first-rate son of a bitch. These people are here for show, Angie. Never forget it. So long, *cara*." He hugged her, then turned to Paavo and shook hands. "Good to meet you, son." He took Janet Knight's arm and walked into the crowd.

Angie leaned against Paavo's arm. "That was one owner. As for others, over there in the purple dress with the white feathers is Eunice Graves. She owns Europa, an elegant continental cuisine restaurant. She's about as elegant as Roseanne Barr."

Paavo glanced at Angie in surprise. She shrugged.

"Over on the far side, the guy in the blue suit with the white carnation—"

"Gray hair?"

"Right. That's Albert Dupries, La Maison Rouge."

This caught Paavo's attention. La Maison Rouge was where the dead cocktail waitress, Sheila Danning, had worked.

"We haven't met, but I did a review of the place and thought it was overpriced," she said. "Then, the tall woman in the green Chanel suit is Hattie Walker of Old South. Her place is said to have the best hush puppies and sweet-potato pie this side of the Mississippi."

"That sounds good," Paavo said.

She looked at him as if she thought he was crazy. "Really? Ah, now talking to Dupries is Vladimir Polotski. His Russian restaurant is doing about as well as the former Soviet Union, and it'll probably share the same fate."

Paavo shook his head. All these owners were starting to swim together.

"The only other competitor of Wielund's that I see here is Greg McAndrews. He's the young guy loading up his plate with pastries. I heard Mark Dustman, Wielund's chef, baked everything you see on the table. Looks like he's trying to find a new boss who's got a sweet tooth. Anyway, McAndrews owns Arbuckle's Seafood Restaurant down on the wharf."

Paavo's gaze leaped from one to the other, taking them in.

Angie smiled. "So what do you think?"

Before he could reply, his attention was caught by a stout older man with snowy white hair done in a pompadour at least five inches high, stepping into the restaurant, waving and barking greetings to everyone around him. Beside him was an elegantly dressed woman with lots of red hair, the ends of one side sticking up as if she'd stuck her finger in a light socket.

"Look who's here," Angie said with distaste. "That's my boss. And with him is his wife the fainter, Lacy."

"Lacy?" Paavo looked at her as if she were joking. "His wife's name is Lacy LaTour?"

"Yes."

He grinned. "Sounds like a stripper."

"Real funny. She's all involved, I learned, in Henry's radio show, as well as his restaurant. To hear her, they're the Fannie Farmer and Wolfgang Puck of the restaurant set, but word has it she knows even less about cooking than he does."

Henry turned his head in Angie's direction and smiled.

"Hello, Henry," she called, in her most charming voice. "And Lacy, darling, how good to see you!"

Once again, Paavo realized he could never successfully move in Angie's social circle. He wasn't that good an actor.

"Oh, no," Angie whispered. "They're actually coming this way."

"Good job, Angie," Paavo murmured as the LaTours turned toward them. Introductions were exchanged.

"Mr. Smith," Lacy said, giving him a delicate handshake.

Henry gripped Paavo's hand. "Angie talks about you all the time," he said, pumping hard. "She was quite worried about you, you know. You're back at work, I hear."

"I'm doing fine now."

"Back at work?" Lacy cocked her head. "Are you in the restaurant business too, Mr. Smith? Like my Henry?"

"I know nothing about cooking."

"Oh, it's not difficult. Just a little of this and a little of that." She nervously patted her hair, as if making sure the upswept fringe hadn't gone limp, while her eyes darted over the room. "Nevertheless, I believe one cook in the family's quite enough. You know what they say about too many cooks, right?"

"They spoil the broth." Henry's belly shook with his loud laugh. Others turned and stared at him.

A waiter carrying a bottle of lightly chilled Mondavi fumé blanc stepped up to them. "May I interest anyone?" They all accepted a glass.

"Speaking of cooks," Henry said, "has anyone heard what'll happen to Wielund's? I suspect it'll sink like a stone. Without Karl, this place is nothing." He looked scarcely able to contain his glee.

"That's why it's so strange he'd go off and leave it when his assistant manager was out of town," Angie said.

Henry pursed his lips. "He might have thought he could be back from the Sierras before the big dinner crowd. Maybe that's why he was driving too fast. Even a little speeding can be dangerous on those twisty mountain roads."

"That's all very possible," Angie agreed. "But why didn't he tell Mark Dustman?"

"Good God," Henry said. "The man's an adult—or *was.* He surely could come and go as he pleased."

"But we just agreed he wouldn't leave his business that way."

"Oh." Henry looked from Angie to Paavo and back again. "Well, I'm sure I have no idea. Won't you excuse us?" He took Lacy's arm and hustled her away.

"He did it, Paavo," Angie said, her eyes merry as she turned to Paavo, waiting until the LaTours were out of earshot. "My boss is guilty! He did it."

Now it was Paavo's turn to look surprised. "Guilty of what?"

"Of whatever happened to Karl. Didn't you hear Henry giving me excuses? Remember the old *Columbo* shows? The real murderer always gave excuses to everything Columbo mentioned. Just like Henry!"

He gave her a sidelong glance. "He was probably just trying to excuse *himself* for being so happy that he doesn't have to compete with Wielund's anymore."

"See? He's guilty. Just like I said."

He took hold of her shoulders and couldn't help but grin. "Just one problem: this is real. It's not TV, movies, or books. So be careful about what you say to these people and what you say about them to others. You don't want to give anyone the wrong idea, especially since they might take you seriously if they find out I work in Homicide."

She put her hands against his waist, keeping her expression solemn. "Of course I'm serious, Paavo. Besides, Henry styles his hair in a pompadour. People with pompadours are always the guilty ones on TV. Didn't you ever watch *L.A. Law?*"

He shook his head, about to draw her closer, when she suddenly spun around, out of his grasp, and took hold of the arm of the debonair gray-haired man passing by.

"Albert Dupries?" she said.

Dupries glared at the hand clutching his arm. But then his eyes raised to hers, and his scowl disappeared. Paavo watched the man's gaze slowly slide from Angie's big brown eyes, to her generous mouth, then lower to her shapely body. Paavo took one step forward. Dupries glanced at him and turned back to Angie.

"*Bon soir, mademoiselle,*" he said. "In *your* case, I am happy to say yes, I am Dupries. You may call me Albert."

For Angie, the force of the man's charm was like being struck by a steam engine. A simple thing like the way he said *Ahl-baerrr* made Angie's own tongue curl up in her mouth. He had a voice smoother than cat's fur, a way of moving his lips when he spoke that made them kissable, and a knowing glint in his eye that told her he could imagine exactly what it would be like to make love to her. To her amazement, she found she suddenly could imagine it too. Yves Montand had nothing on this guy.

"My name is Angelina Amalfi." She couldn't tear her gaze from his, so she pointed over her shoulder with her thumb. "And—uh, this is Paavo Smith."

Paavo gave Angie a look that should have turned her to stone as he extended his hand to Dupries in a greeting.

"So nice to meet you," Dupries said, shaking Paavo's hand, then Angie's. He didn't let go of Angie's hand but, instead, held it in both of his. "Amalfi . . . that sounds familiar. It sounds, in fact, like someone who thought I charge too much for my Chateaubriand." He cocked one knowing, perfectly formed eyebrow.

Angie wanted to sink through the floor. "I must have eaten there on an off-night."

"So much damage, *ma chérie.*" He stroked her wrist. "The pen, as you Americans say, is mightier than the sword. I was ready to run a sword through myself when I read your article."

"I'm so sorry!"

He lifted her hand near his heart, then cupped it with both of his. "Please, come again to my restaurant. Your next critique will be glowing, I promise."

"Well . . . but I have to be anonymous, you see, or it does no good."

"Oh, *ma chérie, ma chérie!* Do you think Bernie is anonymous? Or Nona? *Mais non.* I wonder, in fact, if Nona will run her piece about Wielund's now?" He shrugged. "Why bother? I imagine it will close without Karl and his recipes, unless the new owner gets them. Anyway, take advantage of your power, Miss Amalfi, just as they do. Have a fine meal. With me, in fact. I insist."

"Well, I . . ."

Dupries cast his glance at Paavo, sighed, then looked again at Angie. "You may even bring a friend, if you wish. Call me personally, and let me know when I can make a reservation for you both. Our talk has warmed my heart." He bent low and kissed her hand, then gave a curt nod to Paavo and walked away.

Paavo frowned. "His talk warmed *my*—"

"Stop that! He was just being French. Good God, was he sexy!"

"Don't drool on your pretty suit, *ma shay-rie*." Paavo shook his head, trying to forget the way Angie had eaten up the smooth talk and to concentrate instead on the man who was Sheila Danning's boss. He thought he might very much enjoy having a serious talk with Mr. Dupries. One on one.

Angie glanced at Paavo and then smiled into his eyes. "That kind of man means nothing. It's all mechanics, no heart."

"So you prefer unsexy ones . . . like me."

She placed her hand lightly against his chest. "I definitely prefer you."

The heat from her hand and the warmth that flowed through him at her words singed him all the way to his toes. He took her hand from his chest, letting her fingers curve lightly over his, and slowly lifted it to his lips for a kiss.

Her breath caught and her heart pounded as his gaze met hers, piercing her with his eyes. "Was that what you like?"

She could scarcely believe her tough cop would do such a romantic thing. It took a moment to find her voice. "That's a good start, Inspector. Did you just say some nonsense about *not* being sexy?"

His usually stern mouth spread into an easy grin and she felt her spirits buoyed by the sight. She smiled back and couldn't help but think what a silly pair they must seem, beaming at each other this way in the middle of a memorial.

Paavo ran his fingers through his hair as he turned away, away from the delicate look and feel of her, the perfect smile, the lingering scent of roses, and forced his attention back to the restaurateurs. This was not the time or place to let himself think more about Angie.

"So," he said after a while, "who are this Nona and Bernie that Dupries mentioned?"

She, too, turned, standing side by side with him as she looked over the crowd. "Nona Farraday and C. Bernhardt Eickerman are two of the most widely read restaurant critics in the Bay Area. Nona writes for *Haute Cuisine* and Bernie for the *Chronicle*."

"*Haute Cuisine*—the magazine Chick Marcuccio's girlfriend edits?"

"That's right."

"Doesn't this whole thing seem a little incestuous?"

"Same interests, same friends. Look at the police department. All your friends are cops."

No, he wanted to say, that wasn't quite right. His closest acquaintances were cops. His only real friend, Matt, was dead.

Angie saw the sudden shadowing of his expression, and a pang touched her heart as she realized what he had to be thinking. She slid her arm around his waist. "And me," she added softly, looking up at him.

Cautious blue eyes met her brown ones, and slowly his guard eased. A friend. Yes, he had to admit it. As much as there was about her that was all naïveté and femininity, so too he was finding that he could talk to her about his thoughts, and she never brushed them aside, or his feelings, and she never dismissed them. Angie as a friend . . . the idea warmed him in a comforting way that was as puzzling to him as it was novel. He gazed down at her, at the trust and openness in her face, and even as he forced his expression to remain stern, a lump filled his throat. Quickly, he looked away.

Just then Eileen Powell, Karl Wielund's assistant manager, walked to the center of the room. "I'd like to say a few words."

Everyone grew silent. Eileen was attractive in her black suit and starched white blouse, her black hair sleek and shoulder length. She gave a polite, nondescript little speech, saying what a kind, generous, and outgoing man Karl Wielund had been—all lies.

Then Mark Dustman got up and slowly stumbled toward Eileen. He'd obviously been crying. Angie leaned toward Paavo. "He's been Karl Wielund's chef since shortly after the restaurant opened a year ago," she whispered. "He studied cooking in Paris, wanting to become a master chef in time. Karl had also been a cook before buying his own business. By hiring Mark, Karl could keep his hand in the kitchen as well. Cooks with more experience than Dustman would never have tolerated such a thing."

Paavo nodded, although he scarcely understood the world Angie was talking about. But then, temperamental chefs were the last people he wanted to know better.

Dustman was *GQ*-model handsome, with sandy brown hair, green eyes, and a boyish demeanor. Now that young face was pale and wan, his eyes red and swollen. He looked warily around the room. "I want to tell you all about Karl," the young chef said, his voice hoarse with emotion. "And why he died."

6

The place began to buzz. Angie glanced at Paavo. He took her hand and they inched closer as Mark Dustman began to speak.

"I talked Karl into coming to San Francisco last year. I met him while I was in Paris at a small cooking academy where he was an instructor. He took me under his wing." He dabbed his eyes with his handkerchief. "I could see that his exquisite talent with food might stay buried in Paris for years, one among so many. I'd lived in San Francisco awhile before deciding that I was sure I wanted to be a chef, and before saving enough money to go to Paris.

"I told Karl that San Francisco was known for its fine hotels and restaurants, but that, despite so much competition, Karl would succeed here. I knew talent when I saw it. And succeed he did."

Mark looked out over the group.

"He succeeded too well, you might say. He was

clobbering you—all of you. Wielund's was filled up while you went begging for customers. We never had to offer two-for-one or, God forbid, a 'ladies' night' to get customers. We just provided food good enough to cause jealousy in even the kindest soul—and to make his life a living hell. He was a good, kind, and sensitive man, and knowing how so many of you felt hurt and pained him. And that, ladies and gentlemen, is why he died."

Amid outraged cries, Eileen grabbed Mark's arm to make him sit, but he shook her off. "I'll keep Wielund's open," he shouted at them. "I'll keep Karl's memory alive. And keep the same high quality of food on these tables!"

"Sit down, Dustman!" Chick Marcuccio thundered. "We didn't come to hear this."

"Why did you come, then?" Mark leaned toward him, his palms on the table.

Everyone was quiet, waiting for Marcuccio's reply. "To pay respects to a dead colleague, of course."

Mark's eyes narrowed. "Night after night I've wondered what made Karl go to that lonely mountain area in the dead of winter. I can't help but believe it was simply that he wanted to go back to a spot that reminded him of his home in southern Germany. He wanted to get away from this nest of vipers—from you—to find a little peace and quiet. Why on that day? I'll never know. But I'll spend a lifetime wondering about it." Unable to check his tears any longer, he covered his eyes as Eileen led him to the nearest chair.

The room broke into a flurry of reproach.

Paavo had never seen such a well-dressed group

get so ugly. He'd carefully watched the various mourners all evening as they came by to speak with Angie and talked among themselves. Dustman was right about one thing—not one of them seemed truly sorry that Wielund was dead. Yet Dustman's description of Wielund as a caring, sensitive man was completely contrary to what everyone else said about him.

The Wielund of the other restaurateurs wouldn't have cared what any of them thought. But if he hadn't gone to the mountains seeking peace and quiet, why was he there?

The restaurant owners were furious that Dustman had called their bluff and openly pointed out their hypocrisy in pretending to mourn. Paavo silently took them in, one by one, committing their words, their expressions to memory. Something strange was going on. The detective side of him knew it was good he'd come here tonight, very good.

"You're looking pleased with yourself," Angie said, tucking her arm in Paavo's as they watched the angry people file out the door.

He nodded. "Very. Next time I go to a restaurant, I'll make sure the knife's beside my dinner plate, not in my back."

Paavo carried a full-to-the-brim cup of Maxwell House Choice Blend to his desk. He needed it. Last night after the memorial service, he and Angie had stopped at the Buena Vista Café for Irish coffee to wash away the bitter taste of Mark Dustman's eulogy and the group's reaction to it, before going back to Angie's place. It was quite late before he made it to his own house. Difficult as it was to leave her, it seemed like less of a commitment than to spend the entire night with her . . . in her bed. He ran his hand through his short wavy hair and rubbed his eyes with a weary sigh.

He cared about commitment, on both their parts. It would have been a lot easier if he didn't. Angie glibly told him she loved him. She wore her heart on her sleeve, and if anyone were too blind to notice it there, all they had to do was look at her big, expressive eyes. But if words of love came easily to her, did the feelings as well? And if so, how could they endure? The last thing he needed in his life was a failed love affair. He'd spent years avoiding them. At thirty-four, he was too old to get caught in one now.

He turned his attention to the stacks of papers and folders on his desk. He had all the cases he could handle, yet what he'd heard and seen at Wielund's last night preyed on his mind. He couldn't simply drop it. Something was wrong. All those people were supposedly friends, yet there was an undercurrent of dislike and distrust. Wielund had lived in a snowy mountain area in Europe, yet he drove off the side of a major U.S. highway because of what, ice? Did that make sense? What it did was make Paavo uneasy. He'd worked in Homicide long enough to have developed a sixth sense about death. And his sixth sense had gone into overdrive on this one.

One way to put this whole no-brain idea to rest

was to go to the source. He called the Placer County Sheriff's Department and eventually was connected with a Sergeant Osbourne. "I'm calling about a DOA you had last week: Karl Wielund. Looked like an auto accident—guy went off a cliff. I'd like to know the results of the autopsy."

Osbourne's voice suddenly hardened. "The guy was a traffic victim."

"That's what's being said."

"His neck was broken in a fall down five hundred of feet of rock. That was enough for a death certificate."

Paavo's grip tightened on the phone. "No autopsy?"

Osbourne's long, weary sigh came across the phone wire before he spoke. "Look, we've got more tourists than anything else up here, and they're forever killing themselves on the roads or on the ski slopes. Even if we *wanted* to autopsy every victim, there's no money. Got the picture?"

"I got it. But I've also got reason to suspect this was more than an accident."

There was, again, a long silence on the other end. "I see. Let me find out if we still have the body." He put Paavo on hold for a few moments. "This guy must have been really loved. His body's still in the morgue; no one wants it. His attorney's contacting relatives back in Germany. You need an autopsy, Inspector, just give the word."

"Thanks. I'll get back to you." He'd have to talk this over with Hollins.

As Paavo hung up the phone, Yosh walked into the squad room. Bellowing hellos to people in the farthest corners of the floor, he headed toward Paavo's desk.

"Hey there, partner," Yosh said, pulling a breakfast burrito out of a white bag. "You need this more than I do."

"No, thanks," Paavo said.

"I got four more in here." Yosh laughed as he emptied the bag. "I even have dessert." He held up some small, dry, cellophane-wrapped chocolate chip cookies.

Paavo groaned.

"Hard night, huh?" Yosh asked.

"A late one." Paavo picked up a stack of memos from his IN tray and tried to looked interested in them.

"It's tough, hanging around with a woman like that." Yosh took a mouthful of burrito and washed it down with Diet Coke. "I mean, you know the guys here gossip worse than old women. Heck, what else do we have to talk about? They tell me she used to show up on the society page regularly, and always with a new guy. I guess she must have a lot of charm."

The last thing Paavo needed was to hear this. "I guess," he muttered.

"She probably knows how to make you feel real important, like you're the only guy in the world for her, wouldn't you say?"

She sure did yesterday . . . and last night. His mouth felt a little dry. "Could be."

"Yeah. One time in my life I went out with a gal like that. Money, looks, good sex—class all the way." Yosh gave a long sigh. "Then, after a couple months, she stopped returning my calls. I learned she was engaged to a brain surgeon. The least she could have done was pick a guy with an interesting job. Jeez, he probably comes home and talks about stuff that looks like albino earthworms. Who could eat dinner after that? Oh, well, serves her right, that's what I say. My Nancy is worth a dozen of her. Hell, she's worth a million of her. Nancy's good, down-to-earth."

"Is she?" Paavo didn't want to hear any more. Yosh's words expressed thoughts Paavo wouldn't let himself dwell on, yet they were always there, dark and malignant, waiting for the opportunity to force their way into the light.

"Damn right," Yosh said. "These other women, they start interfering in your work. Make you see skeletons in every closet, see danger where none is. They even make you run around like some blue knight, trying to protect them instead of the people who really need you—the ones you're paid to protect."

A sick feeling hit Paavo's stomach. Had Angie's dark hints about Wielund's death caused him to see trouble where none existed? All he could do in answer to Yosh was nod.

"You're a good guy, Paavo," Yosh said unexpectedly. "I like you."

Paavo glanced at Yosh. Now what? he wondered.

"I mean, I can see now why all these guys around here try to tell you what to do. They like you too, and they worry about you."

"Sure they do."

"It's a fact. They don't want to see your head turned by someone who might not be in it for the long term. You know what I mean?" Not missing a beat, Yosh continued. "You're a big tough guy. The jerks we arrest, they shake in their boots around you. But I got to tell you, you're like a babe in the woods around women."

Paavo folded his arms, his body stiff and withdrawn. If this pop psychoanalysis continued much longer, the guy was going to get a fat lip.

Yosh looked long at his partner. "You know what, Paav? I think you ought to meet Nancy."

Yosh reached over as if to slap him on the back, but then, as his gaze caught Paavo's frigid eyes, he withdrew his hand and did nothing more than smile.

"Look," Yosh continued. "I know I open my mouth too much sometimes and say a lot more than I should, but it's because I care about you, partner. I don't want to see you eating your heart out. None of us do. How about tomorrow night?"

"What about tomorrow night?"

"Didn't you know? It's Hollins's twentieth anniversary with the force. He tried to keep it quiet, but I found out anyway. Everyone's coming by the house. Nancy's cooking. You don't have to stay. Don't even have to eat dinner. But, maybe just a minute to give congrats to the chief. What do you say?"

Paavo respected Hollins. If it were a gathering for anyone else, he wouldn't hesitate to refuse. But Hollins was different. "All right."

"Terrific! Oh, by the way, Rebecca can make it too. She's a great gal. All the guys think so. Solid, dependable, like my Nancy. And she really likes you. So what if she doesn't have lots of money? Money doesn't buy happiness."

"Yosh!" Paavo stood up. He'd had it. Yosh had spouted one cliché too many.

Yosh grabbed his jacket and headed toward the door, shouting to Paavo as he went. "Nancy'll be glad to meet you both!"

7

Angie's elbow rested on the work station filled with radio paraphernalia, her hand cupping her chin as she despondently looked at the array of lights and switches on the call monitor in front of her. Henry had decided this was the day she'd begin to do the call screening for him. The trouble was, today she didn't feel like talking to anyone.

Since Paavo had gone back to work there'd been a strange undercurrent of something wrong between them. But what? Maybe she'd just imagined it. Still, when he left her Sunday night, everything seemed fine—or as fine as things ever got when dealing with a neurotic male—but when he telephoned Monday evening, he was a different person. He'd even sounded strangely guilty that he'd gotten the okay from Hollins for the Placer County Sheriff's Department to do an autopsy on Karl Wielund.

Then he said he couldn't come by to see her, and when she asked if he could make it tonight, he said he was going to Yoshiwara's house. Yoshiwara! Paavo gave her the impression that eight hours of his new partner was as much as he could take in one day. But he'd chosen Yoshiwara over her.

Why didn't he want to see her?

He was crazy about her, wasn't he? He should be. She ticked off her attributes: money, wit, good looks. But then, Paavo didn't place much importance on money as long as he had enough for his simple lifestyle; he had a dry wit of his own and scarcely needed her smart-alecky one; and good looks wasn't nearly as important to him as good character. So what *did* he like about her?

Lunch with Henri's new theme music, "The Teddy Bears' Picnic," ended and Henry began talking to the people who made up his radio audience. All five of them.

Forget worrying about Paavo, she told herself. Concentrate on screening Henry's callers. It should be simple enough. She'd find out what the caller's question was, look it up in a cookbook, mark the page, and hand it to Henry. Talking to callers off the air was better than not talking to them at all, she reasoned—and a step closer to talking to the callers *on* the air, besides.

There was just one problem. So that she could talk to the callers and not be heard on the air, she no longer sat with Henry in the glassed-in soundproof studio booth. She now sat just outside it, beside a sliding window that she had to open and shut quietly to hand him pieces of paper with names and notes as well as helpful cookbooks.

She felt ostracized, like a poor relation left out in the cold, forced to peer in at the golden age of radio—

almost as ostracized as she felt with Paavo, in fact.

Why think about Paavo? There was nothing she could do if he didn't want to see her. Everything had been fine between them once and would be again. She couldn't be so dull he preferred other cops to her. Could she?

Henry's opening monologue was winding down. Quickly, she pushed the button on the phone system. "*Lunch with Henri* radio show. Are you calling to speak to Chef Henri?" she asked.

"Hi, there! I sure am," an exuberant voice answered.

Why would anyone sound so happy to talk to Henry? "Your first name and where you're calling from, please." She felt like Ernestine, ready to burst into "one ringy-dingy" at any minute.

"My name's Barbara, and I'm calling from Novato."

Angie wrote down the name and location on a big yellow tablet. "Hello, Barbara. I'm Angie, and while you're waiting to talk with Chef Henri, I'll jot down the question you're planning to ask him."

"Okay. Let's try it. My question is: I've got a recipe here that I want to use to make some oyster beef. It says to put in a teaspoon of five spices, but it never tells me what the five spices *are.* I have no idea what I'm supposed to do."

Her life was in an upheaval, and someone wanted to talk about oyster beef? Angie sighed. What was she supposed to do when the man she loved . . . her eye caught the question she'd written on the tablet. With a start, she forced her thoughts back to the radio show, tore off the paper, slid the window open, dropped the paper into Henry's tray, shut the window, and sat back down with a sigh. "Actually, there's no problem,

Barbara. The recipe doesn't mean to use *five* spices. It means, use the seasoning called 'five spices.' It comes in a jar already mixed for you. You can find it in any grocery store with a well-stocked Chinese food section."

"Oh? That's all? Geezo-petes, why didn't the recipe say so? Well, let me hang up, I don't want to ask Chef Henri something so dumb. Thanks so much, Angie."

Angie stared at the telephone. *Geezo-petes?* Suddenly, she hit the phone line button again. "Barbara, wait!" All was silent.

Damn! That did it. She'd lost a caller. And *Lunch with Henri* had so few of them, losing one was a minor disaster. Never again could Angie allow some stubborn, moody, unwilling-to-discuss-it-properly man get in the way of her job.

A minute later, miraculously, another call came in. She jabbed the phone button.

"Hello!" she shouted.

"Is this the radio?"

She forced herself to sound cheerful. "Yes, lucky caller. This is the *Lunch with Henri* radio show. I'm Angie, and I'm here to write down your name and your question for Chef Henri. Welcome!"

"Oh, why—um, my name is Anthea."

Angie wrote it down. "What's your question for Chef Henri?"

"Am I on the air?"

"Not yet."

"Oh. Good. I want to ask about pizza bread dough. I like to make my own pizza toppings, but I hate making the bread. Yeast is so much trouble. Does Chef Henri have any simple recipes?"

"Oh, that's a great question. Let me just finish writing it here." She jotted it down, then dropped it in Henry's tray. "Chef Henri will love it. I'm sure he's got lots of ideas. I'll never forget the time my boyfriend—my sort-of boyfriend, that is—brought me a pizza. He thought he was bringing me Italian food— which is like coals to Newcastle, as they say—but really, it's so American, I had to laugh." She remembered Anthea's question. "I used to make pizza for him using frozen bread dough."

"What a great idea!"

"After it was defrosted, he would help me stretch it over the pizza pan. That was fun. We'd talk, and as the yeast warmed up, the dough would rise, and he'd warm up, and he'd rise. . . . Oh, well, I'm sure Henri will have lots of good ideas for you."

"I can't imagine anything easier than what you just said. Thanks."

To Angie's surprise, the phone went dead. She shrugged, then glanced at the monitor. No one else was waiting to have their call screened.

"And now," Henry said, "it's time to go to our phones so that you, our callers, can ask me anything your hearts desire about cooking. Our first caller is Barbara from Novato. Hello, Barbara."

No answer. "Barbara?"

Angie vigorously shook her head. Henry noticed and frowned. "Uh, Barbara seems to have been cut off. How about Anthea from . . . hmm. Anthea? Hello. Hello? *Hell*—oh."

Angie's head shaking was a little slower this time. Henry's face turned purple.

"We seem to be having a bit of trouble with our

phone lines." His voice was choked. "Let me give you the numbers to call once more, then we'll take a little station break, and when we get back I'm sure everything will be fine."

He looked ready to break Angie, rather than a mere station broadcast.

"You didn't have to come by, Paavo," Angie said, as she opened the door. "I know you have to go to Yosh's tonight."

"It's all right." He put his arms around her. "How are you doing?"

She leaned against him, enjoying the comfort he offered. "Better, I guess. That man is so hateful, I should just quit! In fact, I think I will. First thing tomorrow."

"It can't be that bad."

"It is. One—well, *two* little mistakes, and the way he carried on you'd think I'd murdered Betty Crocker."

"You can't have done anything that terrible."

She lifted her head and met his gaze. "I didn't." Then she stepped away and paced, her steps faster and her arm movements wider as she spoke. "I just answered questions. I mean, I've *always* answered questions. Even when I was in kindergarten and the teacher would ask the class a question, and most kids would sit on their hands, guess who always raised her arm?"

"Angelina?"

"You're darn right. My teachers expected it of me. They praised me for it. So did my parents. Everyone could count on me to say *something*. Well, no more.

I'll be mute. A regular Marcel Marceau. Charlie McCarthy without Edgar Bergen. Milli without Vanilli."

"Who?"

She breathed a weary sigh, then plunked down in her yellow antique Hepplewhite chair. "It doesn't matter. I'm quitting tomorrow."

"I'm sure Henry will get over it."

"I doubt it."

"Give him another chance, Angie."

"Give *him* another chance?"

"He needs you, remember?"

"He does?"

"Why else would he have hired you?"

She perked up. "That's right. To think, I'd forgotten. You're absolutely correct! How could I forget? Paavo, you're wonderful."

He didn't quite know what to say. *Wonderful* wasn't an adjective he'd often heard applied to him. Maybe never before, in fact.

"There's something else I almost forgot," she called, as she dashed into her bedroom. "I was so upset today that I went shopping. I found something for you."

"For me? You went shopping?"

She came back carrying a large City of Paris box and handed it to him. "I didn't go shopping *for* you, but when I saw this I couldn't pass it up."

He stared at the box in his hands. "It's sure big."

"Open it, silly."

"It's not my birthday or anything. And Christmas just passed."

"And all I got you for Christmas were those silly

suspenders. I mean, I should have known you don't wear suspenders, but they were so adorable."

He remembered the blue and yellow floral braces. Adorable wasn't quite what he'd call them.

With more than a little trepidation, he took the lid off the box. Inside was a double-breasted camel-hair overcoat. His heart sank and he could only think one thing—it looked expensive. He couldn't stop himself from touching the material along the collar, though. It felt like velvet.

"Try it on."

He swallowed. "I can't accept this."

"Of course you can! Let's see how it looks on you. You can take it back and they'll tailor it, of course, but I described to the man just how you were built. How wide your shoulders are, and how long your arms are, and he adjusted it a bit already. . . ."

As she talked, he put the coat on over his sports jacket. She smoothed his collar and ran her hands over the shoulders and then downward, against his broad chest. "Perfect," she said, adding a sigh over how handsome he looked. "Come see." She took his hand and led him to the full mirrors on the sliding closet doors in her bedroom.

He stood and stared at the rolled collar, the perfect fit of the coat. He'd never worn anything like this before.

"You look dressed for the Top of the Mark on a winter's eve. Wow! I *knew* that coat was you, I just knew it."

He raised his arms, holding them right out in front of him. So often when he did that, the sleeves of his jacket would nearly bare his elbows. This coat scarcely showed the cuff of his shirt. He loved it. Quickly, he took it off and handed it back to her. "It's too much."

"Too much what?"

"Money."

"Money! It's a gift. What do you mean?"

"I mean, hell, anyone sees a cop with a coat like that, they'll figure I'm on the take for sure." He slid his hands in his trouser pockets, not giving in to the temptation to touch the soft material once more.

"That excuse is so lame, Inspector. When fog and biting breezes come in off the ocean, even a cop can get cold. Take the coat. Please." She held out her arms.

He shook his head, unable to find the words to explain that as much as one part of him was warmed and touched by her present, another part was troubled. He rarely received any presents at all. And for sure, no one had ever given him a present this expensive. Not ever.

She laid the coat on the bed, then looked up at him. "Did you know I was beside myself when I got home today? I didn't know what to do. I felt like such a failure . . . again. Then I called you, and despite your plans to go to Yosh's house this evening, you stopped here first. I can't tell you how much that means to me."

"It was nothing," he said awkwardly.

"You're wrong, Inspector. That *coat* is nothing. How one person makes another feel inside, *that's* what's important." She touched his arm. "That's everything, Paavo."

He gave her a long look. She was right. She was being generous and warm and caring; he was the one

being petty. He glanced again at the coat, then nodded. "I guess I can wear it if I ever take you to one of
those operas you're always talking about."

Her face lit up. "You'd go with me to the opera?
That's wonderful. In fact, I've got a friend who's
offered me a couple of tickets to *Götterdammerung*."

"To what?"

"Wagner. The twilight of the gods. Four and a half
hours. Valhalla's destroyed and Brunhild rides a
horse into her lover's, who's also her nephew's,
funeral pyre. There's so much loss, it's wonderfully
emotional!" She waltzed out of the bedroom. "I'll go
check the schedule."

Paavo picked up his new coat, not quite sure how
they went from a heart-to-heart to the twilight of the
gods. The time on the clock-radio showed it was time
to go to Yosh's, but Paavo gave a quick glance at
Angie's lacy comforter-covered bed before following
her into the living room. "I can understand loss," he
murmured. "I sure can."

The Placer County Coroner's Office identified
Aconitum columbianum, a poisonous plant found
along the Pacific Coast, as the cause of Karl
Wielund's death. As little as seven drops could
cause a burning sensation, followed by swelling of
the tongue, then paralysis and death in ten to sixty
minutes. Consciousness, though, often continued to
the end. The plant was commonly known as monkshood.

The coroner also noted that, undigested in Wielund's
stomach, were eggs, Gruyère cheese, piecrust, and

honest-to-God truffles. The man went out in gourmet style.

Wielund had been dead for at least five or six hours before his body began to show the effects of being in the snow. Most likely, Paavo reasoned, he'd been killed in San Francisco and then dumped in the mountains, where the heavy snows meant there was a good chance he wouldn't be found until the spring thaw. But even if he was found, everyone would think he'd been in an auto accident and not pursue it any further. That's almost what had happened.

Paavo put down the phone and waved at his partner, who was getting a morning cup of coffee. "Just got word that an autopsy on Karl Wielund showed he'd been poisoned."

"An autopsy on who?"

"A big restaurant owner. I went to his memorial service with Angie, and a lot of people there talked about the guy being disliked. They were right."

"Is this our case?"

"His house was in San Francisco. He was dead hours before his car went off a mountainside in the Sierras."

"Unless dead men drive, sounds like it's our case." Yosh listened while Paavo called Missing Persons.

Within a half hour the report from Missing Persons was on Paavo's desk. He ran off a copy for Yoshiwara. Karl Wielund was a German national who'd taken up permanent residency in this country and owned a popular restaurant. No news there.

Wielund had been reported missing by his chef, Mark Dustman. Dustman said Wielund never went off without leaving strict orders on running the restaurant, plus word on how to reach him in case of emergency. Dustman had thought Wielund was ill and, when he got no answer by telephone, went to his house to check up on him. Wielund wasn't there. After twenty-four hours, Dustman had called the police.

"Where do we start?" Yosh asked.

"His house."

Paavo located Wielund's landlord, Hank Greuber, and broke the news of Wielund's murder. Greuber's only question was whether that would mean he couldn't rent out the house as soon as he'd planned to. Greuber offered to meet the inspectors at the small house on 45th Avenue in the Sunset District.

Yoshiwara slowly steered their unmarked police car, a tan Chevy, across the city. As he cruised into a parking space on 45th Avenue, Paavo saw a wispy thin man, with a clump of Woody Woodpecker stand-up straight white hair on the very top of his head, waiting beside a big green Buick in the driveway of the house Karl Wielund had rented: Hank Greuber. He was jiggling his key chain impatiently.

Paavo and Yoshiwara introduced themselves. Greuber returned the greeting but kept glancing at the house and rubbing his arms as if he expected Wielund's ghost to spring out of it.

Some people did get spooked by houses in which someone had died—or may have died, as in this case—Paavo thought. Wielund's place was four small rooms built over a garage and sandwiched, literally wall-to-wall, between two houses that looked exactly the same except for the color. Blue, pink, and yellow— just like babes in blankets. Nothing to feel uneasy about.

"This is just great, Mr. Greuber," Yosh said, patting the landlord on the back as they walked toward the house. "Great of you to join us. Cooperation makes all our lives easier."

Paavo could hardly wait to see Yosh make an arrest. *Hey there, Mr. Murderer, how ya doin'? It's sure great of you to let me read you your rights.*

"I can't believe it about Wielund," Greuber said nervously. "Good tenant. Clean. Nonsmoker." He put the key in the lock and opened the door. A stairway up to the living area, built over the garage, was directly in front of them, and to the left was a small door that led to the garage.

"Good tenants are hard to find, I hear," Yosh said.

"You better believe it!" Greuber led the way up the stairs. "He always paid his rent on time. Quiet. The neighbors never complained. Wait!"

He stopped so suddenly they nearly bumped into him. Paavo whipped out his gun, pulled Greuber back and behind him, then inched forward to see what had alarmed the landlord. He didn't see a thing. "What's wrong?"

"It wasn't like this before," Greuber whispered.

"Before?" Paavo asked.

"I . . . I checked the house right after word came of Wielund's death, just to make sure everything was okay. It's even neater now. As if . . . as if Wielund came back and cleaned it up."

"You'd better go outside, Mr. Greuber."

With bulging eyes, Greuber looked from Paavo's

gun to his face, then ran down the stairs and out the door.

Standing in the square hall at the top of the stairs, Paavo looked around. To his left was a narrow living room beside a narrow kitchen, to his right two small bedrooms, and before him a bathroom.

"I've never heard of dead men coming back to clean house," Yosh said.

"Let's make sure no one's still hanging around and then get the crime unit out to dust for prints."

The front door slammed shut, loudly, making the windows rattle the way a door does when left open and caught by a burst of wind.

Paavo glanced quickly at Yosh, then took the stairs two at a time. He ran out the front door and onto the sidewalk.

Greuber was starting his car's engine. Paavo raced toward him. "Greuber, wait!" he yelled, grabbing the passenger-door handle. Greuber sped backward off the driveway, nearly pulling Paavo's arm out of the socket. His bad shoulder felt like a hot poker had pierced it. Grimacing, he clutched his arm tight against him, doing all he could to stay on his feet as a fierce, throbbing pain made his stomach turn and the sidewalk seem to sway like a rowboat in a hurricane.

In the far reaches of his mind, he saw Greuber's white face watching him; then Greuber jerked the transmission into drive, gunned the engine, and tore down the street.

"Damn!" Paavo said through clenched teeth, both at his shoulder and at the uneasy feeling that filled him as he watched the car disappear.

Yosh's face showed his concern. "You all right?"

Paavo slowly eased his hand off his arm. "Sure. It's nothing." He drew in a breath. "Jammed my finger on the door handle."

Something flickered across Yosh's eyes before he turned from Paavo to glance down the now-empty street. "Some men just spook easy, I guess."

"I guess," Paavo echoed. The two looked meaningfully at each other. If they believed Greuber wasn't running from some very real, very tangible fear, they were ready to believe in the tooth fairy.

Paavo stared back at the house, brows locked. "He must have seen or remembered something. I think we better have a long talk with Mr. Greuber real soon."

Yosh nodded. "I'll check out the garage soon as I radio the crime unit."

Slowly rotating his shoulder, trying to make it feel somewhat normal again, Paavo went back into the house. He opened doors, closets, and even cupboards as he passed them. Standing by the desk, he used his handkerchief to flip through papers—bills, for the most part, and a few letters from Germany. He spotted an address book and opened it to the first page. Arbuckle's Seafood . . . Andy's Barbershop . . . *Angelina Amalfi*. He stared at her name a moment. She'd said Wielund was a friend. Could he have been more, or wanted to be more? But she was only twenty-four, and Wielund was double that. Much too old for her. Wasn't he?

"The garage is full of stuff," Yosh called from downstairs. "I'll poke around, see if I find anything."

Hearing him, Paavo covered the address book with his handkerchief and slipped it into his pocket. He crossed under the archway between the living room and the kitchen. "I just thought of something," Paavo said.

"What's that?"

"In the missing persons report Dustman filed, he said he didn't see Karl *or any sign of where he'd gone* when he came to his house looking for him. Nobody asked Dustman how he got into the house to search."

"Guess we'll ask him."

After a short while Yoshiwara called out, "Paavo, you better get down here."

When Paavo stepped into the garage he thought he'd entered a sporting goods store: skis, snowshoes, fishing poles and gear, a life raft, and three bowling balls, plus enough tennis rackets and golf clubs to stock a country club. Tin after tin of tennis balls vied with boxes of golf balls for shelf space. Wielund had been more than an enthusiast; this was a tribute to obsessiveness.

Yoshiwara was kneeling next to a large carton, holding photographs in his hand.

"Check these out, Paavo," he said, waving the photos in Paavo's direction. "Our victim was into indoor sports of a different sort."

Paavo looked at the photos—some in color, some in black and white—of women, girls, men, and even animals engaged in activities beyond the imagination of even most *Hustler* devotees. One woman in particular showed up again and again.

Paavo shook his head and let the photos drop back into the oversized carton. "The guy was a real sick one."

"The photos aren't all of it." Yosh pulled reels of film from underneath the photos. "All this was in a box marked GOLF BALLS. Nobody has a box this size full of golf balls. Even manufacturers don't ship in boxes this big. That's why I opened it."

"This stuff isn't commercial, either. We're talking originals." Paavo stood.

"Maybe Wielund made more than one kind of cheese-cake?"

"The question is, was he a special customer, a distributor, or a producer?"

Yoshiwara hoisted himself to his feet. "Messing around with the people that handle this stuff is a good way to get yourself killed."

Paavo began to look around the garage. "Let's see if there are any more surprises here or upstairs. I've got a bad feeling about this whole thing." The memory of Greuber's white face came to him once more.

8

By the time Paavo left the Hall of Justice late that night to go across the street for a quick chiliburger for dinner, it was raining lightly. He turned up his jacket collar. The night ahead loomed long and tedious, to be spent going over the bits and pieces of information he and Yosh had picked up at Wielund's house, along with the files on Wielund that had been sent over by Immigration.

It was rare to have a homicide victim who had a file or a history of any kind. Too many of them were kids from small towns who'd come to the big city looking for excitement and found more than they could handle, or old people killed by accident during a mugging for a few dollars of their Social Security, or innocent passersby caught by stray bullets from a gang-related drive-by shooting.

The city glistened as lamplights cast their glow on streets washed clean and slick by the winter rain. Winter in San Francisco was mild. The rain actually warmed up the weather a bit and washed away the fog so that the streets were clear. Having rain but no snow was one of the benefits of life in this town. There weren't many others anymore.

As Paavo walked toward Charlie's Kitchen, a favorite spot for cops to get a fast meal, he glanced over at the phone booth that stood near the front door. Karl Wielund's address book had been burning a hole in his pocket all day, but he had put off thinking about it. Now though, it refused to be put off any longer.

A man with original photographs in his house like the ones Paavo had seen also knew Angie, phoned her, talked to her . . . about what?

Surely it was about his restaurant, or about food, or about one of her restaurant reviews, nothing more. But Angie was an attractive woman, and Karl Wielund, he'd learned, was a man with a lurid interest in women. What if he'd wanted more from Angie than a few favorite recipes?

His mind flashed to the pictures. No, he couldn't even imagine such a thing. No one could think of Angie that way. Not Angie, with her bad jokes and puckish smile. She lit up empty corners of his life and filled him with her laughter and generosity. He'd been a quiet, normal homicide detective, dealing every day with murder, cruelty, vengeance, and seediness, before she entered his life and turned it completely upside down. Now he couldn't think straight. He argued with his friends, talked to himself and . . . oomph! . . . walked into parking meters in the dead of night.

On top of that, he suddenly realized it'd started raining again.

"Hey, mister." A ragged, scraggly-bearded man huddling in a doorway with an oilcloth over his head and shoulders held out a pint whiskey bottle toward Paavo. "Looks like you need this more than I do."

The guy was probably right, Paavo thought. He handed the man a couple of dollars, squared his shoulders, smoothed his tie, and walked on, as if this little jaunt in the rain were a part of his usual routine.

The night beacon on Alcatraz that once swept the dark waters of the bay searching for escaping prisoners now acted more as a warning and reminder against wrongdoing for all San Franciscans as it revolved. Not that they paid much attention. The sharp beam of light flashed toward the rain-dappled windows of Angie's apartment every five seconds. She sat in front of the windows addressing invitations for a baby shower for her fourth sister, Francesca. Frannie and Seth had been married three years, and their first child was due in April. The youngest of the five daughters, Angie was the only one still unmarried, much to her mother's dismay. Angie hadn't given marriage much thought until a tall and very single homicide detective entered her life. Now she thought about it far too much, and Paavo, it seemed, didn't think about it at all.

But then, she'd only known him three months, and two of those months he'd been recuperating from a bullet she'd caused him to get. Maybe that wasn't the most propitious start for a long-lasting relationship.

At least he loved her. So he said. Once.

There was a loud knock on the door. Paavo? But

he'd told her he had to work tonight. Something must be wrong. She hurried to the door, looked through the peephole, and pulled it open.

"What a surprise," she said. He looked like a drowned rat.

"Sorry to bother you."

Uh-oh, she thought. The deep, serious sound of his voice told her Inspector Smith, not Paavo, had come to call. "No bother. Come in. Were you working tonight?"

"Yes. I'll have to go back."

"At this time of night? Let me take your jacket." It was soaked. His hands felt like ice and she saw his slight wince as he pulled his arm from the sleeve. "What have you been doing, playing in the rain? You've got to take better care of yourself. That shoulder isn't completely healed—"

"It's fine."

"But it won't be. It'll stiffen up in this cold; you'll catch pneumonia. Then the department won't have any choice but to wait a very long time for you to solve all its cases. Nine o'clock at night is late enough to work."

"Angie—"

As he turned to talk to her, she tossed a big bath towel over his head and began to dry his hair with it while singing "He's the Sheik of Araby."

"Angie."

He tried to stop her, but she was on a mission to get him warm and dry.

"*Angie!*" He pulled the towel off. "That's enough!"

She backed off. "I was just trying to help."

"I'm not a child. I stopped by here for a reason."

She folded her arms. "I should have known there was a reason. Not that you wanted to see *me.*"

His lips tightened. "Right." He ran his fingers through his hair to smooth it back down after Angie's terrycloth assault.

"So, how was your boys-night-out at Yosh's?"

An eternity seemed to pass before he answered. "Fine."

Something in his voice made her take a second look at him. "Oh? Who else—"

"Listen, Angie, I've got to talk to you about a case."

Her glance went to the gun and shoulder holster he wore. Usually, she could make herself ignore them, but other times, like now, she was forced to remember them and all they meant: a case. She nodded, walked over to the Hepplewhite chair, and sat. "Okay."

He sat on the sofa near her. "A while back when I came over you thought it was to investigate Karl Wielund's death, and I said I didn't see anything mysterious about it."

She nodded, holding her breath.

"I was wrong."

"My God." He had all her attention now.

"Today I was given the results of his autopsy. He was poisoned."

She felt her face drain of color. "Poisoned! You mean he ate some food that had turned bad?" She shuddered at the thought.

"No. This was no accident. Someone deliberately poisoned him."

"How horrible! He was so happy the last time I saw him, and his restaurant was doing so well."

"How long did you know him?" Paavo asked.

"Eight—nine months, I guess. Chick Marcuccio introduced us. I'd done a review of Karl's restaurant for the *Bay Area Shopper.* It was a favorable review— I loved the place—and Karl asked to meet me."

"That's all?"

"Well . . . yes."

There was a pause. She realized he must have noticed her hesitation. "I found your name and phone number in his address book," Paavo said.

"Oh." Was nothing private with this man? "Well, he did ask me out a couple of times."

"Ah. I see." Silence.

Although who she had or hadn't dated certainly wasn't Paavo's business, something made her say, "I didn't go."

"Why not?"

That, even more, wasn't his business. "I don't know. I guess I just didn't much care for him."

"Oh?"

"Something about him struck me wrong. That's all."

"What do you mean?"

"What is this? Am I a suspect because he put my name in his address book?"

"I just want to know."

She wished that at least once she could fully understand what went on in that complicated head of his. "Why? Because he's your case, or is this something personal?"

He didn't answer right away. "I'm trying to understand what kind of man Karl Wielund was, that's all. Strictly business."

"Strictly business, I already told you I didn't go out with him."

"You also told me he asked you out twice. That means you encouraged him enough to call you back."

"I *what?*" She stood up.

"Did he say what he wanted? What these dates with you were all about?"

"You've got your nerve!"

"Why are you so mad? I just want to know why he kept calling you."

"Maybe he loved my body!"

He stood too. "That's exactly what worries me."

"What?"

He sat again, drew in a deep breath, and spoke softly. "Did he ever—uh, mention anything to you that might have sounded a bit . . . indiscreet?"

Enough was enough. "Good God, Paavo. The bottom line is he just wasn't my type."

"In what way?"

She clutched her hair. For a cop, he was sure obtuse. "Maybe in that he wasn't nosy and didn't grill me for no damn reason whatsoever."

"Relax." He leaned back casually on the sofa, his legs crossed at the ankles.

She sat with a huff. "I am relaxed. I mean, if I'd known he was going to get killed, I *certainly* would have dated him. Then I could tell you all about him, all his little peccadilloes. Is that what you want to hear?"

"Calm down."

"I *am* calm!"

"Good, that's all I needed to know." He glanced at his watch, then stood and reached for his wet jacket.

He threw it over his arm instead of putting it on.

She stood too. "Do you have the overcoat I gave you?"

"It's in the car. I didn't want to get it wet."

Did that make sense, she wondered? Did any of this? "What is it you're trying to learn about Karl?"

He gave a long, resigned sigh. "I guess I owe you some explanation. I had to find out if you knew anything about a possible connection between Wielund and . . . something illegal. But I can't go into any details, all right?"

She stepped closer. "Did you say illegal?"

"I don't know that there's anything to it. Just a few signs that make me curious, that's all."

"Tell you what, I'll make a few phone calls. After all, I'm practically in the same business as Karl Wielund—or close to it. We just may be on to something."

"No. Absolutely not. And no more of this 'we' stuff."

"Why not?"

"It could be dangerous. You don't know who might be involved."

"None of the restaurant owners had anything to do with Karl's death. I know those people. Some might be jealous, vindictive, and even petty, but they're not murderers."

"Someone is, Angie."

"Don't worry. I wouldn't dream of doing anything dangerous. It's just that I knew Karl Wielund. I did a review of his restaurant. And you and I ate there together. I'll always remember it for that reason." God, how could the man argue with her after a mushy statement like that? "Anyway, the last thing I want to do is get involved with a murderer. I learned my lesson already. All I'm talking about is a few phone calls."

"Angelina—no!"

She smiled, then crossed her fingers behind her back as she walked with him to the door. "Whatever you say, Paavo."

"Thank you for coming by to talk with us. We really appreciate it," Yoshiwara said, as he and Paavo led Mark Dustman into the small interviewing room across the hall from the Homicide Section.

"I'll do anything I can to help. I was surprised to hear from you, though, I'll admit," Dustman said with a nervous quiver.

The three sat around a metal table. Paavo looked squarely at Dustman. "Karl Wielund's death wasn't an accident. He was poisoned."

Dustman's face turned chalky. "Poisoned? You mean someone . . . purposefully . . ."

"Yes."

"How? Where?" He pressed his hands to his face, covering his mouth, his green eyes wide and filled with horror. "Oh, God! I can't believe it."

"You said many people were jealous of his success," Paavo said.

"But not enough to *kill* him!" He gave a shuddering sigh, his voice hoarse. "Are you sure? I thought he'd been in an auto accident, that his neck had been broken, the car demolished after flipping over into a deep ravine. That was horrible enough—but this!"

"There was an autopsy."

Dustman looked more closely at Paavo, his eyes narrowing slightly. "I saw you at the memorial service, didn't I?"

"Yes."

"So there was already some suspicion?"

Paavo studied Dustman, every nuance of expression, every gesture. "Not by me."

Dustman rubbed his forehead. "You were with Angie Amalfi, weren't you? She must have said something . . . or one of the others." He lifted his chin. "Well, good! That means it isn't only me who suspects something. They know someone wanted Karl dead." His eyes darted from Paavo to Yosh. "That must be what I felt. That must be why I knew, in my heart, there was more to this than a harmless trip to the mountains. Karl was killed by some bastard! Some jealous, rotten son of a bitch! Damn it to hell!" His eyes filled with tears.

Yosh touched Dustman's arm. "Take it easy, Mr. Dustman. We'll do all we can to find whoever did this."

Dustman squeezed his eyes shut, nodded, and hung his head. "Thank you."

Paavo spoke. "We need to ask a few questions of everyone we talk to in this case."

"Of course," Dustman murmured, trying to compose himself.

"Where were you on Monday, January seventh?"

"On Monday? I went to work at Wielund's as usual."

"Time?"

"Around noon. Oh, I didn't go straight to the kitchen. Karl's assistant, Eileen Powell, was in Paris, so I shut myself in her office to place some orders, pay bills, that sort of thing."

"Did anyone see you?"

"All the kitchen help."

"What was Eileen Powell doing in Paris?"

"Restaurant hopping: seeing what was popular, what's new, who's in trouble, who's not. In short, looking for ideas for Wielund's."

"What's happening to Wielund's now?"

"We've had to close the doors. Karl's brothers in Germany won't release money to run it. Eileen made them release enough money to pay the staff two weeks' severance, and that's it."

"How long did you know Karl?" Yosh asked.

"About two years. We met in Paris, at L'Ecole Cuisine, a culinary institute."

"So he knew the business from the inside of the pot, so to speak," Yosh said.

"He did. He was always in the kitchen, working on new recipes, improving old ones."

"But *you're* the chef. Didn't you care that he was in your domain?"

"I was always a student in Karl's eyes. He was, as you'd say in Japanese, the *sensei*. Do you see what I mean?"

"Yes. The master, or master chef. I understand." Yosh glanced at his partner.

"Do you know Lacy LaTour?" Paavo asked.

"Mrs. LaTour? A little. Just to say hello."

"Do you know if she and Mr. Wielund were close friends?"

"Close? No. I always thought they didn't even like each other."

"Tell me," Yosh asked, "how did you get into Wielund's house before you reported him missing?"

Dustman's head snapped back toward Yoshiwara. His voice was growing more shrill with each reply. "I didn't think anyone would care. I just used the spare key in the Hide-A-Key stuck underneath the mailbox."

"How did you know it was there?"

"I stayed at Karl's house a few days when I first came to the city. We were very close, like brothers, or father and son." His eyes turned red and watery. "I loved the man! Why are you asking me all these questions?"

"Did you ever go back into Wielund's house after that first visit while he was missing?" Paavo asked.

Dustman shook his head. "No. I had no reason to."

"What was the condition of the house when you saw it?"

"The condition? Neat, of course. Karl was fanatical about his house. I'm sure it was exactly the way he left it."

Angie put on her headphones and gave a thumbs up to Henry as "The Teddy Bears' Picnic" played to open the show. She promised herself she'd do her job well today. She'd concentrate, not answer any questions, and be everything Henry could ever hope for in an assistant.

A call was coming in. She sat up straight in her chair and pushed the open-line button. "Welcome to *Lunch with Henri.* This is Angie. How may I help you?"

"Hi, Angie. I'd like to talk to Chef Henri. I love listening to him."

Is this person for real? "Great! What's your name and where are you calling from?"

"I'm Dinah, from St. Helena."

"Okay, Dinah. What's your question?"

"I'm preparing a small but very formal, elegant dinner, and I want to cook something really special. Any advice?"

Yes, don't ask Henry. She bit her tongue. "That's a great question. Chef Henri will have lots of fantastic ideas for you. He'll be with you in a minute."

She sat through the commercial but received no more calls. When Henry saw that only one call was waiting for him to answer, he gave his phone number again. Angie waited, so did he. Finally, he took the call.

After introducing himself, he made small talk with Dinah and asked her about St. Helena. Her answer took about three seconds. Exasperated, he listened to her question.

Still, no one else called.

"Well," he said, stalling, "something special but elegant for four people. . . . Ah, why not Filet of Lamb in Puff Pastry served with Gratin Dauphinois?"

No calls came in. Angie grew panicky. Should she pretend to be a caller herself?

"That sounds absolutely delicious, Chef Henri. Thank you so much for taking my call." Dinah was clearly ready to hang up.

Henry glanced at the empty call-waiting queue. "I know a wonderful recipe for the lamb filet," he said hurriedly.

Angie was horror-struck. That man didn't know a lamb chop from mutton stew. Whatever was he thinking of? She grabbed for his cookbook, *Luscious Licks,* and began wildly thumbing through the index.

"You do?" Dinah asked.

"Grab a pencil and paper and I'll tell you about it."

Angie's heart sank as she dropped Henry's cookbook—quietly. Nothing even close to the elegant recipe was in it. She reached for *Mastering the Art of French Cooking.* STALL! She wrote the word in huge letters and held it up so Henry could see it.

He winked at her. She gawked.

"You start by cutting the filet from a three-pound rack of lamb. Or, better yet, have your butcher cut it!" Henry laughed.

"Good idea," Dinah said.

"Chop two shallots, six ounces mushrooms, and eight slivered pine nuts, then cook in butter and lemon juice until the liquid evaporates. Then stone ten kalamata olives . . ."

Angie looked up from the cookbook. What did Henry know about kalamata olives? He only knew Spanish olives in a martini. Kalamatas were Greek to him!

". . . and blend with a teaspoon of anchovy paste and a half teaspoon of rosemary. Add six ounces of olive oil, drop by drop. Don't hurry it."

"All right."

As she listened, Angie's jaw slackened.

"Lightly fry the meat to seal it, place it on a rolled-out piece of puff pastry of the same size, then spread it with the mushroom and anchovy mixtures. Roll the pastry to encase everything, press the edges together, brush with egg, and cook at four hundred and fifty degrees Fahrenheit for ten minutes, then lower the heat to three hundred and fifty and bake another twenty-five or thirty minutes. That should do it."

Angie couldn't have been more surprised had Henry turned green and sprouted antennas. How could he possibly know a recipe like that? What was going on? She couldn't have misjudged him these past weeks, could she?

When her phone monitor began to blink because another call had come in, it took her a long time even to notice it.

9

"*I give up.*" *Yosh tossed* Karl Wielund's porn photos in Paavo's little-used briefcase onto the back-seat of the tan Chevy, then got into the passenger seat. "For all we know, we've already been to the place these films and shots were made, but everyone denied ever seeing any of them, and we have no way to prove otherwise."

The car was parked in front of Wielund's, Paavo behind the wheel. As he drove toward the Hall of Justice, his frustration built over the pitiful lack of evidence and clues they had so far. Dirty pictures, a poisoned restaurateur, and, on top of that, Greuber's wife said the landlord hadn't come home after going off to meet the detectives at Wielund's house. They'd issued a bulletin for him, but so far had heard nothing.

Wielund's car hadn't been tampered with and was lousy with fingerprints, as was his house. For a loner, this guy had a lot of people in his life.

Paavo and Yosh had interviewed Eileen Powell and, as Dustman said, she had been in Paris at the time of the murder, talking to restaurant owners and chefs—with the receipts to prove it. She, like Dustman, had no idea who would want to kill Wielund.

Waiters, waitresses, and kitchen help at Wielund's corroborated that Dustman went in to the restaurant the day Karl was killed, then went off to handle Eileen Powell's work.

Neighbors had seen nothing strange about Wielund. Relatives were interviewed with the help of translators and expressed shock at Wielund's death. He'd given no indication of any problems to any of them. Shop owners up and down Grant Avenue were questioned about anyone or anything near the restaurant that seemed odd to them. Another big zero.

That's why Paavo and Yosh had turned to the photos and films. At least they were something to put their hands on.

"What if the pictures weren't even shot in San Francisco?" Yosh continued. "What if they're from New York or LA or even Podunk?"

Paavo stopped at a red light and rubbed his shoulder. It had begun to throb again. "The films look too professional to have been taken in someone's house, but studios that do this kind of thing don't necessarily register with the Chamber of Commerce. Still, we might be just wasting time."

Yosh began to chuckle.

Paavo frowned. "What's so funny?"

"I was just remembering the expressions on the faces of Wielund's staff and the restaurant owners when you whipped out those pictures and asked if they knew any of those men or women or ever saw Wielund with any of them."

Paavo shook his head. "They were something."

Laughter bubbled up in Yoshiwara. "Vladimir Polotski looked like he didn't want to give the pictures back, Mark Dustman didn't want to touch them, and Dupries scarcely gave them a glance—not very French of him."

Paavo nodded.

Yosh laughed harder. "I almost lost it when Henry LaTour stopped to put his reading glasses on to see better—'as a public service' he said. Considering the pictures, maybe he meant to say 'a pubic service'?"

"Ohhhh," Paavo groaned; then despite himself, he too was laughing.

Their laughter stopped abruptly, when a call came over the car radio. They found the patrolman who called in the report leaning against his black-and-white, his complexion the same color as Hank Greuber's green Buick, nearby. The car had been parked along the tree-lined drive through Lincoln Park, near the Palace of the Legion of Honor. Although tourists visited the beautiful museum by day, at night it stood secluded and empty. Not until Patrolman Crossen noticed the car had been parked there for over twenty-four hours did he slow down to investigate. He hadn't yet read Homicide's bulletin.

An oddly shaped white object sticking against the windshield had intrigued him enough to get out of his car. Only as he got closer did he see it was hair—human hair. The rest of the man's body was sprawled across the front seat, the back of his head gone.

"So now we know why no one saw Greuber after he left Wielund's house yesterday," Yosh said.

"Damn!" Paavo wanted to shake the old man awake again. He could only figure that someone must have been hiding inside Wielund's house when they arrived. Then, when Greuber got spooked and ran outside, the person must have grabbed him to make a fast getaway. He might have been in the back seat of Greuber's car, inches away from Paavo as he tried to stop it. "We shouldn't have let Greuber out of our sight. This never should have happened."

"You nearly lost your arm trying to stop him."

"But he lost his life."

"I'm glad you called, Angelina." Chick Marcuccio's gaze was subdued yet wistful as he looked at Angie from across the table at Italian Seasons.

"It's been a long time, *padrino*," she said. "I'd forgotten how long until I saw you at Wielund's Sunday night. Our families ought to get together sometime, like we used to years ago."

"The families are so big, spread out. It's not like the old days, Angie. Ever since Teresa got married." He sighed. "But my Joey's still single. He's always had his eye on you, you know."

"So I've been told. But Joey's like a brother. I couldn't go out with him."

"Maybe someday you'll look at him with different eyes and see his true worth."

I should live so long, she thought, but didn't say it. "Maybe."

"In the old days, me and Salvatore would have

made sure you and Joey fell in love. Today, though, things are different. Kids don't listen to their parents anymore. Nobody listens." He glumly poured more wine in his glass. "And people get killed for no good reason whatsoever."

She was ready to object to his saying that he and her father would have "made sure" she and Joey fell in love, but she saw the change that came over him as he spoke his last words. As he picked at the *taglierini* on his dinner plate, his face took on a worried cast. "What is it?" she asked.

He started, then glanced at her. "*Niente.*"

"You were thinking about Karl, weren't you?"

"Does that boyfriend of yours, the cop, have any idea who killed him?"

"Not yet. Not that I've heard, anyway. He doesn't tell me much about his cases."

"What about your boss?"

"Henry? He doesn't know anything about Karl's murder."

"I didn't think he knew anything about cooking, either, but that was some hell of a recipe he gave for lamb in a pastry shell today."

"You listen to *Lunch with Henri?*" Angie could scarcely believe it.

"Every chance I get. It's the best comedy around."

Angie frowned. "Not since I've been working there, I hope."

"No. I have to say you're doing a good job keeping him honest. Was the lamb your recipe?"

"I wish it was. It surprised me as much as it did most of his listeners, I'm sure."

"Hmm." Chick stared at the zucchini on his fork,

as though surprised to find it there, and put the fork down with a preoccupied impatience. He'd always been an energetic, busy man, his mind working through a dozen different projects at once. "I expect it did."

"He knows a little about cooking, of course. But he's not great in anything, not like Karl."

Chick sat back in his chair and took a sip of his pinot noir. "No. Karl was . . . *uno maestro.* A perfectionist. Everything he touched turned to gold, in the bank or on the tongue."

Angie finished the last of her manicotti. "*Delizioso.* You're *uno maestro* as well, *padrino.*"

"Not me. That's the cook. I'm too old for all this. But Wielund, he still worked on his recipes."

"It sounds like you knew him pretty well."

"Not that good. He was a strange one. Nona Farraday worked on a story about him for *Haute Cuisine* magazine. My friend Janet, you remember, is food editor. Do you know Nona?"

"Do I? I know her *too* well. She's been trying to one-up me ever since high school. I swear she became a food critic just because I became one. Then *she* ends up with *Haute Cuisine* and I end up on a newspaper that goes belly up. I could spit!"

Chick gave her a bemused smile, but she didn't care. She felt too strongly about some things to pussyfoot around.

Chick cleared his throat. "She said Karl spent many days on one recipe, early morning and late at night, whenever he was home and alone. He wouldn't let anyone know about it or even try it out until he was sure it was right. He was an absolute perfectionist that way. Nona thought he was mad." He leaned back and pushed the plate aside.

"I wonder what happened to them?" Angie asked.

"To what?"

"Karl's recipes. They'd go a long way toward helping make a good restaurant a lot better. Maybe even worth killing for. I wonder if his estate realizes how valuable they are."

"I'm sure they do. It's nothing to worry about, Angelina. So, what would you like now? *Dolce? Frutta?*"

"*Grazie, no.* I'd better get going. It's almost time for the class I'm teaching."

"A class? About what?"

"San Francisco history."

"Oh." He didn't say anything more. That was the typical reaction to her class, she was sorry to admit. At least the eleven people in it enjoyed it.

They both stood. "Say hello to your father for me. It's good to hear his heart's doing so well. Modern medicine. What a miracle!"

She smiled. "The doctors say he'll be fine—as long as he takes it easy, of course."

"When's he coming back from Scottsdale? He's going to turn into a prune down there in that hot dry sun."

She laughed. "He'll probably be back in the spring. I'll say hello for you."

"Good." He patted his stomach. "I ate too much. I think I'll go for a walk. Maybe up to LaTour's, check out the competition. Any words for your boss?"

"Not really. Just tell him to keep out of the kitchen."

"I wish." Chick smiled.

She leaned closer and kissed his cheek. *"Ciao, padrino."*

"Ciao, cara mia."

Paavo stopped off at Homicide on the way home from visiting the young son and widow of his old partner, Matt. He liked to check in on them a couple of times a week. He owed Matt that much, at least.

Rebecca and Never-Take-a-Chance Bill had night duty this week. Paavo wanted to talk to Bill, the inspector in charge of the Sheila Danning murder investigation, on the off chance there might be some connection with Wielund's death. He'd asked for the file but it hadn't been sent to central records yet. As Paavo entered the squad room, a call came in that there'd been a shooting in the parking lot of a Mel's Drive-In in the Richmond District. A couple of gangs were involved.

Bill suddenly developed a racking cough and thought he'd better stick to inside duty instead of standing around on the street looking at a gang shootout, so Paavo volunteered to accompany Rebecca.

Flashing red-and-white lights filled the street as they reached the scene. Paramedics were already there.

"My God,"Rebecca whispered as she got out of the car. "They're just kids."

They looked fifteen, sixteen at most. One boy had been killed outright. Rebecca knelt by another, whose eyes met hers as the paramedics worked on him. She took the boy's hand.

A third, too, had been shot. He was sitting up, leaning against the tire of an old Mustang. His teeth chat-

tered as his hand clutched his side while blood oozed
between his fingers and onto the street. "This kid
needs help too," Paavo called.

"We only got two hands," one paramedic answered.
"And this one's sinking fast."

Paavo could see the beginnings of shock on the
boy's face and knew he had to be kept warm if he
were to have any chance of making it. He ran to his
car and pulled out his as-yet-unworn camel-hair overcoat. What the hell, he thought with a sigh, he probably wouldn't have felt right wearing it anyway. He
laid it over the boy like a blanket, tucking it between
the boy's shoulders and the tire so that it wouldn't
slide off him. "Hang on, kid," he said.

Wide, frightened eyes met his. Paavo lightly touched
the boy's shoulder, and the boy gave a slight nod, his
fear easing a bit as gratitude softened his features.
After a moment, Paavo stood and looked at the small
crowd watching the little drama. "All right, folks,
we're going to talk about what you saw and heard."

A couple of people started backing away.

Paavo pointed at them. "I mean everyone. We can
go inside the drive-in and make this as fast and pain-
less as possible, or you can come down to the station
and we'll have a real long talk."

The people backing up froze in their tracks. Taking
in the authority and icy glare of the big detective, they
meekly followed orders. Paavo stayed with the boy until
a paramedic took over, then went into the drive-in.

Despite having the name of the alleged assailant,
the make, model, and license of his car, and four
witnesses, it was nearly three hours later when he and
Rebecca could leave the scene. Before they were

through, a call came in that the boy whose hand Rebecca had been holding had also died.

As they left the drive-in, she saw Paavo's coat lying across the hood of the Mustang, where it had been tossed after the paramedics took the boy to the hospital. She held it up and looked at the blood stains, grease, and dirt on it. "This must have been beautiful," she said. Her voice shook, and he could see her begin to tremble as the intensity of the crime scene investigation passed and the cold harsh aftermath set in.

He nodded. "It was."

"Maybe a good dry cleaner—"

"It doesn't matter."

"No." She shook her head, then lowered her gaze as silent tears began to fall.

His chest tightened. He remembered how bad it could hurt, how some cases got under your skin, and no matter how much you told yourself this was just a job you had to do, you reacted to it like a civilian, not a cop, and you shut your eyes and saw the ugliness and cruelty that men could inflict on each other. "Hey, you okay?" Paavo took her arm.

She shook her head. "I'm sorry."

She sounded so forlorn, he placed his hand on her back to lead her to the car. She stopped walking, though, and turned toward him, resting her head against his shoulder as she struggled to gain control.

"They were so young. It's such a waste, so hard to accept. Maybe . . . maybe I'm not cut out for Homicide."

"You did just fine. No one ever gets used to seeing something like this. Some of us just learn to stop the tears from showing, that's all." You're the lucky one, he wanted to add, but didn't. You can still cry. The rest of us just feel the anger and pain and emptiness.

She glanced up at him, wiped her tears, and got into the car for the ride back to the Hall of Justice to begin the lengthy reports they'd have to complete.

It was two-thirty in the morning before Paavo turned his car onto the street where he lived. A white Ferrari was parked in front of his house. He pulled in behind it. The interior light was on, and Angie was curled up asleep, classical music playing softly on the radio. He stood there and watched her, glad he lived on a quiet street where no one would come by this time of night and bother her—and also where they wouldn't come by and see a big hard-nosed detective with what felt like a sappy look on his face.

He couldn't help it, though. It felt too good seeing her here for him to not pause a moment and enjoy the sight.

He sighed as his more responsible self annoyingly tapped him on the shoulder. It was cold out here, and she was twisted like a pretzel on the seat, probably every muscle aching for relief. He had to get her on her way.

"Angie?" He tapped at the window. Across her lap lay a thick book called *Design for the Rebuilding of San Francisco After the Great Earthquake and Fire of 1906.* No wonder she'd fallen asleep.

She awoke with a start, then sleep-dazed eyes met his and she smiled. He felt a tug to realize that even half asleep her reaction to him was so warm. As she unlocked the car door, he opened it from the outside and gave her his hand. "What are you doing here?" he asked.

Slowly, she let him pull her to her feet. "Trying to make my class interesting."

Did that make sense? he wondered. "You were what?"

She blinked a few times and stretched her arms with a big yawn that made him want to hold her tight. In the dim streetlight, she looked sleepy, warm, and inviting, a sanctuary from the bleakness he'd just left behind. He ruthlessly clamped down the urge.

"I was waiting to see you," she replied.

"Do you know the time?"

"No." She glanced at her wristwatch. "I can't see it in the dark." She yawned again. "I guess I fell asleep."

"It's nearly three A.M. Don't you think you should go home?"

"Okay." She turned toward her car, took the key from her pocket, and tried to find the keyhole on the door to unlock it. The door, however, was already standing open.

The befuddled look on her sleep-softened face broke his control. He took the key from her hand, pushed the car door shut, wrapped his arm around her waist, and led her toward his house.

"What's wrong?" she murmured.

"You're sleepwalking. One cup of coffee, and you'll be on your way."

She snuggled closer and shut her eyes.

Paavo lived in a brown-shingled cottage tucked away in the northwest corner of the city, far from crowds and facing the Pacific Ocean. It was so old it had no garage and was mere inches away from similar cottages on either side.

Paavo led Angie directly into the small living room with its overstuffed, mismatched sofa and chairs. His big, pugnacious tomcat, Hercules, bounded off the patchwork cushion he loved to sleep on and pattered across the red and blue hooked rug straight to Paavo, where he rubbed against Paavo's leg and meowed loudly.

"Hello, Herk," Paavo said. He looked at Angie as he shut the front door. "This cat thinks my sole function in life is to open a can of food for him as soon as I walk in."

"While you do that," she said, rubbing her eyes, "I'll put on some coffee."

"Are you awake enough?" he asked.

"Certainly!" She staggered toward the kitchen like a drunken sailor.

Grinning foolishly, he followed her, with Hercules running between his feet.

The kitchen was as old as the house, and so big Angie felt a twinge of envy every time she saw it. It had high shelves—not one of which slid out or rotated, like those in a modern kitchen, and in which things got buried and lost forever. Judge Crater, Ambrose Bierce, and Amelia Earhart could all have been tucked away in there. The refrigerator had a freezer that required defrosting, and the old gas stove needed a match to light a burner, just like Angie's parents' kitchen when she was growing up and before her father's business started to make money.

Going to Paavo's house for Angie was like going home again, in more ways than one. She liked the feel of the homey surroundings, the easy lifestyle where comfort and function mattered more than looks and price, where a big affectionate cat slept on cushions and trimmed his claws on throw rugs and sides of chairs and no one cared. She liked . . . Paavo.

She'd given him a bag of gourmet Italian roast coffee when she learned he had nothing but Taster's Choice in the house. It lay in the tiny freezer, the seal unbroken. She rubbed her eyes, still yawning. In a cupboard under the counter she found a nearly new-looking Melitta coffeepot, but there were no filters anywhere. Taster's Choice it was.

Paavo put a bowl of 9-Lives on the floor for Hercules. As soon as the coffee water boiled, she made them each a cup and they took them into the living room. As they sat side by side on the sofa, Angie folded her arms against the cold.

"I'll put the heater on," Paavo said, standing and walking toward the wall heater.

"A fire would be nicer." Angie loved the big stone fireplace, the one fine architectural amenity.

He looked at her a long moment, as thoughts of warming themselves before a cozy fire stirred a growing warmth within him. On the other hand, Yosh and Calderon had been doing a pretty good job of warning him about getting any more involved. His practical side told him they were right. "It's a little late," he said finally.

She dropped her gaze to the hooked rug, studying its colors. He'd said what she feared he might. All she wanted to do was to spend some time with him. She'd planned to surprise him with hard-to-get tickets to "Beach Blanket Babylon" at the Club Fugazi, but he hadn't even phoned. So she decided to show up here, and what happened? He wanted to boot her out anyway. She almost laughed, but it wasn't funny. Looking at him, it was all she could do to stop her hand from reaching out to touch his face, the high angular cheekbones, the way-past-five-o'clock shadow on his cheeks, chin, and upper lip, the big baby-blue eyes that made her heart thrum. This must be what withdrawal was like. Was she addicted to Paavo? "Nearly three-thirty," she said. "Some people might call it late, but for others it's very early."

He took her hands in his.

Why not ask her to stay? he thought. His friends and their concerns be damned. "I don't know what to say."

She drew back her hands and folded them. "My goodness, all this angst just because you can't decide if it's too early or too late to build a fire in the fireplace? Next time, I'll bring a Presto-log."

"All right, home with you." He stood, pulling her to her feet, then gave her a quick kiss. She'd shut her eyes for just a moment as their lips met, then opened them again, startled. "What are you doing wearing Passion?"

"Wearing what?" He drew back.

"Elizabeth Taylor's perfume. Department stores used to reek of it. You smell like you took a—" Her eyes narrowed on the sports jacket he'd tossed over a chair as they'd walked into the house earlier.

He looked at it and saw a single long blond hair on the shoulder.

"I thought you were working tonight," she said.

"I was."

"Comforting grieving widows? Passion-wearing blond widows?"

"I—"

"You don't have to say anything." Her cheeks felt on fire. "I feel like such a fool! But you could have told me!"

"There's nothing to tell."

She eyed him. "All right. I'll listen to your explanation." She sat back down.

His thoughts turned to Rebecca and how he'd comforted her tonight. She was a nice woman, but not one he was the least bit interested in. Would Angie understand that? No way. "There's nothing to explain."

Angie stared at his face a long time. "Inspector, that's a bald-faced lie if ever I heard one. Just hope you never get arrested for something you're guilty of, because it's written all over your face."

As she stormed toward the door, the phone began to ring.

He glanced at the phone, then back at her. "Wait. I'll tell you about it."

"Don't bother! It's hardly my business."

The phone kept ringing. "Will you wait one minute?"

"Why? It's probably Ms. Passion Perfume wanting to come over!"

He picked up the receiver and cupped the mouthpiece. "Please?"

She could never resist a homicide detective who said please. "Oh, all right." She sat down on the sofa.

"Smith here."

She watched as his face formed a deep frown. He

glanced at her once, then back at the ground. Only an "I see" or "Um-hmm" punctuated his conversation. Finally, the conversation ended with the words she'd dreaded hearing. "All right. I'll be right there." He hung up the phone.

"It's so late," she said. "They can't expect you to go back to work now."

He sat beside her. "The night inspector called because she thought I'd be interested. She's right. I want to see what happened and where it happened."

Angie didn't like the way he was looking at her, as if he had to tell her something but wasn't sure how. "What's wrong, Paavo?"

"A man is dead. A friend of yours."

"What?"

"I'm sorry. It's Chick Marcuccio."

"No!" She stared at him. "What happened?"

"They said he was shot."

It couldn't be. Chick was like an uncle to her. She'd known him all her life. When she was little, she'd go over to play with Terry, and her father would take them to Swenson's for ice cream, or over to the Helen Wills playground for kickball. Even after he and Flo got a divorce, Chick was always around when Terry or Joey needed him for anything. The thought of his not being there, of being dead . . .

"No one would shoot Chick!" Even as she spoke she could feel the world begin to spin.

Paavo pulled her against his chest, and she shut her eyes as thoughts not only of Chick but of Terry, Joey, and even Flo came into her mind. And her father. He and Chick were the best of friends. Her father had been doing so well since his bypass

surgery, but how would he handle news like this?
What would it do to him?

"I have to go. I'll see what I can find out." He felt
her shiver as he held her. There was no way, now,
that he was sending her home. "Angie, wait for me
here. I'll come back tonight, okay?"

She nodded. "He was like family, Paavo. Find out
who did this to him. For all of us."

Angie tossed and turned, scarcely sleeping,
thoughts of Chick, her family, and her childhood
rushing through her mind. She remembered how, in
the old days, before Christopher Columbus became
persona non grata, the Italian community would
always celebrate the arrival of Columbus Day with a
big parade down Columbus Avenue in North Beach.
It would end right in front of Ghirardelli Square, at
the small beach known as Aquatic Park, where every
year Columbus would "discover" America.

One year, Chick played Columbus and Angie's
father was an improbable Indian. Chick wore a pur-
ple-and-silver floppy feathered hat, purple tunic, and
white tights, a Columbus in need of a diet. Sal was
bare-chested and bare-legged, wearing only a pair of
brown shorts, sandals, some bargain-basement beads,
and two pigeon feathers because they couldn't find
turkey. The two of them sat in a tiny gray rowboat on
the far side of a pier, out of sight of the beach, drinking firewater, supposedly to stay warm, while they
waited for the parade to end.

By the time the crowd had gathered at Aquatic
Park, Chick and Sal were unsure if it was 1492, 1992,

or any date in between. Since there was no wind and no sails, Sal was supposed to row them to shore. Instead, Sal rowed the boat in circles while the crowd hooted. Chick's heroic pose dissolved into a flurry of arm-waving and pleas to heaven. The crowd shouted mock encouragements, along with a few obscenities, as the two landlubbers braved the six-inch waves.

Finally, Chick decided to wade in the rest of the way, but he staggered and pitched head first into the water. Sal tried to pull him back into the boat, only to join his friend. Dripping wet and sick to their stomachs, they crawled to the beach. "Columbus" had to be held up to receive blessings from "Il Papa," while his "Indian" companion began loudly to sleep it off. Angie was eight years old before she realized Columbus didn't land in San Francisco when he discovered America.

The sun was lighting the sky when she heard the key in the lock of the front door. Half asleep, she sat up, holding the blanket against her, waiting for the sound of Paavo's footsteps. What if it wasn't him? What if it was a burglar, or whoever had killed Chick, coming to look for her? But why would she even think of such a thing . . . unless Chick's killer was someone she knew?

"Paavo?"

He walked into the bedroom and sat by her side on the bed, taking hold of her hands. She had put on a pair of his pajamas and had the sleeves cuffed about four times over. "I thought you'd be asleep," he said.

"I couldn't."

"I know." As he bent forward for a light kiss, she

wrapped her arms tight around his neck, holding him with mute desperation and fear.

"It really was Chick, then?" she asked finally. "It wasn't a mistake?"

"No mistake. He was standing beside his car, unlocking the door, just outside Capp's Corner in North Beach. Nobody saw a thing."

She pulled back, her anger mixed with grief. "He was in the street? Gunned down for no reason? It can't be! I mean, why? There's got to be a reason. Some explanation."

"We don't know yet."

"Why not? This is senseless, wrong!" Hot tears flowed down her cheeks. "What's wrong with this city? why can't peaceful citizens—"

"Angie, don't." He pulled her closer, holding her head against the crook of his neck.

"It's not right," she cried. "It's not fair."

"I know." He stroked her back and shoulder, trying to calm her, wishing he could wave some magic wand and make her happy once more. The heat of her body radiated through the flannel covering her. "I know the reason the papers will pick up."

"What's that?"

"He was a restaurant owner too. They'll probably speculate that there's a restaurant-owner serial killer on the loose and cause mass panic among all your friends."

She glanced up at him, her eyes stricken. "You don't think it's true, do you?"

He used his handkerchief to wipe the tears from her face, searching for the smile he loved. "I don't. There's a reason for this, a real reason. We'll find out what it is. Believe me, Angie."

She lifted her head and touched his face just as she'd wanted to earlier, before this tragedy happened. "I believe in you, Paavo. I always have."

His arms tightened as his mouth found hers.

Angie awoke in full daylight to a pounding on the front door. Cops, she thought. Why do they always have to make so much noise? Suddenly, she sat straight up. Paavo was beside her, sound asleep. He'd been completely exhausted last night, and then exerted himself even more before they finally got to sleep. So who was at the door?

She glanced at the bedside alarm. It was eight-thirty. Grabbing Paavo's robe, she put it on as she hurried to open the door before the knocking woke him up.

She looked through the peephole and saw an enormous Japanese man with short cropped hair. Leaving the chain on, she opened the door a crack. "Inspector Yoshiwara?"

"Hey there!" The way his voice thundered she was surprised it didn't set off a sonic boom. "You must be Miss Amalfi, right? Angie, if I may call you that. Say, can I come in? I'd rather not talk on the sidewalk and all."

"Sure." She stared at him and then shut the door to unfasten the chain. "Come in," she said when the chain was off.

He sauntered into the living room. "Hey, nice to meet you. I've heard so much about you. I thought you couldn't be real. Lots of education, money, real fancy car out there. Va-va-voom!"

She felt more dead than real, standing there with no makeup and her hair a mess, wearing Paavo's enormous bathrobe, and being greeted by Captain Kangaroo. How could anyone have so much energy so early in the morning? "What was it you wanted?" she asked.

"Listen, Angie, I'm really sorry to bother you, and I wouldn't do it if it wasn't an emergency, but I've got to get Paavo down to the station. There's going to be a live press conference, on TV. The newsies are all over Hollins's neck about these restaurant murders, and he needs Paavo there to bail him out."

"Paavo worked all night. He's exhausted."

"So I heard! I learned about it this morning when I went in to the squad room. I couldn't believe it! That Paav, he's a great guy, letting me get my beauty sleep and all. Maybe that's because he can't stand to work with me otherwise. I mean, I'm ugly enough as is."

"I don't think he should be disturbed."

"Now, Angie, we need him. The chief wants him at the Hall." Under the Captain Kangaroo facade was the will of a mule.

"He's not fully recovered yet from the bullet wound, and he needs his rest. I don't care what the chief wants. I know what's best for him."

"I'll drive him down. Believe me, I'll get him back here just as soon as possible. Look, I'll even tuck him in if that'll make you happy."

"If you'll excuse me, Inspector Yoshiwara. I really can't help you."

"You can call me Yosh."

She walked to the front door and held it open for him. "Good day, Inspector Yoshiwara."

He didn't budge. "Look, Angie. You've got to understand—"

"I understand. You don't. I said 'leave.' Is that so difficult?"

"But, Angie—"

"Say, you two." They both turned to see a sleepy-looking Paavo standing in the doorway of the bedroom, wearing nothing but his pajama bottoms. "This stand-off is real interesting, and I'd love to see how it ends, but I don't think I want to see any more bloodshed. Let me just take a shower, Yosh, and I'll be with you."

"Sure, Paav." Yosh smiled and walked over to the easy chair.

"Please excuse me," Angie said, her nose in the air as she swept Paavo's bathrobe in an elegant turn toward the kitchen that would have done Princess Diana proud. "I'm going to make some coffee."

10

They say the first forty-eight hours after a murder is committed are critical to finding the killer. Maybe that was why Paavo worked every one of them.

Angie spent the weekend moping, drinking coffee, reading newspapers and waiting for Paavo to call. He didn't. By the time Monday morning arrived, she had to break the speed limit to get to KYME radio in time for Henry's show.

She opened up a cabinet and pulled out her recipe books and pamphlets. She had just picked them up to carry them to the call-screening desk outside the studio booth when Henry walked around the side of the cabinet and right into her.

"Angie!"

She jumped, and the books flew out of her hands. Henry bent over to help her pick them up, his sprayed-stiff pompadour jabbing her nose as they both bent at the same time. Angie straightened. "It's all right," she said. "I'll take care of them."

"No, no. My fault." He handed her the books. She stared at him, not moving. He frowned. "Are you okay?"

"Yes. I mean, no. Well, you know. . . ."

He nodded. "Yes. It's terrible, isn't it? Some crazed killer. I feel like locking my door and not going out until the police catch him."

"I'm sure you'll be safe."

"I don't know. After all, I'm more than a mere restaurant owner, I'm a well-known radio personality as well. If this is someone wanting to make a name for himself, who better to bump off than me?" He shuddered visibly.

Carrying all her books herself, she followed him to the studio.

"Remember, you're supposed to *screen* the calls, not answer them," Henry reminded her, as he had every day since their new system began.

"I know, I know."

He was shushing her as his theme music ended. She couldn't help but hope the sound went over the airwaves. His audience should know what a bag of wind he really was.

"Welcome to *Lunch with Henri.* It's so nice of you to join me today at our cozy little table for two. Our waiter is lighting the candles now that sit on our starched white linen tablecloth. He's turning over our crystal glasses to pour a Beaujolais—a bright red color, fresh, with the unexpected scent of black currants: a young wine, yet with nothing thin about it. . . ."

Angie stopped listening. She tiptoed out of the studio, shutting the door behind her, and went to her desk. Henri would continue talking for a while, setting the scene for his listeners. This was something new he'd decided to try, thinking it would make his female callers feel more "intimately attached" to him, though Angie had told him he was just wasting time. After that, he would give a monologue about cooking, then read a couple of commercials before going to the phones. It was time for Angie to start screening the calls.

She looked at the telephone monitor. A call was waiting. She pushed the connect button. "*Lunch with Henri* radio show. May I help you?"

A loud whistle suddenly blasted over the phone line and wouldn't stop. Angie broke the connection before it broke her eardrum.

A minute later, the phone light indicated that another caller was waiting. "*Lunch with Henri* radio show. This is Angie. May I help you?"

Again, a loud whistle made the connection unbearable. What was going on here? Angie took off her headphones and tapped them, hoping that whatever was out of whack could be jiggled back into place. She played with the receiver's buttons for a while, waiting for another call to come in. Theirs wasn't a popular talk show by a long shot. More than one caller at a time rarely had to hold.

Eventually, another call came in, but once again, Angie couldn't hear anything but a whistle.

The music jingle playing over the air told her it was time for Henry to begin to take calls from listeners. She poked her head into the studio. "My phone isn't working," she whispered.

"What?"

She pointed at the earphones. "They're not working!"

"Shhhh!" His face turned red. "All right, send the calls straight to me."

"There aren't any."

"That's all I need. A talk show with no callers!" Henry just then became aware that the music had stopped. He cleared his throat. Angie could picture the wheels turning in his head, as he wondered how much of his last comment might have gone over the air.

"And now," Henry said, "it's time to go to our phones, so that you, our callers, can ask me anything about cooking your hearts desire." He glanced at the blank phone monitor, then at Angie, with an ever-deepening frown. "We seem to be having a bit of trouble with our phone lines, so I know it makes it difficult for you to call in. My, my, whatever shall we do, since you know I *live* for our afternoons together, when I can share my knowledge about cooking with you, my dear listeners." Angie cringed as his voice droned on. She'd never been around so much BS outside a cow pasture. "Let me give you the numbers to call once more," Henry said. "Then we'll take a little station break, and when we get back . . ."

The incoming call light began to flash. Angie waved frantically at Henry, then pointed to the monitor. He nodded.

"Good news, ladies and gentlemen. Our phone system is ready to be tested again. Let's see if it works." He hit the on-air button. "Welcome to *Lunch with Henri.*"

"Hello, Chef Henri."

Angie glanced up from the monitor. She'd been debating whether or not to try to take the next call, if and when one came in, when her attention was caught by the caller's strange voice. It was oddly muffled. Angie couldn't tell if the caller was a man or a woman.

"I didn't catch your name," Henry said.

"Pat."

Angie's eyebrows rose. A neuter-sounding Pat? What was this, a *Saturday Night Live* routine?

"Well, Pat, what can I do for you?"

"I was concerned about the restaurant killer in your city."

Henry's eye caught Angie's. "Thank you. I'm sure the police will capture the person responsible in no time."

"I'm glad you think so, because—you're next."

Henry jumped up and slapped the disconnect button. "And now," he said, his voice quivering, "a word from our sponsor."

Paavo was in the KYME studio by 1:30 that afternoon. Henry was much more of a trooper than Angie would ever have thought. The commercial break gave him time to compose himself and he came back on the air all laughs, saying it was a friend pulling a fast one on him. Then he went on to say he regretted the tastelessness of the joke and sent his apologies to the families and friends of those who'd been lost. He did it all in less than thirty seconds and then continued his show as usual.

Angie was less fortunate. She was a basket case.

With her ailing headphones mysteriously working again, it was all she could do to understand the callers, let alone try to screen their questions.

She and Henry told Paavo and Yoshiwara what had happened, but there was really nothing they could do. The station didn't bother to tape Henry's show, and unless a listener had recorded it, the exact words of the caller were lost. Still, Angie had the strangest notion that there was something familiar about the voice.

Paavo was right, Angie thought, as she sat in her living room and read over the afternoon newspapers: the reporters were still having a field day with the story. The headlines blared. MENU FOR MURDER or DINNERS OF DEATH or the less lurid, more chilling CITY'S RESTAURANT OWNERS FEAR FOR LIVES IN WAKE OF LATEST MURDER. A portrait was painted of a crazed killer going around terrorizing restaurateurs.

She saw Paavo on the local news on TV that evening saying he was sure the murders were not random, there was a definite reason the two restaurant owners were killed, the men had known each other, and there was no reason whatsoever for other restaurant owners to be frightened. He appeared reassuring and calm and even smiled pleasantly at the reporters. But she also saw he could scarcely contain his anger when a reporter stuck a microphone in his face and asked if the public should stay away from all restaurants until the killer was caught. The answer he gave was smooth and skillful. Probably only people who knew him really well could see he thought the reporter's intelligence was somewhere near that of a slug.

Earlier that weekend she had called her parents, then her sisters, and finally, the hardest, she put in a call to her old friend, Terry, to express her sympathy.

She finally tracked Terry down at Flo's house. Joey was with their mother too. They were lucky to have each other at a time like this, Angie thought.

Now, though, she remembered someone else Chick had loved, someone who probably didn't have anyone to grieve with. So she called the manager at Italian Seasons and explained who she was and what she needed to know.

Janet Knight lived in a gated condominium apartment south of the city on Highway 1, facing the Pacific Ocean. Angie couldn't help but reflect on the irony of how secure Janet's house was, and yet Chick was gunned down on the street just trying to get into his car. No matter how much you planned, life was full of surprises—mostly bad ones.

God, I've been around Paavo too long, she thought. Because that really wasn't how she felt. As she walked toward the condo, her eye caught the Pacific in the moonlight. She stopped and looked out at the water a moment, and despite the death and dreariness around her she felt a slight easing of her low spirits. She breathed deeply, knowing she was going to need strength to face Janet.

Mercifully, it wasn't as bad as she feared. Janet seemed to be a beacon of strength in a world gone topsy-turvy. Or maybe she was still in shock, but she took Angie's condolences with grace and invited her to have some coffee.

"Thank you for coming by, Angie. No one else has."

Angie nodded. Being so close to Chick's ex-wife, she'd felt a little guilty herself for coming here.

"The thing that hurts the most," Janet said, "is that the last time we were together we fought over something so silly."

"If it was silly, I'm sure Chick didn't take it too seriously."

"He always took his restaurant seriously. Strangely, our fight was about Karl Wielund and an article we were doing on him in *Haute Cuisine* magazine. I'd sent Nona Farraday to interview Karl over several days. It was going to be a big spread. Then, when he was killed, Nona put together an article on Albert Dupries instead." Janet sighed.

"What was wrong with that?" Angie asked.

Janet gave a half smile. "Nothing, except Chick thought the article should have been about him."

"Ah." Angie understood the professional ethics that would have influenced Janet. "I see."

"He wanted to know why I'd publish such trash in my magazine."

"Did he mean the article was trash or Dupries?"

"He might have meant both. He despised Dupries. But he also said the article Nona wrote on Wielund was far superior. It went into what a fanatic the man was about his recipes, as well as how his customers were treated. He thought it was realistic and should have been used as a tribute to a great restaurateur, even if Wielund wasn't especially popular. But if I didn't do that, Chick thought I should at least have written about Italian Seasons."

Angie put her hand on Janet's arm. "Chick would have realized soon enough why you couldn't do an article on him, I'm sure. It's not worth upsetting yourself over. Chick was devoted to you."

"Was he?" Janet asked.

Angie feared that in his old-world Roman Catholic heart, Chick still thought of Flo as his wife, even though their love had died and they couldn't live in harmony together. She hoped she wasn't lying when she said, "Of course."

11

Sal Amalfi didn't like him. Paavo knew that the minute Angie began to introduce him to her father.

Sal was the complete opposite of Angie. He was tall, standing eye to eye with Paavo, hawk-nosed, olive-skinned, broad-shouldered, and with a keen way of assessing people—that sharpness now mixed with sadness over the funeral of his old friend Chick Marcuccio.

Their handshake held cautious appraisal.

"So you're the man my wife and daughter talk about all the time." Sal's words were softly accented, his manner one of elegant sophistication, yet the ravages of his heart condition showed in the gauntness of his cheeks and in the touch of frailty this obviously once-overpowering man now bore.

"I hope what they say is good," Paavo replied.

"It is."

"I've heard a lot about you too. All of it good."

Angie watched both of them, not knowing what was going on.

"You want a drink?" Sal asked.

"Sure," Paavo said.

Angie breathed easier. Everything would be all right. They were going to have a drink together.

"Angelina, go talk to one of your sisters or your friends," Sal said. "We'll be right back."

Her smile disappeared as, once more, she looked from one to the other. "Oh? Okay . . . I guess."

Sal led Paavo across the restaurant to the bar.

Chick's restaurant was packed with the friends and relatives who'd attended the funeral, as well as the restaurateurs Paavo had seen at Wielund's. In contrast to the falseness of the guests at Karl Wielund's service, the people here looked genuinely saddened by their loss. All around, he heard snatches of conversations as people spoke in glowing terms about Chick, telling each other stories of adventures and schemes, usually humorous, that he'd been involved in. The more Paavo heard, the more he realized what a fine man had been senselessly killed.

Over the group, too, was the pall that murder brings. It was a feeling Paavo knew well. Where Wielund's death had been thought at first to have been an accident, Chick's was known to have been cold-blooded murder. And where the restaurant owners had been able to distance themselves from Karl—a newcomer to the city, his body found in a remote area of the Sierras—Chick was a friend to all these people, someone who came here as a young man, married, raised a family, began a business, and then was gunned down right in the neighborhood he loved. His death gave them all cause to be nervous. Why had he been killed? they asked. And who was next?

"What'll you have to drink?" Sal asked.

"Tonic with a lime twist," Paavo told the bartender.

"Jack Daniel's on ice," Sal said, then looked back at Paavo. "So. I was wondering when I'd meet you."

"Same here."

Sal took a sip of his whiskey. "Angelina sounds serious about you."

Paavo slid his hands in his pockets. He was too old to be given a once-over by the father of the bride and made to feel wanting. Besides, he wasn't convinced Angie would even *be* his bride—or that anyone would. "She's a fine woman," he said. "Good-hearted and generous."

"Yes, she is. And ever since I was able to provide for her, I've always given her the best of everything."

Paavo nodded. "I noticed."

Sal's dark brown eyes were stern. "Angelina is special to me. She's my youngest. She knows history, music, and art, and she can write about anything. I sent her to the Sorbonne, in Paris, for a year. Did you know that?"

"She mentioned it."

"You get my drift, then."

Paavo got it, but he wasn't about to let the man off that easy. "No. Not at all."

Sal's expression said he knew exactly what Paavo was doing. "So. You want to hear the words."

Paavo took a deep breath. It'd been a long time—

years—since he'd been told there was anything he wasn't good enough for. The last person who tried it ended up with a broken jaw. He kept telling himself this was Angie's father, who loved her, and Angie all but worshiped the ground Sal walked on.

Sal sipped his drink and stared at the ice. "I don't want her to be hurt. That's what this is about."

"Neither do I."

Sal smacked his drink onto a coaster, hard. "She's been raised to get the best. And that's not a cop. You don't have the money, you don't have the time to spend with her, and as long as she's with you she's going to live every minute you're away wondering if she's going to get a phone call or a knock on the door and have someone tell her you're dead."

Paavo's stomach twisted. "These days, that can happen just walking down the street—or getting into your car after closing up your restaurant for the night."

Sal shook his head. "No. Not the same. You know it, and so does Angelina. Don't take this personal, because it isn't. I think you're probably a charming fellow. My Serefina, she says so all the time. All the time. But I don't want you for Angelina."

"That's for Angie to say, not you."

"Maybe it's for *you* to say. I love her too much to watch her throw her life away. You're a smart cop. You know I say the truth. If you love her, even half as much as I do, you know I'm right. Angelina's strong, she's young. She'll get over it."

Hearing Sal express his own thoughts, his own doubts, made Paavo feel as if he'd been given a body blow. Paavo's expression was rigid, his voice low and firm. "Whatever happens between Angie and me is up to us, not you, to decide."

"As her father, I have a say in what's right or not right for her. And I will speak. Do we understand each other?"

"Perfectly."

Sal walked away.

Paavo stood alone, then ordered a scotch and soda. Sal Amalfi's words gnawed at him. They reinforced other words, those of Calderon and Benson. Even Yosh, good-natured Yosh, looked askance at the possibilities of a lasting relationship between him and Angie.

Paavo downed his drink and ordered another. Angie had always insisted they could make it; she loved him. He wanted to trust her when she said that. Hell, even Yosh said she'd acted like a mother bear defending her cub the way she wouldn't let him wake Paavo up for the press conference the other morning. But all that meant, Yosh also said, was that she didn't understand his job. Paavo had defended her, but deep down he knew Yosh was right.

He wondered, too, if she knew how her father felt. He suspected not. He suspected that Sal, just like Paavo, did all he could to protect Angie from what was harsh and cruel in the world. She adored her father. If she had to make a choice between the two of them, what would she do? And what would *he* do, knowing that asking her to make such a choice would tear her apart? He couldn't bear to hurt her.

He looked at Angie standing in the middle of a crowd of old friends and relatives beside Terry. The intensity of the group could be felt across the room as they gave comfort to one another. Their wealth and position hung about them like a Swiss bank account. She fit right in, while he, always the outsider, didn't fit at all. Why had he ever expected otherwise?

"Refill?" the bartender asked.

"Sure."

A sultry voice behind him said, "Haven't I seen you somewhere before?"

He looked over his shoulder at a tall woman with enormous green eyes, a perfect heart-shaped face, and flowing, shoulder-length blond hair—the kind of willowy, sexy female he'd always thought of as his type until little brunette Angie confused his aesthetics along with everything else.

"Isn't that my line?" he asked.

Her lips curved up in a wicked smile, suggestive of all kinds of promise. "My name's Nona Farraday."

His gaze met hers with interest. "*Haute Cuisine* magazine, right? You do restaurant reviews."

"Oh, you've heard of me. How nice. And you're with the police department, correct?"

"Paavo Smith, Homicide."

"I was right. What brings you here?"

"Friend of the family." The thought of what 'friends' he and Sal were brought a twisted smile to his lips. His gaze drifted over Nona again. The cost of the dress she wore easily ran into four figures. She screamed money. Like Angie. "What about you?" he asked, trying to muster interest.

"I thought I'd do a story on memorial service fare. Which restaurant is the best place to have a 'dearly departed' meal? They've had so much experience lately."

Snooty and cynical. How charming. "Right." He turned away from her and drank more of his scotch.

"We should get together and talk about it sometime." She placed an elbow on the bar and leaned against him, shoulder to shoulder.

"I don't talk about food. I hate food. I may never eat again." He stared at his glass, watching the ice slowly circle.

She laughed, low and wicked. "That's an illness, you know. I bet I have a remedy for it. Oh, dear. Mark Dustman's headed this way. I promised him I'd see him after the service ended. He's extremely anxious to keep Wielund's, you know; he's willing to do just about anything to get it. But he has no money, the poor dear. Never had. He owed his soul to Karl Wielund." She placed her forefinger on Paavo's shoulder. "I'll see *you* later."

He turned and watched her walk away.

"Careful! I don't think I've seen a neck swivel that far since the last time I watched *The Exorcist*."

He spun around. "Angie! What are you talking about?"

"Oh, nothing. I'm ready to leave any time."

"Angelina! Paavo!" The shrill tones of Angie's mother, Serefina Teresa Maria Guiseppina Amalfi, cut through the murmur of voices around them. "It's so terrible, Angie," Serefina cried, her arms outstretched. Her black dress had long wide sleeves, and a black hat sat squarely on top of her five-foot-one hundred-and-fifty-pound frame. "Poor Chick. *Povero me!*"

"I know, Mamma," Angie began, ready to offer her mother comfort, but Serefina kept going, straight up to Paavo.

She put her hands on the back of his neck, pulled his head down, and gave him a kiss on each cheek. "Paavo, *caro,* how nice of you to come here, to share our family's grief. He was such a good friend. Shot down so young. *È terribile.*"

"We're trying hard to find whoever did it, Serefina," he said, his hands holding her full waist. He loved this woman. She was the sort who could take over a room and not irritate anyone, who could be bossy and nosy, yet do it all with an honest bigheartedness that put others at ease.

"I know, *caro mio.* I'm sorry I couldn't talk to you earlier. I've been so busy, so many people I haven't seen in years and years, all come here to pay respects. He was a good man."

"I can see he was well liked," Paavo said.

"Angelina told me you've gone back to work. How do you feel?"

"I'm fine."

Serefina stepped back, gripped his jaw, and turned his face left and right, peering closely at it; then she let him go and turned to her daughter. "He looks pale, Angelina, and too thin. Don't you give him enough to eat? He needs big dinners—liver, some nice blood sausage—to make him strong."

"I don't give him dinner, Mamma. I mean, we're not married."

"Hmph, and you won't be, you treat him like that! *Mange,* Paavo. Get Angie to cook for you. Don't let her be so lazy—"

"We were just leaving, Mamma," Angie interrupted. Her arms were folded, and Paavo could see she was steamed.

Serefina put her hand on his arm, stopping him from leaving just yet, her eyes, so much like Angie's, seeming to read clear through to his soul. "You met Salvatore?" she asked softly.

He nodded.

She gripped his hand tight, encouragingly. "He worries too much, but he means well. You do what you have to."

Her unexpected words, the trust she showed in him with her daughter, meant more to him than all the medals and commendations he'd ever received. Do what you have to, she said. Her simple words, combined with the logic of Sal's, made clear to him what path he must take. "I will," he whispered, then bent over and kissed her cheek. "It'll be all right. *Ciao,* Serefina."

"*Ciao, caro,*" Serefina said.

As Angie stood astonished, looking at the two of them, he took her arm and led her from the restaurant.

12

Angie knew something was wrong as Paavo rode with her in the elevator up to her apartment. He'd been there whenever she needed him since Chick's death, but now he was too quiet, too distant. She tried to ignore the twinges of jealousy that struck her whenever she thought of how intimately he and Nona Farraday had conversed and how he'd watched Nona walk away. If he'd stared any harder, his eyeballs would have seared her backside. But he couldn't be interested in Nona. Angie might not yet understand Paavo all that well, but she knew he wasn't the type to be swayed by just another pretty face. Was he?

On the other hand, why not? He was certainly attractive. She had only her own ideas as to why he'd never married. She thought it was because he was basically a loner. Maybe she'd been wrong. Maybe he was just a gigolo.

She glanced at his profile. No. She couldn't be that bad a judge of people.

She unlocked the door to her apartment.

"I think I'll say good night here," Paavo said.

Again, the brush-off. Was it Nona? Someone else? She spun toward him, ready to ask, then stopped as she saw his closed expression, the reserve he wore like a barrier reef. Suddenly, she was afraid of what he might answer. "I suppose you have to get to work really early tomorrow. Lots of crimes to investigate."

"True."

"Heaven forbid you come in my apartment, then. You don't want to risk exposing yourself to my wiles and not get a good night's sleep."

"That's not it."

"No? Afraid I might lock the door and not let you leave?"

"Angie."

She shut her eyes as she drew in a deep breath. "Tell me."

He looked at her a long while, Sal's words playing in his mind as they had all evening. He put his hand on the doorframe. "This isn't the time. You just got back from a funeral."

Her blood turned to ice. "Seems to me that makes it perfect."

As ever, he warred with himself over her. Maybe because the scotch muddled his brain, he decided he should level with her. "All right. I think this . . . this thing between you and me is a mistake. You need to see other people. So do I."

The color drained from her cheeks. "Is there someone else?" she asked.

"No. Not for me. Not yet, anyway."

Her eyes smoldered. "Not *yet?* Well, that says a lot about how you feel about me, doesn't it?"

He ran his fingers through his hair. He couldn't remember the truth ever hurting more. "I didn't mean anything by it. It's just that we might not be right for each other. Hell, you know it as well as I do."

"I do?" How many times had she imagined saying those same words to Paavo, but not as a question. Now, though, everything was upside down, wrong. So wrong for them both.

"Angie, let's give ourselves a little time, a little space. Okay?"

She bit her bottom lip to stop its trembling. "You really mean it, don't you."

His gaze held hers. "Yes. I mean it."

She wished he didn't look so heart-stoppingly handsome in his dark gray suit and pale blue shirt—a blue that perfectly matched his eyes—as he stood there saying good-bye to her. She wished she didn't remember so well the softness that came into those beautiful eyes when he gazed at her with affection and warmth, instead of with this bleak cold look. She wished she didn't understand how much he cared about people and making things right in the world, or how well he took care of those few people he allowed close to him, like Aulis Kokkonen and Matt Kowalski's son and widow. She wished she didn't know how it felt when he took her in his strong arms, or how, when they kissed, the spicy clean scent of him sent her senses reeling, or how the rapid drumming of his heart felt when he pressed her close. If all that meant nothing to her, it would be easy to say good-bye to him now.

But she was never one to insist that a man stay with her. Quite the opposite, in fact. "If that's how you feel, then fine," she said, forcing her voice to sound strong. "I'm not any more eager to see you than you are to see me. So good night, Inspector Smith. You needn't bother to call me again."

She opened the door to her apartment and stepped inside. He turned and walked toward the elevator. She hurled herself against her door, slamming it shut. Almost immediately, she regretted her action.

She stood at the door a moment, waiting for him to come to his senses, but instead she heard the elevator doors open, then close. She opened the front door a crack.

The hallway was empty.

She couldn't believe it. She stood there a long, long while, watching the elevator door, believing he'd come back to her. Then she shut her eyes, shut out the tears that threatened, and went back inside.

Willing herself not to feel, not to think, she curled up on the sofa. On the floor next to her she noticed Paavo's briefcase, an old-fashioned one, with handles on the top and a wide bottom. He'd carried it up to her apartment because his car doors' locks weren't very good, and nothing left in a car on city streets was safe anymore—not even people. He told her he'd needed it for work that morning; then, since he came straight to her house to go with her to the funeral without stopping at his desk, he brought it to her apartment. Now he'd forgotten it. He'd be back to get it, she knew.

Her gaze went to the briefcase again. Why would a homicide detective need such a thing?

Curious, she walked over and picked it up. It was heavy. She couldn't help but wonder if its contents had anything to do with Chick's murder. That had to be Paavo's main case. Remembering the telephoned threat against Henry made Angie even more nervous. Could someone really want to kill restaurant owners?

She really shouldn't peek, but what if the briefcase contained information that had to do with Chick's murder? or Karl's? Mightn't it give her, an insider almost, a clue to the murderer that an outsider like Paavo wouldn't be aware of?

But wouldn't he have told her everything he knew about Chick's murder, considering that she knew all these people? Who was she kidding; he was the most close-mouthed person she knew. So maybe she *should* look, and that way, if there was something about Chick's murder, she could be helpful to Paavo without his having to ask. In fact, wasn't it her civic duty to look inside Paavo's briefcase to help him out? Of course it was.

She opened the briefcase. A few notes scribbled on small tablets were in it, plus a thick envelope and two reels of film.

She looked at the films with interest. Old eight-millimeter jobs. They had serial numbers on them— 911,974 and 911,221—rentals, perhaps? Nine-one-one. Almost like an emergency hotline. Why would Paavo have rented old movies?

She lifted the manila envelope out of the briefcase and turned it over. A yellow Post-it note caught her eye.

P—

These'll take your mind off your little Italian friend!

Ha-ha!

Yosh

Little Italian friend? What was this all about? Opening the envelope, she peeked inside, stared, then shrieked with fury.

She dumped the contents of the envelope on the coffee table and grew angrier with each photo that passed under her nose. Naked women!

Spreading the photos before her, she took in the full disgusting display. So Yosh thought Paavo had to forget about her, did he? And with pictures like this? She could hardly wait to give him a piece of her mind. Paavo should have just thrown them away! In fact, she'd do it for him.

She scooped up the photos, stuffed them back into the envelope, and stormed over to her garbage chute. "Mrs. Calamatti! Hello!"

No answer.

"Mrs. Calamatti, are you down there?" she called again.

"God damn it!" A deep male voice echoed up from the chute. "Can't you women use the phone like everybody else?"

"You can go stuff it!" What nerve, when she was just trying to be polite and not plaster the old lady with porn. She dropped the photos down the chute.

A loud rap on the door woke her. She knew that knock. Her heart bounded, but then she forced back the feeling. Last night he'd told her they were finished.

She put the pillow over her head, trying to block out the world and Paavo Smith and all he'd ever meant to her.

She sat up. What if he regretted his words and behavior? What if he wanted to apologize?

He knocked again. Tossing back the covers, she put on her robe while running to the door, then skidded to a halt. After all, she didn't want to make things *too* easy for him. Not after the hell she'd gone through last night after his good-bye.

"Who is it?" she called sweetly.

"It's me."

She folded her arms and leaned against the door. "Who?"

She could all but hear his teeth gnashing. "Paavo."

She grinned. "Back so soon?" She glanced at her fingernails. Time for a manicure. "I thought you didn't want to see me."

Silence. Good, she thought. He was steamed. "I left my briefcase," he said finally.

Her smile vanished. "What?"

"I need my briefcase."

Crestfallen, she stared at the door. "*That's* why you're here?"

"Just give it to me, and I'll be on my way."

She grabbed the briefcase, yanked the door open, and shoved the damn case hard against his stomach. "Good riddance!" Her voice was shrill. "You and your smut can keep away from me."

"My what?"

She slammed the door in his face, then cursed herself for being twenty kinds of a fool over this man.

A minute later, she heard another knock on the door. "Angie?"

"Leave me alone!"

"Angie, open the door so I can explain."

"No!"

"Angie!"

"*No!*"

Stan's voice came from the apartment across the hall. "Angie, open the door. I'm trying to sleep!"

She pulled open the door. Paavo stood in front of her, and a sleepy-looking Stan stood in his doorway. "You should be at work," she told Stan.

"I'm sick today."

"Again?" She glared at Stan, who quickly backed into his apartment and shut the door. "All right," she said to Paavo, "come in before my father ends up evicting me for disturbing his tenants."

He walked in and put the briefcase on the coffee table. "It's not what you think, Angie."

She folded her arms. "Oh? Now you're going to tell me what I think and that I'm wrong, right? A little arrogant of you, isn't it, Inspector?"

"Let's start over. Where are the photographs?"

"I can't believe you're asking about them! Why should you care? There are a zillion shops down the Tenderloin where your buddies can buy a whole new set."

"They're part of a case."

"You work in Homicide, not Vice, remember?" Her voice softened to a pained whisper. "Besides, I read Yoshiwara's note."

"He was just joking."

How much of a fool did he think she was? "Joking?

Sure! Since when do cops have a sense of humor?"

He looked heavenward as if for guidance. "Believe me, he didn't mean anything by it. It was tasteless, I agree. But he didn't mean to hurt you or insult you."

Something about his tone told her everything he'd been saying was true. She bit her bottom lip. "Those photos weren't needed for anything important, were they?"

He spoke very, very slowly. "The photos are from Karl Wielund's house. Now, what did you do with them?"

She felt as if an earthquake had struck, an 8.2 on the Richter. "Karl Wielund? Karl had those photos?"

"That's right."

Her mouth felt so dry she could scarcely speak. "And they're part of your case?"

"Angie, this isn't funny. Where are they?"

"Karl Wielund," she whispered, then gasped and placed her fingers against her mouth. "Paavo, when I looked at those pictures, something struck me. I think Karl . . ." She took a deep breath. "One woman showed up a lot in the photos. Do you know who she was?"

"No. We haven't been able to find out yet."

"Oh, God!" Her eyes were wide. "I think I know her."

"What?"

Her breath came fast. "We've got to find those pictures."

"That's what I've been saying!"

"I thought she looked kind of familiar, but then, you know, it wasn't the face I was looking at. But when you mentioned Karl, suddenly it clicked. She was a cocktail waitress named Sheila Danning, and she was killed."

Paavo gripped her arm. "Those photos were of Sheila Danning?"

"I'm pretty sure."

"Unbelievable." Paavo crossed the room. "Unbelievable! I'd heard she was a sweet kid from Tacoma, young and innocent."

"I think you were told wrong. Nobody who went out with Karl was innocent—or stayed that way."

He looked at her as if he couldn't believe what she'd just said. "She went out with Karl Wielund?"

"Yes."

"No one told us that!"

"Oh." She blanched. "Well, maybe they didn't think it was something to tell the police."

"Good God!" He switched from pacing to stomping around the room. "Danning, Wielund, Greuber—"

"Who?"

"Karl Wielund's landlord."

Angie's eyebrows rose. "Was he a cook too?"

Paavo stopped and stared at her a moment, then continued. "And now Marcuccio. The only tie between them is Wielund, but is the connection because of his restaurant or because of his pornography?"

"Chick Marcuccio had nothing to do with porn," Angie answered indignantly.

"We don't know that. Just like we don't know how much Sheila Danning had to do with restaurant ownership."

"What are you saying?"

"All I'm saying is, *I need those pictures.* I want to

find out where they were taken and what connection Wielund had to the place they were made. Now, would you get them for me?"

"I see." She felt sick. When he found out what she'd done with the photos he might die of a stroke or kill her. She wasn't sure which she preferred.

"I have to get dressed." She hurried toward the bedroom. "Then we'll go to the basement and get the photos."

"The basement?" he called.

"I threw them down the garbage chute." She slammed her bedroom door shut but could still hear his mutter of pure fury.

She put on her Liz Claiborne denims, coordinated white-and-blue striped cotton blouse, and Versace boots and ran into the living room. "Let's go."

They rode down on the elevator, each too aware of the nearness of the other. He got in the back and she stayed near the front, keeping her eyes on the floor indicator as they descended. She could feel his gaze on her neck the whole time and was sure he wanted to wring it.

She walked to the dumpster and looked in. It was empty. The Sunset Scavenger Company had just tolled her death knell.

Paavo looked ready to explode. "Damn it, Angie."

"Wait!" How in the world was she going to retrieve those photos? Pay someone to go through the garbage dump for the whole city and county? More likely, she'd have to hire a small army. Oh, God, why didn't she think before acting? If she couldn't get the pictures back, she was sure she'd lose Paavo forever. There was no way he'd forgive this. "Don't worry," she said, proud she could still bluster while her knees knocked. "Mrs. Calamatti probably has them."

"Or the dump."

"No, really. She gets up early before pickup day and hunts for things. Pictures are a real favorite. She's always looking for ones of her daughter."

He stared at her a moment. "No way she'd mix up family photos with porn."

"Maybe she doesn't see it as porn," Angie said. "Maybe she doesn't remember."

"Nobody's *that* old. Let's go see her."

"No! She's not home."

He gave her one of his infamous cold stares. "How do you know? You were asleep when I arrived."

"Today is Wednesday. Her daughter-in-law picks her up Wednesday, very early, right after the garbage-men come, in fact. She'll spend the whole day with her daughter-in-law. Maybe she'll even spend the night."

"Oh?" He eyed her suspiciously. "You're sure?"

"Absolutely. I know her schedule." She was lying through her teeth and suspected Paavo knew it.

They walked back to the elevator. Paavo pushed the call button. "Why don't we go double-check?"

"Oh, no. I don't want to waste any more of your time. I'll just go back to my place, you go to work, and I'll call you when I get your pictures back."

"You seem pretty sure of all this."

"I know Mrs. Calamatti."

The elevator arrived. "That time we found her in the basement," Paavo said, "we took her to apartment three-oh-one. I think I'll stop by there."

"No need to bother." She pushed him into the back of the elevator. "Let's go to my place."

He stepped forward and hit the button with the big 3.

Angie swallowed hard.

He lifted an eyebrow. "Anything wrong?"

"Wrong? No, not at all. I was just wondering if Mrs. Calamatti will see the absence of clothing in those photos as proof that the Depression's already hit."

Paavo gave her a strange look.

They knocked on the door, once, then again. No answer. I must be living right, Angie thought. "See?" She raised her forearms, palms up.

He glanced at his watch. "I have to get to work. Now listen, you call me just as soon as you get your hands on those photos, understand? Not one minute later, and no funny business. Is that clear? Absolutely clear?"

She saluted. "Aye, aye, Inspector."

After seeing Paavo off, Angie raced back to her apartment, ran into the den, found the telephone book, and began calling every Calamatti in South San Francisco, hoping to find Mrs. Calamatti's daughter-in-law so she could learn where Mrs. Calamatti had gone today. Also, she wanted to make sure the old lady *didn't* have the pictures. Angie dreaded having to go to the city dump. Talk about looking for a needle in a haystack—which reminded her of the kinds of needles that would be lurking in the dump of a city like San Francisco. She wondered if she could rent suits of mail along with that army to search for Paavo's photos.

She finally located the correct Calamatti family: Mrs. Calamatti had gone to the doctor that morning and would be home around 10 A.M. A second call to the Sunset Scavenger Company told her that her building's trash was, as she feared, already in the dump.

At 10 A.M. she was standing outside her building, waiting for Mrs. Calamatti to show up. There was just enough time to talk to her before she had to go to KYME to do Henry's show.

Eventually, a taxi pulled up to the sidewalk and the old lady got out. Angie ran up to her.

Mrs. Calamatti looked startled. "Angelina. Is anything wrong?"

"No, not at all. How was your doctor's visit?"

"No problems that youth couldn't cure."

"That's good. I'd like to talk to you about something, if you've got a minute."

"Of course, dear. Let's have a cup of coffee."

Angie knew it would be the height of insult not to accept. "That sounds very nice."

She sat on the avocado-colored Sloan's sofa with its white antimacassar over each arm and waited as Mrs. Calamatti poured coffee into paper-thin china teacups and then placed a small platter of some hard, circular Italian cookies with white icing on the coffee table. The only way to eat the cookies without chipping a tooth was to dunk them into the coffee. Angie did so, just as she'd done with those cookies when she was a little girl.

"I was wondering," Angie said, after listening to a

recital of Mrs. Calamatti's current ailments, "if you happened to find any pictures in the dumpster this morning."

"Pictures?"

"Photographs, actually. They were in a manila envelope."

Mrs. Calamatti's face flushed red. "I did see something like that."

Could she be so lucky? "You did? You're sure?"

"I think I did."

Angie mentally crossed her fingers. "And did you—uh, pick them up by any chance?"

"Me? Pick up something that belongs to someone else?"

"Oh, they didn't belong to anyone. I did throw them away—but it was a mistake, you see."

"What I saw couldn't possibly have been yours."

"Actually, they belong to a friend of mine—for his work. I misunderstood, and I shouldn't have thrown them away."

"His work? My sister's boy does work like that too. It breaks her heart. He used to be such a good boy. An altar boy, even. And now?" She shook her head.

"My friend . . . it's not like that. Anyway, do you have the photos?"

"Don't believe him, Angie! Just like my sister's boy. She thought he was a fashion photographer. Hah! Some fashion. *Un*fashion, they should call it."

"My friend needs the pictures back, Mrs. Calamatti."

"I know why men need pictures like that!"

Angie was ready to writhe on the floor. "Please! Tell me if you have them!"

"Oh, all right." She got up and got the pictures from a bottom drawer in her bedroom. "I didn't want them out where anyone could see them. I didn't want anyone to think I like things like this. I'm surprised you looked at them, Angie. What would your mother say?"

Angie nearly dropped to her knees in thanks. She held the pictures tight, swearing she'd never let them go, would never do anything so dumb as to throw away Paavo's, or anyone's, belongings ever again. Thank you, Lord!

She looked at Mrs. Calamatti, and suddenly everything the woman had been babbling about her nephew came together. "Mrs. Calamatti, is it easy for your sister to contact her son?"

"Her son the zucchini brain? Sure. He's not married, so she makes sure she knows where he is. Even though he's a jerk, she still has to be sure he eats right."

"Could you call her and ask her to ask him a question? A very important question?"

"I guess so."

"Ask him if he knew which studio took photos of a woman named Sheila Danning."

"This Sheila, is she someone he should know?"

"He might. She was murdered. It's her in most of the pictures here. Someone ought to know who took them. Tell him I won't say who gave me the information, and I don't even want to know his name. Okay?"

"All right. Let me write this down, then I'll call Ma—"

"Stop! Don't even tell me your *sister's* name."

Mrs. Calamatti nodded conspiratorially and whispered, "Okay, Angie."

Angie got up to leave. She had just time to drop the photos off in her apartment and go on to work. "Thank you. I'll talk to you later."

"All right, Angie. Oh, Angie?"

"Yes."

"After we solve this problem, maybe we can figure out how to solve the Depression."

13

Paavo stayed close to his phone most of the day waiting for Angie to call to tell him she had his photos. When evening approached, he grew more and more worried that she couldn't get hold of them. As angry as he was with Angie for throwing them away, he was angrier with himself for letting her distract him so thoroughly he'd gone off and left his briefcase. Of course, he had thought it'd be safe in her apartment.

How in the world could he ever explain to Yosh and Chief Hollins why important evidence had disappeared? That was all he needed. He might as well quit his job right now and save the police department the trouble of firing him.

This investigation was getting broader and stranger at every juncture. The press kept up the clamor about the dangers of being a restaurant owner in the city, making it sound as if getting gunned down was as common as getting stiffed with a bad credit card.

The only lead Paavo and Yosh had was that the gun that killed Greuber was also used to kill Chick. Every other aspect they pursued came up empty, even including Wielund; they found no known associations with criminals, no known enemies, no police records, no family troubles, no financial troubles, and no bizarre habits, hobbies, or associations beyond his interest in pornography. But now, if the woman in the photos did turn out to be Danning, that would link her, Wielund and possibly Albert Dupries. But why was Marcuccio killed? Or Greuber?

The press quizzed the mayor and the police chief daily on what was happening. They would question Hollins, and he, in turn, would grill Paavo and Yosh.

Paavo had requested all the account books from both Wielund's and Italian Seasons. Often, when all else failed, following the money trail led to a chink in an otherwise baffling case. Money had been called the root of all evil, and in Paavo's mind that held doubly true for homicide cases.

He pored over the books, carefully studying the income and outgo, looking for patterns, odd sums, imbalances, too much money, he wasn't sure what— but anything that was odd.

"Need help, Paavo?" Rebecca asked.

He glanced up. Ever since the dinner at Yosh's and their investigation of the gang murders, Rebecca had been friendlier than ever, and she'd always been pretty friendly. They got along well, he had to admit. Yosh, Calderon, and the others constantly reminded him of how stalwart Rebecca was. She was a woman he could understand and who understood him. She certainly wasn't the type who'd become angry for no good reason or who'd throw away evidence without realizing what she was doing. She wasn't the type to jump first and ask questions later, nor was she impulsive, whimsical, or zany. She was cautious, logical, and serious. In short, she was much like him.

"I've studied accounting," she said. "I could be helpful."

Was there anything practical this woman hadn't dabbled in? "I didn't know that."

"It was too dull, so I dropped it for this."

"Let's see how much you remember. But first, I wanted to ask about Shelia—"

His phone rang. "Smith here."

"A Miss Farraday to see you, Inspector."

"Give me a minute."

Before he even hung up, the door to the squad room opened and Nona Farraday sauntered in. She spotted Paavo immediately. She wore a plum-colored suit with a short skirt and a V-necked cream silk blouse that showed off her tall figure to perfection. Her long blond hair glistened and swung freely as she walked. Every eye in the place turned her way.

Rebecca picked up the set of books. "Later," she whispered and went to her desk.

Paavo stood. "Miss Farraday, this is a surprise."

She gave him her hand. "Call me Nona, Inspector Smith."

"Won't you have a seat?"

She sat by the side of the desk, flicked her mane of hair, then crossed her long legs, letting her skirt ride up well above her knee. "I have some interesting information for you."

"Oh?"

"Tell you what." She leaned forward, her elbow on her thigh. "It must be near your quitting time. Why don't we go somewhere for dinner and I'll tell you all about it?"

From the corner of his eye, Paavo saw Rebecca staring at him. Benson gave him a thumbs' up. Calderon rose from his desk and, on the pretense of searching for something, moved closer to Paavo. "You can tell me about it now," Paavo said.

"But this is a long story, and I have a restaurant to review. Arbuckle's, on the wharf. It'll be my treat."

Greg McAndrews, owner of Arbuckle's, was one of the restaurateurs at both Wielund's and Chick's memorial services. Might be worth going. He glanced up to see that Calderon's frown had grown deeper. Yes, Paavo decided, it was definitely worth going. It'd give Calderon more to fret about, and it'd help pass the time waiting for Angie to call. If she hadn't left a message by the time dinner was over, he'd stop by her apartment and probably strangle her.

"Sounds good." He picked up his jacket and led her past gaping looks as they walked out of the squad room.

Arbuckle's Seafood Restaurant was small and intimate. After Greg McAndrews greeted Nona lavishly, they were given a secluded table, with a view of the bay, and two waiters who hovered nearby to fill their every whim. Paavo saw what it meant to be a well-known restaurant critic in this town.

Nona perused the menu. "I've been told the food here is elegant. I'll order, if you don't mind."

Paavo shut his menu and leaned back in the chair. "Fine."

"For soup," Nona began, causing the waiter to spring to attention, "we'll have the seafood bisque."

"Ah, excellent choice, Miss Farraday," the waiter declared.

"What do you recommend as a salad?"

"The smoked mussels. Definitely. Served on a bed of arugula with warm goat cheese and roasted red peppers. It is . . . uncompromising."

She smiled. "Fine. For our shellfish, how are the grilled scallops today?"

"Perfection. Wrapped in cucumber, with caviar and saffron sauce."

"And for the main entrée you suggest . . . ?"

"Striped bass filet, sautéed and served with citrus sauce and braised fennel."

She shut her menu. "I leave it up to the discretion of the house to bring wine to best complement each course."

"*Naturellement.* May I recommend our desserts, Miss Farraday? The perfect ending to a perfect meal."

"Dessert! How could I forget?" She opened the menu again and glanced at Paavo, a sly smile toying at her lips. "I think the passion fruit *bavarois* sounds promising. Don't you agree, Paavo?"

He wasn't used to feeling like something on a menu. "Right," he replied.

In no time, the waiter had served wine and brought their seafood bisque, which Paavo discovered was minced squid and tiny brown shrimp swimming in a thin, milky soup. It was going to be a long meal. Where was Angie when he needed her?

He took a few bites and put down his spoon. "What was it you came to the office to tell me?"

She patted her lips with the napkin, then leaned close to him. "Have you heard what Mark Dustman is up to?"

"No."

"He didn't get to keep Wielund's open. The lawyers for Karl's brothers back in Germany shut it down immediately, even though anyone should know an operating restaurant with a large clientele is worth far more than an empty building with a large kitchen. And Wielund's was on the verge of being the best, the number-one restaurant in the city . . . for the moment. Nothing's permanent in this town. All it needed for its fifteen minutes of fame was a truly world-class chef. But the lawyers want to sell it with the least possible trouble. Eileen Powell tried to explain to them what was best, but she's given up."

From his interviews with Mrs. Powell, he thought she'd care more about her life with her husband and young son than how much money Wielund's estate made.

"And Dustman?"

"He's taking a job with LaTour's."

Paavo couldn't hide his surprise, especially imagining Angie's reaction to a respected cook like Dustman going to work for Henry LaTour.

Nona laughed. "Bravo, Inspector! I see you've learned enough about our little restaurant world to be shocked, yet amused, by Mark's behavior. Isn't it ludicrous?"

"It is ludicrous. Why is he doing it?"

"He needs the money. These days, even in San

Francisco, there aren't many openings for a creative chef. For his career, LaTour's is a step backward, even if he can turn the place around."

Paavo shook his head. "You seem to know Dustman pretty well."

"Not really. But I knew Karl Wielund *very* well."

"You did?"

"I spent several days with him practically 'round the clock, a week before he died. I was doing a special article for *Haute Cuisine.* After he died, though, they didn't want to publish it."

"You still have the article, then?"

"It's at my apartment. I can give it to you tonight. After our passion fruit."

Lunch with Henri had been mercifully uneventful that day, and as soon as it ended, Angie telephoned Mrs. Calamatti.

"This is Angie. Did you talk to your sister?"

"Not only that. Her son knew a little about it. He thinks the place you want is in Berkeley. The upper floor of a brick building on Dwight Way near Telegraph."

Bingo! That was easy. Why couldn't the police do as well? "You're a doll! See you later."

Angie could have simply given Paavo this news along with the photos, but considering the trouble she'd caused him, she wanted to be sure the information was correct. How long could it take to find out?

Her Ferrari would have broken the speed limit, crossing the Bay Bridge and then heading north on I-80 to Berkeley, except that there was too much traffic. Berkeley was a place where anything goes, as long as it was politically correct. Compared to Berkeley, San Francisco was John Birch Society country. Angie felt like a fish out of water here; her Italian-Catholic upbringing didn't prepare her for this kind of place.

She rode down Telegraph Avenue until she spotted a parking garage on a side street. It was worth the big tip to the attendant to be sure he'd keep a watchful eye on her Ferrari.

Telegraph Avenue was a 1960s nostalgia lover's dream. Angie had been told by older friends that little had changed there in thirty years. It was a place where the Grateful Dead were still young, Janis Joplin still hung around with Bobby McGee, and the Free Speech Movement was considered the height of daring. Although college bookstores, coffee shops, and very nineties students existed side by side with small colorful shops that sold used records, books, sandals, tie-dyed T-shirts, and all kinds of psychedelic funk, it was the latter that drew her attention. Angie thought the street looked like something one should find in Disneyland. Between Frontierland and Tomorrowland there should be an old-fashioned Hippieland. It could look just like this.

She wove her way through the mass of students and street people and the cacophony of sounds that filled Telegraph day and night.

"Spare change, lady?" *Lady?* Did she look that old already? But then, the girl who spoke to her looked about fourteen. The girl's chubby-faced healthy looks told Angie she was in no imminent danger of starvation. She was the sort who gave beggars a bad name.

"Hari krishna, hari krishna."

Angie glanced at the group of chanting middle-aged men in their saffron robes and Birkenstock sandals. She wondered if these same people had danced in circles on this street years ago. Their shaved heads would hide any gray or bald patches. Maybe that was the secret of their popularity?

"Free abortions, *now!*"

"Got any change?"

"Save the Berkeley Five! Give donations!"

"Falafel! The taco from Morocco. Get your falafel!"

"Love one another, brothers and sisters. We must learn to love, to dedicate ourselves, our bodies . . ."

"Hari rama, rama, rama . . ."

"Sexism sucks!"

"Gimme some change, lady!"

She scurried even faster toward the building on Dwight Way. It was a square two-storied building with a brick facade. The downstairs had storefronts, and a glass side door showed a steep flight of steps.

She pushed open the door and went up the staircase. At the top, in what should have been the hallway, a thin man sat behind a high counter. He looked up and stared at her through black-framed eyeglasses thick as cola bottles. He had a mustache and beard, and his black hair was practically gone on top but long and bushy on the sides. He had it tucked behind his ears, making it look as if he had a whiskbroom stuck to the back of his head.

What in the world is this? Angie wondered. She was expecting some kind of a photography studio, but this looked like a factory office. Past Whiskbroom

Head, a long doorless hallway disappeared in a bend at the far end.

"Hi!" she said.

The man remained expressionless.

"Do you take pictures here?" she asked, stepping closer.

He frowned. "Could say that." The ends of his scraggly mustache reached below his top lip and into his mouth when he spoke, but since his teeth were kind of green, she decided that, all in all, covering them was for the best.

"I was thinking of having some photos taken of me for my boyfriend," she said.

Thin eyebrows popped up over the tops of his glasses. "Oh?"

"Some special photos, if you know what I mean." She held her breath.

He smirked. "Sure. I know."

She could have jumped for joy. This must be the place.

"They cost, though," he added.

"A lot?"

He tugged at his beard. "Sure. Takes a special talent to take photos like that."

"Oh. Well, that's all right. My boyfriend's worth it. And he'll be so happy to get those photos."

"I'll bet he will." Small brown eyes behind his glasses leered as his smirk grew broader.

"I'm sure," Angie continued, "he'll save lots of money not having to buy *Playboy* anymore."

Whiskbroom Head nearly choked. When he stood up from the stool he'd been perched on, she saw he was tall and lanky. "Why don't you come back here, and we'll see what we can do for you."

"Well—uh, I was wondering if I could see some samples of your work first."

"Samples?"

"Sure. I don't know exactly what kind of—uh, pose . . ."

"The photographer will know how to pose you."

"But shouldn't I have some say? I want to do a scene on a rug. Maybe a white flokati type. Do you have anything like that?"

He gave her a strange look. "Could be. Where'd you hear about us?"

"From a guy I work with."

"What's his name?"

"John—uh, Stein . . . beck . . . stein. John Beckstein."

"Never heard of him."

"He sometimes calls himself Jack. Now do you know him?"

"Nope."

"Brown hair, brown eyes, skinny."

"Nope."

"He's got a brother. Maybe you know his brother? His name is . . . Lenny. You know Lenny, don't you?"

He folded his arms. "I don't know any Lenny Beckstein either."

"Oh, well, I guess I came to the wrong place. They said you'd probably take the pictures. That it'd probably cost around five or six hundred dollars for the sitting, but I was willing to pay it. Sorry to have bothered you."

His eyes brightened at the mention of money. He quickly stepped around the counter. "Let's take off your coat and see what we have to work with."

He began unbuttoning her light-gray, double-breasted wool coat. She was too shocked to stop him.

"Very nice," he said as he peeled the coat back from her shoulders, revealing her simple yellow DKNY dress.

She didn't like the way he looked at her one little bit, but before she was able to say anything, he gripped her arm and led her down the hall. When they turned the corner, a large warehouse-like space, alive with activity, opened in front of them.

As they walked through, Angie saw it was a movie studio, a series of cubicles with low walls, making multiple sets. Beds and precious little else were in the cubicles, all arranged for the cameramen to do their work as quickly and efficiently as circumstances allowed. The cubicles were set up so that once a scene had climaxed, so to speak, the camera could swivel around to another cubicle's rising drama.

A woman wearing a short yellow robe stood with a thin pockmarked man, a sheaf of papers in her hand. "Oh, oh, ooooh," she cried. Her voice was flat and nasal. "Do you think that expressed enough emotion? I don't know how I'm ever going to remember all these lines."

Angie nearly backed into a partition.

Off to the right, a group of people were standing around a brightly lit cubicle.

"They're filming," Whiskbroom Head said.

"Filming?"

"Want to see?"

"All right." He led her through the group to a set illuminating a bed with sheets yellowed with dirt and age. On the bed, two naked women knelt. Seated between them was a man, fully dressed in a tuxedo and top hat, with a dopey look on his face. The scene, as best as Angie could tell, was that the women were trying to seduce the man, and one woman had to take off his clothes, while the other was supposed to slip ropes on his hands and feet without his knowing it. The ropes got caught up in the man's shirt, so they had to go through the scene again.

"Action!" the director shouted.

As the women writhed, Angie's eyes nearly popped out of her head. The man's shirt came off and the ropes went around his hands. He lay flat on the bed, then had to scoot closer to the head of it for the ropes on his wrists to reach the bedposts, but Angie figured verisimilitude was the last thing on anyone's mind.

One woman unzipped his trousers.

Angie held her breath as the trousers were spread open. She quickly learned that underwear was not a part of the porn movie world. "Cut!" the director yelled.

Angie jumped, her attention now caught by a chubby, greasy-haired man. "Dammit, when they open your pants, man, we're supposed to see the Statue of Liberty, not the Blob, for cryin' out loud!"

The man on the bed yanked the ropes loose and lifted himself up onto his elbows. "Hell, all these hours, being poked and prodded and shoved around by these broads. I'm tired!" He jutted out his lower lip. "I'd like to see you do better."

The greasy-haired man turned purple. "I'm the director. You're the actor. So act!" He spun around, looking over the crowd. "I need someone who can do something with Don Juan, here. Right now!"

Angie backed out of the cubicle. She didn't know what anyone was going to do about Don Juan's problem, and she didn't want to know. She'd seen quite enough.

Whiskbroom Head followed. He took one look at her face and chuckled. She knew she looked shocked, but she couldn't help it.

He opened the next door they came to. The set wasn't much bigger than a closet, with a frayed once-gold chaise lounge, stained with she-didn't-want-to-guess what, and adorned with old-fashioned pink and white feather boas hanging from its edges. The walls were draped in black cloth, and two big light stands stood in each corner. On the floor was a flokati rug.

Her legs turned rubbery as she stepped inside.

"Get undressed and lay down on the rug." Green teeth behind a scraggly mustache grinned at her. "I'll take these shots myself."

"I . . . I think I'll think about it a bit longer." Angie gripped the edges of her coat tight against her, turned, and ran through the hall, down the stairs, and out the door as fast as she could, Whiskbroom Head's laughter ringing in her ears.

14

Paavo used the phone in the corner grocery store just down the street from Nona's Nob Hill apartment to check his answering machine. He hadn't wanted to stay there any longer than it took to say thanks for dinner and to get the unpublished article on Karl Wielund.

Angie had left a message saying she had what he wanted. In more ways than one, he thought.

As he'd done many times, he parked his car, walked into the lobby, waved at Mr. Belzer, and took the elevator to Angie's floor. As always, anticipation made his heart thump a little harder as he stood in front of her door. But this time he tried hard to squelch the feeling. He would get the photos and films and leave.

He knocked.

She opened the door. "Hello! Why so late? Were you working?"

The smile he'd missed seeing lit her face, but he

also saw the caution in her eyes. He felt his own wariness, despite the emotions that filled him, so he said nothing but marched sternly into the room.

The living room was dark except for the blue glow from her television. Watching TV wasn't like her; she much preferred to read and listen to music. Moans and heavy breathing caused him to walk over to the TV. He couldn't believe what he saw.

"What's this, the *Playboy* channel?" he asked.

She switched on some lamps. "No. I bought three movies. Research." She pointed to the stack of videos on the coffee table.

He turned his back on the television set and picked the videos up. "*Behind the Green Door, Deep Throat,* and *Debbie Does Dallas.* Are you kidding me?"

"The man at the video store said they were the classics, the ones to watch." She grinned. "Hey, if my radio career doesn't work out . . ."

He shut his eyes and took a deep breath. He knew this had something to do with the Sheila Danning photos she'd gotten her hands on, and he knew she was just joking when she implied anything more, but he was steadying himself for what the truth behind this might be.

He shut off the TV. "All right, Angie. Tell me all about it."

"You'll never guess what I found out!" She picked up the manila envelope that had been lying on the Chippendale secretary beside her front door and handed it to him.

He looked inside. The missing photos. Thank God! "I couldn't imagine."

She sat on the sofa, primly folded her hands in her lap, and said with an angelic smile, "These photos are from a studio on Dwight and Telegraph in Berkeley."

One of his eyebrows lifted. He carefully placed the photos on the coffee table, tugged at the knees of his trousers, and sat beside her. In a strained voice he asked, "How could you possibly know that?"

She couldn't stay put. Excitement radiated from her and she nearly bounced off the sofa as she began to explain. "I know someone who knows someone else who knows someone involved with photos like these. All I had to do was ask. Then I went to the address the friend found out for me. I saw the very rug these pictures were taken on. It's a pornographic film studio. I even watched them shooting a movie."

He felt as if he'd been shot again. "Good God!"

She giggled. "Really. It was fascinating—but a little weird."

She had to be joking again, he thought. "Nobody waltzes into a porno studio and gets them to give you a guided tour."

"I did. I simply told them I wanted some photos taken of me and that I'd pay plenty."

She wasn't joking. He stood. Every ounce of his control was gone, vanished. As she sat there looking at him with a huge, beatific smile, all he could think of was the horrible risk she'd taken; all he could feel was anger. "Don't you know those people are dangerous?" he bellowed. "Especially if they realize you're just being nosy."

She leaned back against the sofa. "I realize it. I was even a little scared, at first. But then I saw that it was just a film studio like any other, almost. It didn't bother me at all."

He paced, still shouting. "What if you couldn't get away? What if they tried to force you to . . . to . . . " He couldn't say any of the horrible things that flashed into his mind. He ran his fingers through his hair. She just didn't know, like he did, how ugly it could be.

"Nothing happened," she said. The excitement gradually left her face, replaced by a guardedness unnatural to her.

It tore him apart, but he couldn't stop himself from going on. "I can't believe you'd be so foolish! What in the hell did you think you were doing?"

She folded her arms. He could see red spots of anger forming on her cheeks. He didn't care. "I was trying to help you. And Chick! He was my friend. If those photos had anything to do with why Karl was killed, and if Karl's death had anything to do with Chick's murder, it's my business as well as yours."

He pointed his finger at her. "I want you to stay away from this. Whoever's behind it is very likely responsible for at least three murders—Wielund, Chick, and Wielund's landlord. And possibly four, if he also killed Sheila Danning. It's too dangerous for you to go snooping around."

She jumped to her feet, her nose near his—or as near as possible with a ten-inch difference in height between them. "I'd stay away *if,* Mr. Inspector, you and your police force caught Chick's killer. I don't see that happening, though, do I?"

"I'm warning you, Angie. Keep out of it." He drew in his breath. "I don't want you getting involved in Chick's *or* Wielund's murders any more."

"Involved? But I didn't—"

"I don't want you asking the restaurant owners, or Wielund's employees, or Mark Dustman, or Eileen Powell, or anyone else anything about Karl Wielund. The same goes for Chick's friends and employees."

"What do you mean? Those people are my friends."

"And everyone knows you've been seeing me. I don't trust a single one of them, I'll tell you that right now. If, by chance, you stumble across the one who's guilty, do you realize the danger you could be in?"

"Nonsense!"

"When you talk about the case, they think your words are coming from me or from some other inside information you might have."

"So what?"

"It's happened both to Yoshiwara and to me that when we question them, we later discover that they answered with whatever they'd already told you."

"Already. *Already?* So, that's it! You're mad because I've been ahead of you. I've gotten there first. Well, I guess I must apologize for being so prompt at *your* job!" She turned her back on him and folded her arms again.

"Just keep away."

"Don't worry. I will. Especially if you're there!"

He picked up the photos and walked toward the door, but as his hand touched the knob, it was hard to turn it. He glanced once more at Angie, still showing her back to him, one foot tapping angrily. His gaze slowly drifted up her high, high heels, her shapely legs, nicely rounded derrière, and tiny waist. He looked away, taking in the apartment: richly beautiful, it also had warmth and comfort . . . and Angie.

Hers was a world so different from the one he knew, he wouldn't have believed it real had he not seen it for himself. How cold and lonely his own world seemed in contrast!

She glanced over her shoulder at him, her expression quizzical, as if wondering why he hadn't left yet. As his gaze met hers, he steeled himself against her pull. "Thanks for finding all this out for us. Please, leave the rest of the investigation up to me."

Rebecca looked up as Paavo and Yosh walked into the squad room late the next afternoon. "When's the funeral?"

They stared up at her. "Whose funeral?" Yosh asked.

"I don't know. I figured someone must have died, the way you two look."

"Gallows humor has no place in Homicide, Inspector." Barely glancing at her, Paavo walked straight to the desk.

"Neither does any other kind, I see," Rebecca said. "Don't let me interrupt your fun."

"Wait, Rebecca," Paavo called as she strode away from her desk. She stopped. "I have something here you need to see."

"Oh?" She stepped closer.

Hesitantly, Paavo picked up the envelope lying on

the edge of his desk. Despite himself, he found it hard to hand a woman, homicide detective or not, a pile of pornographic pictures.

"What's your problem, Smith?" She grabbed the bag from him and took the photos out. "Oh, yuck! What are these—oh, my God!" She leaned closer, staring at a photo of a woman sandwiched between two men. "I don't believe it!"

Paavo and Yosh glanced at each other. "What is it?" Paavo asked.

"Where did you find these? This woman looks . . . she looks like the one killed in Golden Gate Park last fall. Sheila Danning. My first case. Let me show you." She hurried to her desk and pulled a file out of the bottom drawer. "I should have turned this over to Central Filing by now, but I just couldn't bring myself to give up on the case."

"So you had it. Never-Take-a-Chance thought he'd misfiled it somewhere. He's been stalling us for days."

"I don't think he ever had his hands on this file," Rebecca said as she ruffled through the pages. "Here."

She dropped an 8×11 photo on Paavo's desk of a shiny-faced, smiling teenager wearing a graduation cap and gown. He picked it up and studied it, then picked up one of the pictures from Wielund's house. Under the heavy makeup, he saw that the face, nose, and lips were basically the same in both photos. But the eyes that sparkled in the graduation picture had grown dull quickly for one so young.

"Her parents sent that picture down to us," Rebecca added, "saying she hadn't changed much in two years. Boy, were they wrong."

"Why did she come to San Francisco?" Paavo asked.

"No special reason. Her parents said she thought it was pretty and she wanted to find a job here."

"Seattle would have been a lot closer to home." Yosh's voice was weary, tinged with the dismay of seeing, once again, the pointless loss of youth.

"Maybe that's why she chose San Francisco," Paavo said.

"'I never could find out what she did before getting the job at La Maison Rouge," Rebecca said. "No one gave us any hint that she could have even thought of posing for pictures like these, let alone done it. The investigation turned up nothing more telling than a nice, wholesome girl who happened to be in the wrong place at the wrong time."

"Who happened to make porn movies," Paavo added.

"And who knew Karl Wielund, who's now also dead," Yosh added.

"And who worked for Albert Dupries, another restaurant owner," Rebecca added.

"Who just happened to deny knowing the woman in the photos we showed him." Paavo stood. "I think it's time we went and visited Mr. Dupries again."

Yosh stood, and so did Rebecca. "It's my case too, remember?" she said.

Paavo and Yosh exchanged glances; then Yosh sat. "I'll leave it up to you two to figure out. I don't mind holding down the fort."

Rebecca smiled at Paavo. "Are you ready?"

"I guess." He threw one last piercing glance at Yosh as he followed Rebecca out the door.

*   *   *

La Maison Rouge was just opening as Paavo stopped his old, battered Austin Healey in front of it. He was surprised a valet didn't run out to hide it in a back alley. Rebecca was out of the car and waiting on the sidewalk by the time Paavo joined her.

The maître d' gave them an ingratiating smile as they entered. "A table for two, tonight?"

"We won't be dining," Rebecca said, pulling her badge from her purse. She held it up for him. "We'd like to speak to Albert Dupries."

The maître d' looked as if they had announced themselves as health inspectors. "I shall see if Monsieur Dupries is available."

In no time, Paavo and Rebecca were shuttled toward the back of the restaurant to a small office. Dupries sat behind a desk but stood as they entered. Paavo noticed his face paled a bit as he gazed at Rebecca.

"Inspector Smith, what a surprise," the restaurateur said, holding out his hand. He glanced at Rebecca as if he didn't recognize her. Paavo introduced her and explained that they had some some questions about Sheila Danning's murder.

"I cannot believe I have more information for you after all these months," Dupries said, looking puzzled.

"We believe you can be quite a help, Mr. Dupries," Paavo said. "I'm surprised you don't remember Inspector Mayfield."

Dupries glanced at her. "Should I? I'm so sorry. I meet so many people, you see. I have no memory for faces." He drew in a deep breath. "Pardon, mademoiselle. It is inexcusable to have forgotten someone who is so lovely."

Rebecca stared at him as if he'd just crawled out from under a rock.

"Well, umm." He waved his arms helplessly, then gestured toward the straight-backed wooden chairs. "Shall we sit down?"

Paavo opened his briefcase and took out the pictures. "There's someone I'd like you to tell us about," he said.

"Yes?"

"This person." Paavo placed the graduation picture on the table.

"But of course. This is Sheila Danning."

"And," Paavo continued, "this one."

Dupries glanced at the naked woman in the photo and jerked back in his chair. "I don't understand."

"Don't you?" Rebecca asked.

Dupries looked closer. "*Mon dieu!* This is Sheila Danning, too?"

"Isn't it?" Rebecca asked.

"Well, I suppose."

"Are you saying you didn't know she made such photos?"

"I had no idea."

Paavo jumped in. "Did she always look like the girl in the graduation photo?"

Dupries glanced up at him. "No. She was not so innocent. Especially after her *amour* with Karl Wielund. But then, I didn't pay much attention. She was a cocktail waitress. Unimportant."

"You had no recollection of anything at all about

this woman several months ago, Mr. Dupries."
Rebecca's voice was cold. "I'm curious about why
you remember so much now."

Dupries pushed out his lips in thought. "It must be
because of my conversation with a mutual friend of
Inspector Smith, Angelina Amalfi. She and I had a
most enjoyable lunch together today. She said Karl
Wielund had been seeing one of my waitresses. Since
Sheila knew most of the staff at Wielund's, I assumed
it must have been her."

Blood rushed to Paavo's head. Hadn't he just told
Angie to stop talking to people about these cases?
Hadn't she listened at all? "Angie told you about
Danning and Wielund?"

"Yes. I hadn't paid much attention before. Sheila
Danning was a bit . . . cheap. Angie thought so
too."

Paavo's throat began to tighten, his breathing grew
harsh. "Did you remember any of this before talking
with Miss Amalfi?"

"I'm not sure. I don't think I'd heard it before. If I
had, I paid no attention. I'm not one to gossip."

"Where shall I drop you?" Paavo asked as he and
Rebecca got into his Austin.

He could see the curiosity but also the hesitancy in
her eyes.

"How about dinner?"

He glanced at his watch. He had to admit he was
hungry. It was nearly eight o'clock. "Want to eat
here?"

"No. I'm more a Jumbo Jack kind of girl."

He nodded. "As you wish, Inspector."

They ate their cheeseburgers and fries in the car, washing them down with large black coffees-to-go. When done, Rebecca asked to be dropped off at her place. She lived in a tiny flat built behind a garage on the ground floor of a three-story building.

Paavo walked her to her door and waited as she opened it.

She held the doorknob in her hand as she turned to face him. "Why don't you come in? It's not very late," she added, a little too quickly.

Her offer shouldn't have surprised him—he knew she found him interesting, knew she must have heard about his split from Angie—but it did. A part of him said he should take her up on it. He needed to see other women, needed to forget about Ms. Society and all she ever meant to him.

Rebecca was a nice person. She was attractive. A good detective. That was why he couldn't be anything less than straight with her.

"No, thanks."

She looked at him a long moment, as if waiting for an explanation. He knew better than to make excuses, and she didn't need to hear the blunt truth.

"Okay," she said. "Maybe next time."

"Probably not, Inspector Mayfield."

Her face flamed. "You make yourself clear, Inspector Smith." She caught his gaze, then smiled sheepishly. "I guess I should say thanks for that."

He looked uncomfortably at the fog-misted night-lights lining the street.

She stepped into her apartment. "Well," she said, her voice heavy, "Good night, Paavo."

"Good night, Rebecca. Good job with Dupries tonight," he added, then felt like an ass. She didn't want to hear, right now, about being a good cop. He knew the feeling.

The door shut. He turned his back on the house and the woman in it and got into his car for the lonely drive home.

15

Angie had received calls for the past two days from so-called "friends" wanting to tell her about Paavo's dinner with Nona Farraday.

So that was the situation. One little meeting with the woman, and he was so smitten with her he'd dumped Angie like a fallen soufflé. It hurt. She'd never really been in love before, but she guessed she must be now. That was the only explanation for feeling so miserable.

But Nona Farraday, of all people! Just because she looked as if she stepped from the pages of *Vogue* was no reason for Paavo to have his head turned like this. Nona would lead him a merry chase, toss him aside, and break his heart. It'd never work. Nona was only interested in good times and money—and not in that order. One evening out with her would blow Paavo's paycheck for a week.

Poor guy. Angie folded her arms and paced around her living room, just as she'd seen Paavo do time and again. She was going to have to save him from himself, she decided. She was the cause of his meeting Nona, after all. Naturally, she'd feel responsible for his misery. And a miserable Paavo wouldn't be able to concentrate on his cases.

She had to come up with some distraction, some way to keep Paavo's attention on his work and off Nona. For Paavo's sake, for Chick's family's sake, for the police department's sake—and for her own.

Paavo was typing up a useless interview with Eunice Graves, owner of Europa, when Yosh came into the squad room. He tossed his notebook onto his desk.

"She's done it again," Yosh said.

Paavo looked up. "Who?"

Yosh took a deep breath. "Angelina."

"Angie?"

Paavo had never seen Yosh scowl at him before. It wasn't a pretty sight. "Don't play innocent, Paavo. You know that every time we talk to a restaurant owner about Karl Wielund, she's already been there. I was at Perestroika trying to get some information out of Vladimir Polotski, and he all but answered my questions before I even asked them."

"She knows these people. It's just small talk."

"Small talk with someone who's going out with the detective working on Wielund's and Marcuccio's murders."

"*Was* going out, Yosh. I'm not seeing her anymore."

"You're not? Well, I guess that's good. But these people don't know that. They remember what they say to her and make sure they tell me the same thing.

They all talk to each other, Paavo, you know that. Ask one a question, and fifteen of them chime in with the answer—and it's always the same answer. God damn. If I didn't know better, I'd think this was *Murder on the Orient Express,* where they're *all* guilty."

"I know the feeling."

"Paav, you got to do something." From time to time, like now, Yosh's jolly facade would slip. His face would grow serious, his dark eyes penetrating, and Paavo could almost see the wheels turning in his logical mind. And now, Paavo knew Yosh was right.

"I can't very well stop her from talking to her friends, Yosh."

"Don't you hear what your partner is telling you, man?" Calderon said as he stepped nearer. "You got to do something about her. You can't let your personal life mess up a murder investigation."

"My personal life isn't messing up a damn thing."

"No? That's not what I just heard Yosh say."

Paavo looked at his partner. He could see Yosh's hesitation. While Yosh didn't want to get involved in the constant bickering between Paavo and Calderon, at the same time, it seemed, he couldn't dispute Calderon's words. Paavo turned back to his desk, sat, and began going through some papers.

"You got to face it, man," Calderon said. He pulled out the chair by Paavo's desk and straddled it backward, his hands clutching the top chair rail.

Paavo just stared at him, the muscles in his jaws tight.

"Look, man, hanging out with a cop is like a lark for her. She can have everything money can buy, but one thing it can't buy is excitement. She's just some bimbo who finds murder exciting. She wants to be in the middle of it—gives her a thrill, you know? Maybe more than you do."

"Get the hell away from me, Calderon." Paavo's voice was icy.

Calderon stood and slammed the chair back against Paavo's desk. "Just remember when you get dumped after she learns the filth and ugliness this job's really about, remember we told you that you were being played for a sucker. *This* is the only family you got, the only one that matters. And don't ever forget it."

"She's not like that."

"They all are, damn it! I'm warning you."

Paavo slowly rose to his feet, eyeball to eyeball with Calderon. If possible, his voice had grown even colder. "Who made you my goddamn savior?"

"Go to hell, Smith!"

Yosh quickly stepped between the two. He put his hand on Calderon's shoulder and turned the man as he spoke. "Thanks, Luis. It's five o'clock. Time for us to go home. It's been a long day. A long week."

"Well, I still got work to do," Calderon said, as he walked toward the door. When he reached it, he turned and looked at a still-seething Paavo. "You know, man, *pavo* means turkey in Spanish. You're really livin' up to your name." With that, he stomped out.

"The problem's with his wife," Yosh said.

Paavo spun around to stare at his partner. "Carlota?"

Yosh nodded. "She said she's had it. Same old story."

Yosh didn't have to say any more. With a sinking heart, Paavo knew. All cops knew. Too much loneliness, too many nights Calderon's wife had to stay alone when she needed him with her, too many promises that things would change that never did, too much danger, too much worry. "She walked?"

Yosh nodded. "Took the kids and went to her mother's near San Diego."

Paavo remembered the pained expression on Calderon's face. He'd thought it was anger. Now he knew it went a lot deeper. "Hell."

If Carlota Calderon couldn't handle this life, Angie didn't stand a chance. He was glad he was no longer seeing her. It was much easier this way.

"All right," he said quietly. "I've got Angie out of my private life. Now she has to be out of my public one as well."

Yosh looked taken aback by his sudden change. "That's what I was saying."

"I'd like you to tell the next restaurant owner you see that Angie and I split. Word will spread and they'll believe you. You won't have to worry about her interference anymore."

Yosh gave him a long look. "You sure about this, partner? I mean, she'll hear as well."

"Maybe this way she'll believe me. And yes, I want it done."

"Okay, it will be. Listen, Paav, why don't you go home on time for once? Take it easy. It's five o'clock now, anyway."

Paavo glanced at the pile of lab reports he had to read and notes he had to write up. "What the hell? Why not?" He grabbed his jacket and struggled into it as he walked toward the door.

*   *   *

Angie's heart pounded as she pulled the Ferrari into the red towaway zone in front of the Hall of Justice. Once she got over the shock of Paavo's going out with Nona Farraday, she'd figured out what to do. Nona had gone too far this time, and Angie wasn't about to sit back and play dead.

Nona had always wanted whatever Angie had. That woman was the curse of Angie's life, the bane of her existence, the dead fly in her chowder. Well, not this time. Paavo was hers—sort of—and she wasn't about to let him forget it.

To her surprise, she saw Paavo coming through the big brass doors. Was he getting off work at quitting time? He never did that. The thought that he might be doing it to go out again with Nona wasn't beyond the realm of possibility.

He was walking down the granite steps when he looked up and saw her. Whatever she expected or wanted, it wasn't the aloofness in his blue eyes.

She got out of her car and forced herself to smile, a bright smile, as if her heart didn't feel like lead. She waved, her arm high. "Perfect timing!" she called, hurrying around the car to the sidewalk.

He continued slowly down the steps. "What are you doing here?"

"I wanted to see you." She held up her car keys, the Ferrari key ring glistening between her thumb and forefinger in silent invitation.

But instead of taking them as he usually did, his shoulders stiffened. She wondered if he preferred Nona's Mercedes 450SEL. How stodgy of him.

"What's this about?" he asked.

"I haven't seen you for a week. You've been working too hard. It's Friday night. You have the weekend off; so do I, so . . ."

"So?"

Her high hopes sank. She took a deep breath. "I— well, do you remember when I rented a house in Bodega Bay a couple of months ago? And you said how much you liked it?"

He nodded. No fond memories lit his eyes, only wariness and reserve.

She swallowed hard and went on. "Well, I was able to rent it for the weekend. So I did."

His brows furrowed. "You rented the house?"

She nodded.

"For us?"

She nodded again.

"Without asking what my plans were?"

She twisted her hands. "I wanted to surprise you."

A meter maid came zipping down the street toward them on her motor scooter, the book of parking tickets in her hand flapping in the breeze. She looked like the witch on the bicycle in *The Wizard of Oz*.

"You'd better get out of here," he said.

"It doesn't matter. Anyway, you can always fix a ticket."

"No, I can't, and no, I won't."

Her cheeks burning, she put her keys in his hand and slid into the passenger seat. "So what are you waiting for?"

He frowned but climbed into the driver's side and started the motor just as the meter maid stopped behind them.

"Hey!" she yelled, standing in the street, as they pulled away from the curb. He waved and kept going.

Angie sighed and leaned back against the plush leather seat. "I'm all packed."

"Is that so?" Paavo knew his voice was cold and emotionless and disliked himself for it. But wasn't this for the best?

He glanced over at her. Her eyes were questioning, and a worried frown puckered the space between her brows. Seeing her look that way ate at him like an ulcer. It wasn't her fault she was the way she was. He knew her intentions were good and impulsive. She was just being Angie.

The truck in front of him suddenly stopped and turned off its motor, double-parking in the middle of the street. Almost too late, Paavo saw it and stomped on the brakes. Swearing under his breath, the thought struck him that he couldn't even *drive* right when this woman was around. He looked at her, ready to vent his frustration and unhappiness, but with her nearness the words stuck in his throat.

He pulled around the truck and continued toward . . . what? He didn't know or care. He took a deep breath. Concentrating on the road, he said, "Look, Angie, I know you meant well, but I was planning on working this weekend. It's a good time to catch up on the paperwork."

"But you're still getting over being injured. You need to rest, not push yourself. We can go away and try to forget about death and cooks and restaurant murders for two days. Just be together." And in love, she wanted to add, like before, like the one time you told me you loved me.

She leaned closer and ran her cool fingers along the side of his hair, lightly brushing against his ear, then settled them along the back of his neck. An electrifying reaction shot through him and settled somewhere below the seat belt.

He drew in a shuddering breath. "I'm fine."

"Fine enough to spend the weekend at a beautiful house in Bodega Bay?"

"I'm too busy."

"Can we at least have this evening together? Dinner, perhaps? Is that too much time for you to spend with me?" She smiled, but he heard the slight catch in her voice.

Her fingertip traced his hairline. The rose-petal perfume on her wrists smelled stronger now. Roses would always remind him of Angie. He glanced at her. He liked the subtle brown and gray blend of shadow on her eyelids, the winged effect of her brows, even the mascara that made her already thick and long lashes look more so. He could get hopelessly lost in her large Mediterranean eyes.

"I've got to work tonight as well."

"Do you?"

His hands tightened on the wheel. She was sexy, flirtatious, and could be maddeningly coy, like now. But he also knew she loved him—or thought she did. For the moment at least. She'd get over it. "I'm sorry," he said softly.

The realization that he felt sorry for her stung more than she wanted to admit. She blinked back tears. There had to be another woman. He was sorry that she'd be alone and miserable while he was . . . she shut her eyes against the vision of him and Nona in bed, twisted in those disgusting black satin sheets Nona found so sexy. And heaven only knew what kind of Frederick's of Hollywood negligee Nona would—

"Stop the car!" she shouted, twisting around to look out the passenger side window. They were in the right neighborhood. *Yes!*

He slammed on the brakes, causing the car behind him to do the same. "What is it?"

"I need to buy something." She could scarcely hide her smile.

"What?"

"Even though we're not going to Bodega"—she gave him a look she hoped was filled with innocence—"I don't want this trip downtown to be a complete waste of time."

"Look, it's impossible to find parking around here. Your car could be towed."

"They wouldn't dare." She raised her nose. "My father's good friend owns the city's towing service."

He shook his head. Around the block, he saw a couple of cops sitting in a squad car in a legal parking place. He pulled up beside them, lowered Angie's window, and, leaning close to her, flashed his badge at the officers. "You leaving here soon?" he asked.

"Right now, Inspector," the driver answered. Then, eyeing the Ferrari, he asked, "Is this a remake of *Miami Vice* or what?"

Paavo didn't say a word but simply backed up a bit to give the squad car room to pull out, then parked.

"This will just take a minute. Come on," Angie said as she leaped from the car.

He took a deep breath before following her. They walked along at a good clip—he was a fast walker—and they were almost past Le Peignoir when Angie grabbed the sleeve of his jacket and pulled him into the shop and right up to the counter.

"Oh, my God," he whispered. She watched his chin sag as he realized he was surrounded by women's silk, satin, and lace underwear. He glanced at the left wall and moved back one step. On it were displays of underpants, dozens upon dozens in white, black, paisley, floral, and every color and pattern in between. High-cut, bikini-cut, flutter-cut, and some string versions that were so skimpy they might have been called no-cut. He turned his head to the right to see rows and rows of bras. All around him were racks of teddies, camisoles, negligees, dressing gowns, robes, and on and on until Paavo appeared dizzy from looking at them all.

The shop reeked of floral sachets. The scent of dried flowers mingled with the air so thickly they could almost taste it. Paavo turned a little green.

"I love this store," Angie announced as she lifted a lacy see-through bra and ran it against her hand. "I buy all my underwear here."

His frantic gaze told her he'd noticed.

"Look at this." She picked up a white satin garter belt, held it up to look at it, then lowered it to her hips. His eyes followed. She turned to face him, still pressing the garter belt against her. "These are so much sexier than pantyhose, don't you think?"

"Ah, well." His voice seemed to catch.

A pretty young saleswoman came by, looking from one to the other. "Would you like some help?"

"You have my size on file. Angelina Amalfi. I think I'll take one of these." Angie handed her the garter belt. "My friend, Inspector Smith here, has no opinion. But he's in Homicide, so I guess he only knows about *dead* bodies."

The saleswoman looked with interest at Paavo, then smiled broadly. Angie saw the color drain completely from his face. She almost felt guilty.

"Actually," she continued. "I really came in here to pick out something especially pretty to wear to bed. A black negligee, I think. Or maybe a red one. Hip length. In case I go away for the weekend."

"Miss Amalfi," Paavo said, "I think it's time you tell the lady the truth."

Angie glanced up at him. He'd spoken the words in a voice too full of glee at his own cleverness. She held her breath. One shoe had dropped. The next was poised for a fall. "The truth?" she asked.

"That she needn't bother to fill your request. In fact, she may as well throw away your file. You know San Quentin has standard issue for its prisoners." He pulled out his badge and showed it to the shocked saleswoman. "She's right. As you see, I am in Homicide. And now that I've caught up with her, she's under arrest."

"He's joking!" Angie squawked.

"It was so nice meeting you," he said to the saleslady as his grip locked on Angie's arm. The saleslady's shocked expression leaped from him to Angie, then she turned and ran into the back room of the store.

Angie got in the car beside Paavo. He could almost see steam pouring from her ears after being embarrassed in one of her favorite shops. And the damned part was, she'd managed to make him feel guilty about it even though every part of him knew he'd been justifiably provoked.

The car seemed even smaller than it had on the trip over here, and he knew why. She knew exactly what she was doing in dragging him into that high-priced boudoir. His thoughts were on her and how those damned frilly pieces would look and feel—how she'd look and feel with them on—and how he'd feel taking them off her. Damn woman. It wasn't right she should get under his skin this way. Clever and manipulative—wasn't that what Calderon and Yosh and Rebecca all said about her? And those were the *good* things.

They were probably right. What did he know about women anyway? *Turkey,* Calderon had called him. Well, at least he was aptly named.

In silence, he drove back to the Hall of Justice and pulled Angie's car into the parking lot near his own. He was ready to open the door and get out when she turned to him. "Paavo, why don't we talk?"

He folded his hands, staring out the windshield instead of looking at her. "No. It's no good, Angie. Everybody knows it. It's time we faced it too."

"Because of Nona?"

"No, damn it! I don't even *like* the woman. It's because of you and me and how different we are."

"I don't care."

"But I do care." Saying that, he got out of the car. He glanced back at her and saw her eyes glisten with unshed tears. Quickly, he hurried toward his small Austin. He heard the roar of the Ferrari's engine and didn't even turn around as Angie drove away.

*   *   *

"I don't know what to do, Papa," Paavo said, look-ing at the small white-haired man seated across the wooden table from him. Aulis Kokkonen, born in Finland, had left for the West during the 1950s. He traveled to San Francisco, where he found a job work-ing for a carpenter.

Paavo always felt Aulis would have done a lot better for himself in this country if Paavo's mother had not dropped him and his sister off at Aulis's apartment one day and never come back for them. Aulis had raised them from that day on and always said he never regretted it for a moment.

"If Angie says she loves you, son, why not believe her? Why not give her, and yourself, a chance at happiness?"

Paavo stood and rubbed the back of his neck. "She doesn't know what it means. Everything comes too easy to her, even love. How can I believe she'll feel the same way in a year? Hell, in a month? Breaking it off now is probably the best thing I can do for her."

Aulis's turquoise eyes studied the proud man his ragged little boy had become. He, more than anyone else, understood where Paavo's reserve came from and why he feared so much to open his heart. He still remembered how, years ago, four-year-old Paavo had sat by Aulis's apartment door day after day, his jacket in his hand, insisting that his mother would come back to get him. Jessica had never waited for their mother's return. She was only nine but already much too wise about the harsh side of the world. She never expected anything from it.

Then, one day, Paavo stopped talking about his mother, stopped asking about her. That day, Aulis realized, Paavo had decided not to put his faith in anyone anymore. It took years for Aulis to get Paavo to trust even him. The only person Paavo truly loved was Jessica. And then she died.

Aulis put his hand on Paavo's shoulder. "There are no guarantees. But sometimes you have to put your heart at risk. Only you can decide if she's worth it."

"That's not the point."

"What is, then? You worry, I think, that you'll just be together a short while. That what you have now won't continue for eternity. But tell me, do you wish Jessica had never lived at all? Because if she hadn't, you wouldn't have had to lose her, either."

"Of course I don't feel that way." Paavo ran his fingers through his hair. After Jessie's death, it had taken nearly ten years for the nightmares to stop, the visions of Jessie as she'd been at age nineteen, laughing and beautiful, going on a date with a strange man, a man he'd never seen before, a man with small brown penetrating eyes and a large black beetlelike mole on the side of his face, a man whose hand lingered a little too long on Paavo's hair as he ruffled it when they met. Then Paavo's uneasiness when Jessie didn't return that night, his search for her and, finally, finding her dead from an overdose of heroin. "She died and, much as I wish I could have done something to stop it, there was nothing. This is different. I've got control. But I'm not sure what I should do."

16

Straight through the weekend, Paavo and Rebecca worked together on the books for Wielund's and Italian Seasons. They didn't find a single thing in the Italian Seasons accounts, but Wielund's were another story.

"Look at this, Rebecca," Paavo said. "I may have finally found something. Look at this increase in money going into Wielund's personal account. Where does it come from?"

"It isn't coming from the restaurant, that's for sure." Rebecca scooted her chair closer to his to study the figures Paavo had before him. "In fact, look at this: a couple of weeks after money goes into his personal account, his restaurant shows a profit at the same time as his personal account takes a dip."

"So what's going on?"

"He's moving money into the business—laundering it, perhaps, by running it through his operation. Who knows where it's coming from? But when you look at all he's buying for the restaurant, it's pretty clear where it's going. He might not, in fact, be laundering it at all. It might be that to run a top-notch restaurant and make it big in this town, it simply takes this much time and this much money."

They turned their heads back to the books, watching carefully for that money, and in time a pattern developed. For the past three months, a ten-thousand-dollar increase would show up briefly in Wielund's personal account; then, a week later, his business would have an upsurge in receipts. But only one week out of the month did he do so well, and that week was always the week after money went into and then out of his personal account. The amount wasn't huge but it was steady.

Nothing at all was unusual in Chick Marcuccio's books.

On Monday, Paavo and Yoshiwara talked again to Never-Take-a-Chance Bill, reminding him that he'd been the lead inspector in the Sheila Danning murder investigation. Her death could be the key, but the man remembered far less than Rebecca did about the case. According to Bill, if witnesses and friends could be believed, the woman had been such a loner she must have raped and strangled herself.

So far, every one of the restaurant owners, workers, and chefs that Paavo and Yosh talked to had an alibi for the hours when the midday murders of Wielund and Greuber took place, and almost none had an alibi for the early morning murder of Marcuccio. There had to be some fact he was overlooking. What could be the connection between the death of a porno actress, Wielund's pictures, and those two restaurateurs?

It didn't take Paavo long to realize that Never-Take-a-Chance had done a piss-poor job of investigating Danning's death. Paavo and Rebecca would have to start over.

First, Paavo looked over Danning's birth records, then contacted the authorities in Tacoma to ask if they could find out anything about her life there that might connect her to the murders taking place here now.

The police in her hometown, fortunately, had done a thorough job investigating her background at the time of her death. Family, school friends, employers, old boyfriends—the picture that emerged was of a wild, ambitious girl with above-average looks and below-average brain power, who wanted to make her mark in the world if it killed her. And it did.

Her life had become a blank after she moved to San Francisco. Paavo and Rebecca went to Danning's rooming house to interview the landlady who had reported Danning missing. Danning had been found in the morgue and, with no fingerprints on file, had been listed as a Jane Doe.

The landlady remembered that Sheila received many phone calls, but she never had visitors. At times, though, the landlady did notice that Miss Danning would get a ride home from a man in a big blue car.

Karl Wielund had owned a big blue Lexus.

Paavo and Rebecca went to Dupries's restaurant once more to talk to the other cocktail waitresses.

Tiffany Carson said Sheila's main interest was to make it big in movies, and she seemed willing to do anything to get a break. And she did mean anything.

She was quite sure Sheila would willingly make sleazy pictures if she thought it would help her career. Once, Tiffany had invited Sheila to a party because she felt sorry for her not having any friends, but she never asked her again.

"Why was that?" Paavo asked.

"I don't like to talk badly about the dead, but I'll make an exception here. We went to the party, as I said. We weren't there ten minutes when a good-looking fellow who said he was writing a movie screenplay asked her to dance. Now, I know this fellow. He's been working on the same screenplay for six years and doesn't have a chance in hell of selling it. It's awful! Of course, Sheila didn't know that. From what I could see, they didn't even finish the dance but went into the bathroom—together. Well, that didn't leave anything to my imagination. I'm a liberated live-and-let-live woman, but that was a little too much for me. So I never invited her to anything else. Never felt sorry for her again, either."

Paavo took the name of the ersatz screenwriter, Jared Albright, and went to pay him a visit.

Albright lived in a small apartment on Twin Peaks. He remembered Sheila Danning, all right, and wasn't surprised she'd been murdered. "She lived on the edge. I dated her a couple of times, but after the second date she asked for money. I thought she did what she did because she liked me. She laughed and said she didn't think anyone living in this town could still be so naïve. I gave her some money and never saw her again. Last I heard she was having a torrid affair with her boss."

"Her boss?" Rebecca asked. "Don't you mean Karl Wielund?"

"No, her boss. Albert Dupries."

*   *   *

"Henry," Angie said, after their lunchtime show ended and they were in the studio putting things away until the next day.

"Yes?"

"I've been thinking about how much you know about food and its preparation." What she didn't say was that the restaurant world was abuzz with the news that Mark Dustman had gone to work at LaTour's.

Henry glanced smugly at her. "Oh, really? That's very complimentary of you, Angie. Yes, I do have quite a store of knowledge. But then, look at how white my hair is. Had to learn something in all those years."

"I can't help but wonder if having a restaurant isn't the key to learning so much."

"You want to buy a restaurant?"

"Maybe someday. But for now I wouldn't mind working in one." Especially one with a fine chef like Mark Dustman, she thought, but didn't dare say. After all, Dustman had worked with Wielund; Chick went to see Henry the day he was killed, and now Chick was dead. Perhaps from inside the kitchen she could learn what was behind all this. Once, a lifetime ago, she would have relied on Paavo to figure out who killed Chick. But no more. The mere thought of Paavo made her heart contract. She had to focus her attention, her energy, on finding Chick's killer.

"It's hard work, believe me," Henry said.

"How about as an apprentice for a little while? For you, Henry. I wouldn't expect you to pay me anything. Just let me come into the restaurant's kitchen from time to time and soak in the knowledge and atmosphere that surrounds you and Mark Dustman. I'll chop, clean vegetables, even wash dishes if it'd help."

"That's very flattering, Angie, but surely that's not the sort of thing for a young woman like you to want to get involved in."

"I certainly would. All the best chefs in Europe have apprentices, don't they?"

"I don't know."

"Well, whatever. Let's try it for a day or two, okay? If it doesn't work out—well, that'll end it. Is it a deal?"

"If you really want to."

She smiled and quickly turned around so he wouldn't see her face. Angie was sure the restaurants were a factor in the murders of Karl Wielund and Chick Marcuccio. And she was going to find out why.

Another week dragged by. Paavo and Yosh spent hours talking to Chick Marcuccio's friends and associates, just as they had previously spent hours talking to Hank Greuber's and Karl Wielund's.

Wielund was egotistical, secretive, greedy, ambitious, a womanizer, and he had a nasty streak besides. Everyone hated him. Although Dustman said he liked him, he seemed more upset by the closing of the restaurant than by Wielund's death.

Marcuccio was clever, hard-nosed when necessary, but fair, and everyone loved him. He was divorced, and his girlfriend was a food editor who'd commissioned an article on Wielund. Nona, who wrote the article, might play the femme fatale, but she was sharp and shrewd. If Wielund had been involved in something weird, she'd probably have noticed.

Greuber was retired, cranky, and a busybody. Everyone said he probably stuck his nose where it didn't belong and got himself killed. They were surprised it hadn't happened years earlier.

Paavo had passed the name of the porno studio Angie had visited to the Berkeley Police Department, but that too was a dead end. The Berkeley PD announced the place made legitimate dirty movies. There was no crime against that activity. At least, not in Berkeley.

The studio's owner, Axel Klaw, admitted that Danning's photos were taken at his studio but said she was known to them by her professional name: Sharon Sharalike. He didn't know her real name and didn't know she was dead. No way to prove otherwise.

Paavo asked the Berkeley PD to keep an eye on the place anyway—especially if a certain small, mischievous, brown-haired woman driving a white Ferrari showed up. He could tell by the silence on the phone that the officer thought he'd taken leave of his senses, but then, that man hadn't met Angie.

17

Mark Dustman pulled tin after tin of canned food off the shelves in LaTour's kitchen and tossed them into the industrial-size garbage can beside him.

"Excuse me." Paavo stepped through the side alleyway door that led straight into the kitchen. Yosh followed behind him.

Dustman spun around, peas in one hand and canned peaches in the other. "I didn't hear you. Look at this! Cans! How does the man expect to serve quality food with inferior ingredients? This is totally unacceptable!" He dumped the cans into the trash along with all the others.

"Where is everyone?" Yosh asked, walking around the big kitchen.

"We're closed Tuesdays. I just came in to get the stock in some kind of order. I guess Henry did his own buying, but he let his pocketbook get in the way of his menu."

Locks of sandy brown hair fell on Dustman's forehead, and he flicked it back, off his face. In marked contrast to his demeanor just a few short weeks ago, he looked calm, at peace with himself and the world despite Henry's cheap food.

"Good of you to take the time to see us today, Mr. Dustman," Yosh said. "We appreciate it, we really do."

"I always have time to help find whoever killed Karl. You do still think he was murdered?"

"We know he was murdered, Mr. Dustman," Paavo replied.

"Call me Mark, please. It's such a terrible thing. I keep wishing someone would figure out that it was a mistake, but now, with Chick dead too, I guess that'll never happen. Has there ever been a serial killer of cooks before?"

"There's no indication of a serial killer yet," Paavo answered.

"Well, leave it to San Francisco to come up with another first." Dustman glanced at the rows of canned foods on the shelf. "Do you mind if I continue working? I've got to get rid of these abominations and restock if we're ever to be a competitive restaurant."

"Sure," Yosh replied. "Can I help?"

Dustman chuckled. "I doubt it." He got on a stepladder to reach the highest shelf. He pulled down a dusty can of chopped black olives and made a hook shot right into the garbage can. "Two points."

"Can you tell us," Paavo began, "when you last saw Mr. Marcuccio?"

Dustman stopped rummaging. "I wasn't expecting any questions about him. I hardly knew the man. Let me think. I guess it was at Karl's funeral service."

"Do you know how well he and Mr. Wielund knew each other?" Paavo asked.

"They were on friendly terms but had little interaction."

"What about Mr. Wielund's assistant, Mrs. Powell? Did she know Mr. Marcuccio very well?" Paavo continued.

"Eileen Powell had the title of assistant manager, but she was really a glorified secretary. I doubt if she knew Marcuccio well enough to do more than say hello."

"Why would a secretary be sent to Paris on a buying trip?" Paavo asked.

Dustman shugged. "Her competence was more in her own mind than Karl's, but she has an eye for what's popular and for what sells in this country. Also, of the three of us, she was the most expendable. Naturally, Karl sent her to Paris. Not to buy, though, just to look." He said this with an air of hauteur that exaggerated his own importance and diminished Eileen Powell's. He seemed to have gotten over the trauma of Wielund's death quickly enough, Paavo thought.

"Did she keep the restaurant's books?"

"Karl did his own bookkeeping."

"Did he ever have a partner?"

"Not that I know."

"Did anyone ever want to go into partnership with him?" Yosh asked.

"Well, I heard once that Greg McAndrews, who owns Arbuckle's, suggested some kind of partnership. German seafood? I have no idea. Anyway, Karl told him in no uncertain terms that he was nuts. McAndrews never forgave him." Dustman looked from one inspector to the other.

Paavo took the next stab in the dark. "How long did you work for Wielund?"

"About nine months."

"That isn't very long, considering how well you say you know him."

"As I've mentioned, I met him in Paris. Here, when Karl first started the restaurant, he did his own cooking. He was a master chef, you know."

"You've mentioned that, too."

"He was the most superb cook. I learned so much from that man."

"Didn't Wielund's grow popular awfully fast?" Yosh asked.

"That's the way it is in this business. Either you make it right away, attracting customers and at least breaking even for a while and then starting to build a profit, or, in most cases, you simply die on the vine and fall off without ever making a splash. If you're lucky, like LaTour's, instead of dying off because you've got a lousy restaurant, you can keep going by doing radio shows and plagiarizing cookbooks, just to keep your name in the public eye. Of course, no one goes to LaTour's more than once. Things will change soon, though. I'm in charge of this kitchen."

"I thought you'd wanted to keep Wielund's open?" Paavo asked.

"I did. I should have. But Karl's family wouldn't cooperate, the fools. I have the last laugh, though, because without me the place is worthless."

"Why did you choose to work at LaTour's?" Yosh asked.

"I wanted a job where I could run things my way. I can do that here, since Henry LaTour is a lousy cook and he knows it."

A female voice rang out from the doorway. "Isn't that a little harsh, Mark?"

Paavo felt his blood pound. Angie. It'd been ten days, fifteen hours, and approximately forty-five minutes since he'd last seen her. Not that he missed her. Not that he wondered every day and night what she'd been doing, or if she'd been doing anything with anyone in particular. He turned slowly. She was wearing a jaunty white pants suit with a nautical look. The gold buttons and braiding on the double-breasted waist-length jacket caused him to notice that she filled out the jacket in a way sailors never did. Her short hair was a tumble of curls today, falling onto her forehead and framing her face. They made her lashes seem longer than usual, her eyes wider and more shiny. He'd somehow forgotten how small and straight her nose was, and how her top lip had a deep dip in the center between two peaks, and how the fullness of the bottom made it easy for her to look like a child when she pouted, which she tended to do with some regularity, at least around him.

She ignored him now, though, and kept her attention on Dustman as he crossed the room toward her, his arms outstretched. "What a surprise! I didn't think you meant it when you said you'd come by to help." He gave her a hug. Paavo's teeth ground watching them, and a volcanic swelling in his chest told him this wasn't something he could put up with for long. Luckily, they broke it off soon, and Dustman turned to face the inspectors, his arm still around Angie's shoulders.

Dustman? Could she be seeing Dustman? If she said she'd come by to help him, this wasn't a chance meeting. They'd met before, talked, or more. Suddenly, he was seized with a desire to grab Dustman's hand, which was holding Angie's shoulder a little too snugly, a little too possessively, and make sure LaTour's new chef didn't ever lift anything again, not even a soup-spoon.

"I'm being quizzed here by two of San Francisco's finest," Mark explained. "But of course you already know them."

"I do," Angie said, "although I haven't seen them in a *very long time.* How have you been, Inspector Yoshiwara?" She held out her hand.

Yoshiwara glanced at the set expression on his partner's face and then shook Angie's hand. "Fine, thanks," Yosh said. "Yourself?"

She stepped back, and Dustman again took her in the circle of his arm. "Just ducky," she replied. "And you, Inspector Smith? How have you been?" She raised her brows ever so superciliously as she gazed at him.

He had the sudden urge to wipe Angie's smile off her face. "Never better," he replied. He should have felt satisfaction at seeing her cheeks pale and her brown eyes dim. He didn't.

Yosh's head swiveled from Angie to Paavo; then he moved closer to the refrigerators, as if he feared being in the line of fire.

"Gentlemen, I must tell you, this is the best little restaurant critic in the country," Dustman said to the detectives. "She was the first to give Wielund's the recognition it deserved in a wonderful newspaper article about us. I still have it on the wall of my den, Angie."

"I didn't know I was your *first,* Mark." Her voice was filled with innuendo as she leaned closer to him.

Paavo's teeth clenched.

"I'd always loved Weilund's," she said, with a radiant smile that lit up her face and also Paavo's heart—except that the smile was directed at Dustman. "I might even give some thought to buying it myself. Would you want to share it with me, Mark?"

Dustman smiled and gave her another hug. "Oh, Angie! Would I ever!"

Slowly raising her long lashes to look into Dustman's eyes, she asked, "Am I interrupting anything?" Paavo swallowed hard, remembering how she used to give *him* those looks.

A slow, lazy smile creased Dustman's face. No grown man should have dimples, Paavo thought uncharitably. "No. I don't have anything new to say. I think we're done. Am I right, gentlemen?" It was a smooth hustle out the door.

"I guess so," Yosh said. "If we think of anything more, we'll give you a call."

"Very good. Good day."

Yosh started toward the door. Paavo turned abruptly and followed.

"If you need to ask me anything about Karl or Chick," Angie called, "I'll probably be here for many, *many* hours."

Paavo's step faltered. His jaw tightened as he gazed straight ahead. But then he saw, reflected against the blackened glass of the kitchen doors, Angie and Dustman behind him. They were watching him, not each other. Angie stuck her elbow in Dustman's ribs, and he nodded and put his arms around her waist.

A ruse? Was that what this was? Was Angie purposely torturing him, making him think she had something going with Dustman just so he would suffer, so he would realize he still cared about her enough that he'd feel jealous? The volcano that smoldered when he first saw her with Dustman began rumbling again. He glanced over his shoulder to see Mark beaming down at her like the fox who's just had a chicken walk into his den.

"Fine," Mark said softly. "I've got lots of ideas for filling time."

"Paav." Yosh put his hand on Paavo's shoulder, trying to nudge him to continue out the door.

He saw Angie quickly jerk her head toward Dustman. "We *do* have to work, though."

Dustman pulled her close. The front of their bodies were plastered together, while his hands started sliding lower than her waist. That did it!

Yoshiwara's hand dropped as Paavo took slow, deliberate steps toward the couple. Angie took one look at the expression on his face, dropped her arms from Dustman, and backed up. "Now, Paavo."

"Playtime is over, Miss Amalfi." He came closer. "Time to go home and let this man get on with his work."

"Playtime! I'll have you know we need to discuss some important business."

"Let's go." He tried to take hold of her arm, but she pulled it away. His anger, which he'd always managed to contain, was at the boiling point. "Business deals over murdered men can put that sassy little butt of yours in a ringer."

"What! That's a horrid thing to say!"

Seeing her hands on her hips and her pert nose going once more into the air drove him right over the top. He grabbed her wrist and started to pull her out the door.

"You're going home."

"Home? Stop! This is harassment! Police brutality!"

"Wait! What's going on?" Dustman called, but Paavo ignored him and stomped out the door, dragging Angie behind him.

"He's a psychopath," she yelled. "A real life Hannibal Lecter. Don't let him—"

The door banged shut behind her. Mark Dustman didn't come running to save her virtue or anything else.

Yosh followed them out the door. Paavo let go of a still-shrieking Angie once they reached the sidewalk. "I think I'll leave you two alone awhile," Yosh said.

"No need. I have nothing private to discuss with her. She just needs to clear her head about who she wants to spend her time with. And it's not with murder suspects!" Paavo glared at her.

She got right in his face. "It's not with meddling cops either, Inspector!"

He was beside himself. "I'm not the only one who's meddling around here, Miss Amalfi!"

"Excuse me," Yosh interjected. "I think it's time I got going."

"Good-bye already!" Angie said, her eyes never leaving Paavo's.

He glared back, his lips a grim line. Neither noticed Yoshiwara's departure.

"He's telling the restaurateurs it's over between us." She spat the words at him.

"I told you myself. You wouldn't listen."

"I guess I should have realized, after your dinner with Nona at Arbuckle's, and then going to La Maison Rouge with a lady detective—"

"Who's the detective around here, Miss Amalfi? I think you should take over."

"I only hear about these things because mine is a small world, Inspector, and your case has landed smack in the middle of it. I'll try not to meddle any longer. Good-bye."

He watched her march away from him on her high heels, head up, shoulders square, backside swinging, and felt his stomach tighten. It was all he could do not to go after her. A vision flashed before him of her with Mark Dustman leering down at her with his arm around her.

"Angie!"

She stopped and looked over her shoulder at him. "Yes?"

He stared at her a long while. "Those times with the women you mentioned."

"Yes?"

"They were for business reasons. For my work."

"Work, Inspector? Or were you just hiding from life?"

He stepped toward her, but she turned and walked away.

*   *   *

Angie splashed herself liberally with perfume and put on a slinky black satin jumpsuit with a long past-the-navel gold zipper. It was eight o'clock.

If she knew Paavo at all, if he really cared about her at all, he'd come by to see her tonight. If he could stay away after this afternoon, if he didn't care enough to try to patch up this San Andreas fault–size rift between them, it was truly over.

She put Wagner's *Tristan and Isolde* on the stereo. The long, sad, emotional opera about star-crossed lovers suited her mood perfectly.

At eleven, she made a fresh pot of coffee. Paavo would probably need it, if he showed up.

What would she do if he didn't stop by? How could she ever let go?

But if he didn't still care about her, he wouldn't have acted like Cave Man Clyde at Wielund's today. He cared. He had to.

By midnight, she knew she'd been wrong.

She removed the sexy jumpsuit and changed into her comfortable old football jersey nightshirt and washed off her make-up. She shut off the lights, got into bed, and stared at the ceiling.

At 12:30 A.M. she got up again, made herself a cup of warm milk, and took it back to her bedroom along with a book about San Francisco's rough Barbary Coast during the 1880s and 1890s, when people were shanghaied right off the city streets. All in all, it sounded like child's play compared to these days.

She put the milk and the book on her nightstand, got into bed, then sat back against the pillows. Her head bumped the wooden headboard. She got out of bed, plumped and turned the pillows on their ends so they stood upright against the headboard, and got into bed again. Comfort. She reached for her book and milk, and the pillows fell over. When she sat back, her spine rapped the headboard sharply.

She leaned forward, knees bent, and wrapped her arms around her legs. It took all her strength not to cry.

At one o'clock in the morning, the knock she'd waited for all evening sounded. She sprang up and fairly floated to the door. There was no reason to feel happy, she warned herself. He might be coming by to quiz her about Mark Dustman, for all she knew. Still, the spring in her step was unmistakable.

He stood there with his sports jacket unbuttoned, his tie and shirt collar loose, looking more weary than a human being should. But his blue eyes brightened as they took her in, and the granite-hard look he wore so often eased. She stared at him, afraid she might, as she did so often, say the wrong thing and drive him away again. So she said nothing.

He leaned one hand against the door frame. "I know it's late."

"Come in." She let go of the door and stepped back, letting him enter the apartment. He seemed to fill the room, and to fill the emptiness she felt inside.

He walked in, and the uncertain pause in his steps made her catch her breath. She had never known Paavo to be unsure. What were they doing to each other? Why were they wasting so much time?

"Coffee?" she asked, standing before him. "Or maybe you're hungry? Would you like a sandwich? An omelet, maybe?" She bit her bottom lip. "I could see what I've got. Or we can call out. Pizza, maybe? Or Chinese?"

"I'm not hungry."

"Oh . . . Well, do you want to wait a moment? I know I look a sight."

As she turned to go to the bedroom and put on something more enticing, he stepped closer to her, putting his hand on her chin and lifting her face to see it better. "You look fine."

She trembled at his touch, her body suddenly alive. "Fine?" She tried to sound casual. "Little old ladies look 'fine,' Paavo!" Her voice was breathless.

He dropped his hand and gave a slight smile. "I'm not staying. I just stopped by to make sure you were all right."

She sat down on the Hepplewhite. "Have a seat, please."

He sat on the sofa. "Neither one of us was exactly on our best behavior this afternoon."

She steepled her hands, then pressed them to her lips. "I can't imagine what your new partner must think of me! I pray I never see him again."

Paavo grinned. "Actually, he was quite impressed with your lung power. He said he hadn't heard anything that loud since a Grateful Dead concert at the Oakland Coliseum."

She covered her face with her hands. "Oh, God."

He put his hand on her knee. "It's all right."

Her breath caught. Her skin felt seared, as if his hand were a branding iron. As she glanced up, their gazes met.

He pulled back his hand and stood. "I should go."

She stood and nodded.

"Hiding from life, hmm?" he said, repeating the charge she'd hurled at him that afternoon; then he walked toward the door.

She took his hand, stopping him. "Yes, until you learn to trust someone besides Aulis."

She could see him bristle. "I've trusted other people," he said.

"Oh? Who?"

"Matt."

His partner, who had been killed. "And?"

"My sister."

Who had also been killed. "And?"

Blue eyes hardened. "That's enough."

Her heart ached for him. "No, Paavo. It isn't."

"You?"

There was a pause. Angie's eyes felt shadowed, and she spoke softly. "No. I know you don't trust me."

He took his hand away, his eyes cold. "I know what you expect me to say, but I'm sorry, I can't do it. I don't trust a father I never knew or a mother who walked out on me. If that means I don't trust much, it's true. But I've got good reason."

"Maybe you could find them. There might have been a reason they left. Then you could forgive and—"

"Hell, Angie! Stop dreaming. The bastard never even married my mother. I know it." He gave a derisive snort. "And well I should, considering I just called *him* what he made *me*." He looked hard at her, then cupped her chin. "Don't let it upset you, Angie. It was a long time ago. They're probably both dead by now. They have nothing to do with this—with you and me."

"What does, then? Why must I always be saying good-bye to you?"

Because everyone says it's best, he wanted to shout, *including your own father! And, damn it, because I know they're right!*

But when he looked down at her, saw the glimmer of tears in her eyes, he couldn't say it. He touched the sides of her face, then moved closer. "I don't want to hurt you, Angie. Believe me. All I ever wanted was to do right by you. Logically, rationally right."

Her arms circled his shoulders as she looked up at him. "Don't you know love doesn't work that way?"

"Good Christ, woman!"

"Don't!" She pressed her fingers to his lips. The heat of her hand, the silken softness of her fingers, burned where she touched him. He stayed absolutely still, knowing that to move would be to lose all his resolve.

She felt his warm breath on her hand, felt the firm but smooth skin of his lips, edged by the bristle of tiny whiskers just appearing above his upper lip and on his chin. Her hands quivered as her breath caught. Ever so lightly she moved her fingers along the outline of his lips, memorizing their shape and form and feel, as if she were blind and would never be able to touch him this way again.

His mouth opened, as she traced along the inner edge of his bottom lip.

His mouth was pinched with terse lines, the skin below his lower eyelids dark and hollow, his broad high brow lined with tension. Slowly her gaze met his, and in his eyes she saw the full ache of his longing and of his loneliness.

"Hold me," she whispered.

Grasping her shoulders, with a delicate pressure he drew her closer. When her face lifted to his, he lowered his lips, meeting hers in a kiss that held all the love he would never speak of.

The kiss deepened. With long, slow, deliberate pressure, his hands moved to her back, then lower, over her waist, her hips. Wherever he touched, she came alive, each nerve end singing. She gripped his shoulders as need rocked her.

He picked her up as easily as if she were a doll and carried her to her bed. There he tossed her football jersey onto the floor. Shucking his own clothing, he lay beside her. She raised her arms to circle his neck, but instead of moving closer to her, he took a moment to stay back and simply look at her. He ran his forefinger lightly over her dark brows, her small nose, along the edges of her generous lips, then over to her ears until she smiled from the tickles. Then his hand traveled downward, over her breasts, her small waist, wide hips, and, lower still, to her dark, inviting warmth. As much as he'd tried to break away from her these past days, seeing her with another man, even though they meant nothing to each other, made him realize how he'd feel if he lost her, how much she meant to him and always would.

To have her here, now, was suddenly more important than any plans or wishes for a future that might never be.

Before dawn, she awoke to find the back of her body pressed against the front of Paavo's, the two of them fitted side by side like soupspoons in a drawer. The problem had to do with commitment, it seemed.

But she wouldn't let herself dwell on that, she decided, snuggling closer. He was here now.

His hand cupped her breast. "You move against me like that one more time, and you'll get more than you bargained for."

"How do you know what I bargained for, Inspector?" She wriggled again.

"Is that a dare?"

She rolled onto her back, her eyelids heavy with sleep, her lips still puffy from his kisses. Then she gave a long, languorous, full-body stretch, just the way a cat might while lying in the warm sun. He waited impatiently for her answer, his body heat rising with every seductive move she made.

"What happens if I lose the dare?" she asked.

He kissed her shoulder, her chest, her breast. "I make love to you."

"What happens if you lose?"

His kisses continued to her ribs, her waist, her belly. "Same thing."

"I like your rules, Inspector."

Paavo was quiet when they finally got out of bed, but she hadn't expected him to be otherwise. She looked at him in amazement when he called his office and said he wouldn't be in until after lunch. She didn't understand it, but she wasn't about to question or complain.

It didn't sound as if he'd gotten any complaint from his boss, either. Angie couldn't help but wonder if the other officers might not be glad he was staying away, if he'd been as moody and bad-tempered around them as he'd been around her.

For breakfast she made him a Belgian waffle, topped with a scoop of whipped butter and a choice of real maple syrup or homemade boysenberry jam, bacon and scrambled egg on the side, fresh-squeezed orange juice, and strong Italian roast coffee.

Paavo stepped up to the dining table after showering and then shaving with the Lady Shick she used on her legs. Luckily, she had a fresh blade for it. He looked at the feast, then glanced at her uncertainly. "Looks good enough to eat," he said, and smiled awkwardly.

Paavo rarely smiled. She knew he was uncomfortable, unsure of what last night had meant to her, to himself. "Don't let it get cold!" She tried to make her voice light, then quickly sat down, knowing he was too much of a gentleman to sit while she still stood.

He pulled out the chair across from her and busied himself with the meal. She watched him instead of eating. Time and again she'd imagined him there with her, the morning sun brightly filling the room. How did he feel? she wondered. He came last night to apologize, then to leave. Was he upset his plans had been altered, or happy? He looked up, and she quickly dropped her gaze.

"Aren't you eating?" he asked.

"I am." She grabbed the syrup and poured it on top of her waffle before she realized she'd already taken some. The waffle floated in the sticky mess.

"Angie." He reached over and squeezed her hand. "You and I both know it'd be a hell of a lot easier if when I came over last night you were with Mark

Dustman and showed me the door. But since that didn't happen, at least not yet, we'll take things slow."

"Last night wasn't slow."

"I don't mean that. I mean . . ." Blue eyes held hers, and he couldn't seem to find the words.

"Going our separate ways?"

"Exactly."

"You expect how I feel about you will slowly wither away?"

Her heart skipped several beats. Then he said, "It might."

It hurt that he still wouldn't accept the way she felt about him, but he'd spent a lifetime of having people he loved leave him, everyone but Aulis Kokkonen. She couldn't demand that he change. That would only drive him further into his shell. She had to be content, at least for now.

She ate some of her waffle, then pushed the soggy mass aside and sipped some coffee. "I'm glad I ran into you with Mark yesterday," she said brightly. "Even though you hadn't planned it that way."

"Planned it?" he replied. "I had no idea you'd been in contact with him. Or that you two had grown so chummy."

She smiled. "Don't worry. I've been working at LaTour's, and I got to know him there. He's pretty quiet, all in all. His dream is to be a master chef. When he told me you called him, we got the idea of making you a little jealous."

"Who, me?"

"More surprising things can happen, though not many. Anyway, Mark was certainly a good sport."

"He seemed quite taken with his role, if you ask me. The only problem is, we didn't get to ask him all our questions."

"He's not going anywhere." Her expression grew mischievous. "On the other hand, he might have been using me just to stop your interrogation."

"I wouldn't be surprised."

"What?"

"Just kidding, Angie." Or was he? What better way for Dustman to throw him off the track than to involve Angie? Would Dustman know that? And if so, why do it?

"Anyway," Angie said, "how did you know to find him at LaTour's? I didn't think word had gotten out yet that he was going to work there."

"Nona Farraday told me."

Her face turned white. "Nona! So you're still seeing her!"

"Not at all. She's a good source, that's all."

"Nona doesn't know anything to help your case that you couldn't find out from twenty other sources," she announced. "And in particular from me."

"She did, though."

"Hah!"

Paavo nearly laughed aloud as he thought of how irate Angie would be if she realized how much she sounded like her mother just then. "She was writing an article for *Haute Cuisine* about Wielund when he was killed. She couldn't get it published, but she showed it to me."

"But it's about cooking. It's not as if Karl was killed in an eggbeater duel. What could it tell you?"

"I'd hoped it would give some clues to his personality. But you're right. It was about cooking, and how fanatical he was about new recipes."

"Hmm, that actually sounds more interesting than most things Nona writes." She stood and began to stack their dishes. He helped carry them into the kitchen.

"Not to me, I'm afraid. I've got it out in my car if you'd like to read it."

"Sure."

"I'll go get it."

"You don't have to make a special trip." She picked up the jam and syrup and was carrying them into the kitchen, her head high, when he touched her arm, stopping her.

"You don't even realize how little there is that I *can* give you," he said softly. "When I come across something like this, let me enjoy it."

His words made her heart twist. It wasn't in her to think in such materialistic terms about the two of them, and probably never would be. The fact that he did still surprised and dismayed her. "All right," she said. "I'd like that very much."

"And don't touch those dishes! I'll be right back." He headed toward the door.

"But Paavo," she called, "all I was going to do was load them into my new Maytag." She went back into the living room to sit down.

Shortly, he returned and handed her Nona's typed, double-spaced article. While Paavo straightened the kitchen, Angie leaned back, a fresh cup of coffee on the table in front of her, and read.

When he came back into the living room, he saw her with the article on her lap, one finger lightly resting against her cheek, staring intently at the far wall. Silently, he sat down beside her and waited.

"Something's very strange here," she said eventually.

"Strange?"

"From what you know about Henry LaTour and Karl Wielund, do you think the two of them could come up with the same recipe for anything short of how to boil water?"

"No."

She rubbed her head. "It seems they did, though."

"I don't follow."

"It's here, in the article. It tells how Karl was working on a recipe for filet of lamb in puff pastry before he died. It talks about what a perfectionist he was, and how secretive. How he wouldn't let anyone see his recipes until he was completely satisfied with them. Karl never finished that particular recipe. Recently, though, Henry gave a lamb filet recipe on his radio show, and the ingredients were exactly the same as Karl's."

"Can't it be coincidence?"

"Not when two of the ingredients are Greek olives and pine nuts. Oh, my God!" Angie gasped.

"What's wrong?"

"I'll bet Chick knew!"

A strange uneasiness was on the periphery of his subconscious, as if something she had said struck a wrong note or memory, but he said calmly, "Knew what?"

She grabbed his hand. "That Henry stole Karl's recipe! Janet Knight told me Chick had read Nona's article. He'd have noticed the strange ingredients. Plus Chick always listened to Henry's show. Said it was the best comedy on radio. He heard Henry spouting Karl's recipe."

"Let's not jump to conclusions, Angie." But they were both remembering that, on the day he died, Chick went to see LaTour at his restaurant.

She covered her mouth and echoed his thought. "Chick might have confronted Henry with the theft. Oh, my God! It can't be my boss!"

"You do know how to pick 'em," he said wryly, his mind again sending up a faint alarm.

"I'll keep an eye on Henry. Observe every strange move and report to you."

Paavo nearly choked on his coffee. He remembered the last time she promised to "observe and report." She could have been killed and he nearly had been; he carried the scars to prove it. "I suggest you stay away from his restaurant, just in case."

"I'll consider keeping away from the restaurant, but I can't give up the radio show."

"I don't know, Angie. If Henry's involved—"

"But I love radio!" Then she clasped her hands, her gaze intense and her voice soft yet almost pleading. "I'm really hoping to make something of this job, you know?"

He knew. She had brains, education, money, energy, but for whatever reason had never really clicked with a job, career, or profession that she could make a go of and devote her talents to. And until that happened for her, it was yet another reason for him to be wary of involving her in a lasting relationship. When she was uncertain about everything else in her life, could he really believe her when she said she was certain about him?

His fingers tightened on his coffee cup. "I guess it'll be all right. Just make sure there are always lots of others around." At least he'd never heard of anyone being done in by a microphone.

18

Angie knew the janitor would let her in, even though she had no business being in LaTour's kitchen early in the morning before anyone else was there, and sure enough he did. She'd learned her skill with janitors after a few times of forgetting a book for a homework assignment while in high school. The janitors at St. Cecilia's were pushovers.

Henry's office was in a converted storeroom just off the kitchen. While she might not know what she was looking for, she had confidence she'd know it when she found it. The windowless room was dark. Without turning on the lights, she hurried across it.

"Good morning, Angie," Mark said, holding a large carving knife as he walked toward her from around a large cold-storage locker.

She jumped. "You're here early."

"I could say the same about you." He reached over and flicked on the lights. "What are you doing here?"

"I have a class to teach this afternoon. I thought I'd come by early and see if there were any notes about today's menu, so I'd know what I could do to help prepare the food."

"Your dedication is most commendable, Angie." His voice was coated with sarcasm. "Where's your friend the cop?"

"He's working. I don't think he'll be back for some time."

"Good. He plays a bit rough, wouldn't you say?"

She patted her hair. "Not always."

"Ah, I see." He opened the cooler and began to take out vegetables. "You can assist me today. I'm preparing breast of roast duck on a bed of julienne carrots, green peppers, and mushrooms."

"It sounds magnificent."

"Good. You can julienne the carrots."

"Cut carrots? That's all?"

Ignoring her, he opened a black leather two-inch-thick binder and began to write in it.

"Oh, is that your chef's log?" Angie asked, peering over with professional interest, but Mark gave her a suspicious glance and moved it out of her view. It seemed he was as secretive as Karl had been.

"That's right. I'm writing about today's meal, saying that you helped and what you did, so that if the meal is especially successful or causes criticism, I'll know what was different about it."

"How far back does that go?"

He made a note and closed it with finality. "About a year."

"Before you began working for Karl?"

"True. But there wasn't a lot of creativity involved

at the Purple Sandpiper. It was good basic fare, and I needed a job. I was new in San Francisco."

"Like Karl."

"Exactly. We came here from Paris together."

"So you must have known all his friends very well."

Dustman chuckled. "There weren't many to know."

"Did you know Sheila Danning?"

"Danning? Never heard of her."

Paavo was in a foul mood. Benson snickered, Calderon glared, and Rebecca looked hurt as word spread about his dragging a bellowing Angie out of Mark Dustman's clutches two days earlier. Yosh had no business writing it in his report, and Hollins had no business talking about the report loud enough for Benson to overhear it.

Everyone figured Angie had set it up so he'd catch her and Dustman together. The maddening part was, they were right.

Angie finally found a chance to assuage a bit of her curiosity—in the name of culinary professionalism—and look at Dustman's log. He went off in a huff over the poor quality of the fresh vegetables delivered to LaTour's, saying it was no wonder Henry had used canned ones, since the so-called fresh ones Henry bought were farmers' market discards. Henry insisted he'd spent good money for them, but Dustman refused to use them and refused to cook. Henry finally gave him the okay to buy whatever he wanted.

"Don't touch a thing in this kitchen!" Dustman shouted, then left.

His log sat open on his worktable. Everyone else, including Henry, had found other things to do, far from the spot where the temperamental Dustman had been, so Angie sat down to go through the log page by page, wanting to learn all she could about how a practicing cook adjusts recipes and temperatures.

She turned to the front, and suddenly the handwriting was Germanic script. She stared: Karl's! These were Karl's notes! She'd wondered what had become of them when Wielund's was closed, although she suspected Dustman or Eileen Powell must have gotten them. It would have been a shame for a bunch of lawyers to take them. They'd either overrate the log's value and lock it up, or underrate it and throw it away. Either way, the notes would be lost.

She tried to read them, but they were mostly in German, French, or a combination of both. Angie knew French but only a smattering of German. Turning the pages, she was stopped by a recipe all in English. She read it over, and her mouth was watering by the time she'd finished.

Fresh Cream Truffles

4 oz. whipping cream

1 vanilla pod

1 egg yolk

4 Tbsp. coarse granulated sugar

5 oz. Valrona chocolate, broken into bits, plus 4 oz. for coating

1 oz. unsalted butter

1 Tbsp. Grand Marnier
pure cocoa powder
1 tsp. polyunsaturated oil

Boil cream with split vanilla pod. Remove from heat
and remove pod. Beat egg yolk with sugar until thick.
Add to cream. Heat through, whisking continuously,
and being careful not to boil. Remove from heat. To
hot mixture, add 5 oz. chocolate and blend well.
Refrigerate for $1/2$-hour, until set but not hard, then
beat in softened butter and liqueur. Put into a piping
bag and pipe little balls onto plate or foil. Refrigerate
until hard (about 2 hours). Melt remaining chocolate.
Using two toothpicks, dip each truffle into the melted
chocolate, coat on all sides, then roll in cocoa powder. Refrigerate until ready to serve.
911,394.

What? She read over the end of the recipe once
more. It sounded delicious and complete, but what in
the world did the number at the bottom of the page
mean? Nine-one-one . . .
Emergency! She remembered—the films Paavo had
in his briefcase. Of course. Was it the same as one of
those numbers?
She copied down the number. Could it be another Sheila Danning film? Why would Karl write it
down on this recipe? Should someone take a look
at it?
She could tell Paavo about it, and he could tell the
Berkeley PD.
On the other hand, she probably could get back
inside the studio without much trouble. She'd done it

once and no one bothered her. It wasn't as if the place was dangerous or anything.

But then, Sheila Danning was dead. And the people at the film studio admitted knowing her.

"What do you think you're doing?"

Angie jumped a mile as Mark Dustman's voice boomed out at her. She'd been so lost in thought she hadn't even heard him come back in. "Nothing." She shut the log and stood.

Dustman's jaw twitched. "So you found my little secret."

Karl's recipes. "I don't suppose you told his family about them," she said.

"I was more like family than any of them! Besides, none of them cook."

"So it doesn't matter, then."

"Look, Angie, I need these recipes to turn this restaurant around."

"Probably so."

"These gems will give me—and Henry—a chance to make something of ourselves. Something big. Okay?" Passion blazed in his eyes.

It wasn't her business to get into this. Particularly since she could sympathize with his ardor. To a chef, recipes were creations, works of art, and Karl was a great artist, whose work might have been lost if it weren't for Mark. "I'm just glad you're keeping Karl's work alive."

He shut his eyes a moment, then turned around and gave the vegetables he'd just bought to a kitchen aide to wash.

*   *   *

Angie stood outside the plain glass door on Telegraph Avenue, the number she'd found in Wielund's notebook clasped in her hand. She looked at it one more time, memorizing it. Surely, she needn't worry about going inside again. There hadn't been anything frightening about the place. Not really. It was a legitimate business establishment, a type she'd never dealt with before but legitimate nonetheless. There was nothing for her to be frightened about. Why then was her stomach jumping maniacally?

Whiskbroom Head sat at the counter again. She shivered but kept walking toward him.

He pushed his thick glasses higher on his nose, following her every step. "Well, I didn't think I'd see you again."

"I realized the last time I was here that I didn't know what I was doing or what I was supposed to ask for. I talked to my friend some more, and now I do know."

"You know what?"

"Do you rent movies?"

"Rent them? Does this look like a Captain Video store?"

She placed her hands on the counter and gave him a heartfelt look. "My friend just loves all this stuff, you know, and he told me I should look at some films you folks have put together to learn everything I need to know."

"Where'd you say this friend found out about us?"

"I don't know. He doesn't tell me too much." She gave him a vacant grin.

The expression on the guy's face told Angie he wasn't surprised.

"You know, I was thinking," Angie continued, "maybe we can watch some of these films together."

"Together?"

She gave him what she hoped was a sly, knowing look. "Do you have someplace we could go?"

It worked, because a grin slowly spread over his bearded face. "Sure I do."

"I'd like to pick out the film, though. I've got some idea of the kind my friend wants me to see."

"So do I, baby."

"Do you have a catalog?"

"No."

"No? You just keep canisters of film lying around without knowing what's in them?"

"We've got some write-ups. And outtake photos."

"That sounds fine. I'll look at those."

"Great. Let's hang your coat here. I want you to be comfortable."

Angie quickly unbuttoned it herself this time, remembering how creepy it felt when he did it. She handed it to him and stayed far back.

He led her to a dusty back room filled with boxes of films. File boxes on a table were labeled with folders. "Here you go."

"Great." She started to look through them. They were sort of in numerical order, though someone had done a pretty sloppy filing job. She flipped through them until she found the one labeled 911,394, the number in Karl's cooking notes. She couldn't go to that one first, so she started elsewhere, randomly picking out files, opening one file after the other, all showing men and women having sex in a variety of combinations. After the initial shock, much to her surprise, the vacant emotionlessness of the photos quickly grew strangely boring.

Finally, she decided enough time had passed and picked up folder 911,394. She opened it, stared, then quickly shut the folder. Her mind refused to accept the face, the body, she'd just seen. Trying to control the sudden shaking of her hands, she pulled out one photo, turned it face down, then shoved the folder back into its spot in the file. "Thank you. I believe I'd simply like to buy this one shot. Before we watch a whole movie, I'd like to show my boyfriend and see if this is what he wants."

She left the room and started down the hall toward the desk.

"Wait a minute. We were going to watch some films together."

"I'm sorry. I've changed my mind."

He stood in front of her, blocking her path. "You don't get to just waltz in here and look at all this for free, you know. You got to pay, one way or another."

She looked him straight in the eye. "I will. For this one photo. How much?"

Whiskbroom Head glanced at her clothes and her shoes as he stroked his beard. "Two hundred bucks."

"Two hundred! That's outrageous!"

"It's a bargain. Less than a pair of shoes, even."

"Oh." She glanced at her feet. "Well, if you put it that way. Do you take plastic?"

"A personal check will be fine. I trust you." He smiled wide, the green on his teeth turning Angie's stomach.

As she filled out the check he said, "Make it out to Dwayne Cartwright."

"Wrong, Dwayne," a deep booming voice said.

Angie spun around to see a flashy-looking character: medium height, trim but muscular, somewhere in his forties. The first thing Angie noticed was his short bleached-blond hair, worn forward, Napoleon style, framing a darkly tanned face. With his scarcely buttoned shirt, turquoise and silver rings, and Indian necklace and bracelets, he looked like someone who should be on the beach in Los Angeles, not a studio in Berkeley. But then, Berkeley attracted all types.

As he approached, Angie thought he had some kind of a bug on the side of his face. When he came closer, she saw it was a large black mole.

The man smiled at Angie. "Cross off his name and make the check out to Axel Klaw, with a K."

"Oh?" She looked back at Dwayne. When she saw how pale he was and how rapidly he nodded his head, she didn't hesitate. She completed the check and handed it to Klaw, then turned to leave.

"Not so fast." Powerful fingers gripped her wrist firmly as he glanced at the name and address on her check. "Tell me, Angelina, whatever makes a sweet young thing like you interested in these eight millimeters?"

"My boyfriend—"

He released her wrist but slowly shook his head as she spoke. "Uh-uh. You aren't the type for boyfriends like that."

She blanched. "Bad taste in men, I guess." Her laugh was hollow. She stepped back from him. "I've got to go. Thank you for your help."

Klaw grabbed the picture from her.

"Hey!" she cried.

He turned it over, his eyes narrowing as he glanced from the picture to Angie. "Why this one?"

"I don't know. We looked at a bunch. I took one."

"You know her, don't you?"

The world seemed to shift. "Me? No. Should I?"

Klaw chuckled. "As a matter of fact, yes. She's become somebody now. The wife of a hotshot restaurant owner. Her name's Lacy LaTour."

Angie kept her face immobile. "Oh? Well, I never heard of her. I don't have to take that photo. Any one will do, as long as it's old. 'Oldies but Goodies,' that's what my boyfriend says. But then, he's sixty-five, so that's probably why he feels that way. I don't care myself. Any age is—"

"Shut up!" Klaw turned to Dwayne. "This the first time you've seen this broad?"

"No. She was here once before, saying she wanted to be in a movie."

"Be in a movie?" He looked her up and down, then burst out laughing. "Don't that beat all?"

"On second thought, I don't want to anymore. My boyfriend's a big fan of these movies, that's all."

"That so? And what's this boyfriend's name?"

Her mind went blank. Some big writer. Started with an S. Shakespeare? Shaw? Shelley? Sartre? What the hell had she said? "Steve," she answered.

Dwayne looked puzzled. "Wait a minute, that doesn't sound right."

Angie could have sunk through the floor. Who'd have thought a porno counterman had nothing better to do than remember her tall tales?

"You're lying," Klaw said. "All this boyfriend jazz is nothing but an excuse."

"An excuse?" Her voice was tiny. Klaw couldn't possibly know about Paavo or her restaurant background, could he?

He folded his arms. With his tan, muscular upper body and short fair hair, he looked like Mr. Clean. "You're just some rich bitch who wants a little fun. A thrill. You want to make one of these movies, but you don't have the nerve to come right out and say it. I've seen your type before. Plenty of times. And I can be *very* accommodating."

She felt herself pale. "It's not true."

Klaw laughed, then wrapped his arm around her waist and led her down the long hallway. "I know women get cold feet all the time. But looking at you, I know you got what it takes to be a star. You got class, something lacking in lots of these films. Let's see how you do on camera."

Angie couldn't even believe this man was touching her, let alone taking her anywhere. She dug in her heels. "Let go! I've changed my mind."

"So you want to get rough? I can oblige you in that, too."

She was shocked. "This is no game."

"You're good. I like the tone. You'll be great on camera. The equipment is ready and waiting for us. Freddie will take you to a set. I'll be right behind you."

Angie paid no attention to the mountain of a man who stepped her way but did get the fleeting impression of a Vegas casino bouncer. "You can't do this to me!" she yelled at Klaw.

Klaw yanked her in front of him so hard and so fast she nearly fell over. He gripped her neck with his long, hard fingers. She froze as they began to tighten.

Panic filled her as she stared into eyes as flat and devoid of feeling as those of a dead fish. She pushed hard against him, but it was like hitting a steel door. Suddenly, laughing, he relaxed his grip. She drew in deep, gasping breaths, unable to think but only to feel complete disbelief and panic.

He waited only a few seconds before he shoved his thumb under her chin and roughly lifted it, forcing her head back, her face upward. He leaned forward, his nose almost touching hers.

"I'm the director. That's like God around here. Life and death are in my hands." His fingers ran along her neck again, then dipped lower to stroke her collarbone. "So remember, I can do anything to you I damn well please."

19

Paavo knew a waste of time when it kicked him in the face, and this was a waste of time. The accounting books from Italian Seasons were spread over his desk. Leaning back in his chair, he rubbed his eyes. Clearly, Chick Marcuccio hadn't been cooking his books, and from the profits he saw coming in, Chick hadn't needed to.

His gaze moved from the accounting books to a stack of folders from files about cases that had been closed out, plus a few magazine articles. His review of the Sheila Danning case had led him into general reading about the world of pornography from both sides of the camera as well as a number of case studies from Vice, Homicide, and Missing Persons.

The women in these stories were universally so incredibly naïve he had trouble believing they were real, until he remembered that a certain miss he was close to also surprised him with her naïveté. Even the hard ones, though, the ones who grew up with abuse and drugs and sold their bodies from the time they learned they were salable, still seemed to have some hope that acting in these films could offer a way out, a way to riches or an escape to the kind of life they could only dream of. They were in it for the money, only to find that the money was hardly enough to buy the escape offered by drugs.

The male actors in these films, on the other hand, Paavo found to be a complete enigma. He couldn't begin to comprehend what kind of sickness might lead a man to perform on camera like that.

His telephone rang.

"Smith here."

"Officer McGifford, Berkeley. We just spotted aforementioned female going into building on Dwight Way. Reporting as instructed, sir."

"The woman with the Ferrari?"

"Yes, sir."

"She's there now?"

"She just walked in."

"Thank you."

Paavo hung up the phone. I'll kill her! he thought. He'd told her not to go back to that place. Did she listen to him? Did she *ever* listen to him?

He looked at the files he'd been reading and a shudder went down his back.

"She's all yours, Freddie." Klaw pushed her into the bearlike arms. She tilted her head back to see a man about her age, curly brown hair, dark eyes, wearing a white sports jacket and a red shirt open at the neck, showing off a thick gold chain. A scar across his top lip caused it to pucker at one side, as if in a perpetual sneer.

"I want to leave," she said.

Freddie really did sneer as Klaw smirked and waved his hand, telling Freddie to take her away. The big man began to lead her, but when she pulled back, he took her arm and dragged her along as if she weighed no more than a rag doll. She yelled at him to let her go, but he paid no attention.

He pushed her into the cubicle where they'd been filming the last time she'd been there and flipped on the light switch. Angie could hear the expected sounds from the other cubicles as she faced Freddie. An eight-millimeter camera stood in the center of the room, while tall spotlights pointed down at the big brass double bed.

"You've got to be joking," Angie said.

"Mr. Klaw never jokes," Freddie answered.

She was impressed he could say so many words at once without drooling. "I hate to tell you, but I get stage fright. I'm leaving."

"You can't go until Mr. Klaw says."

"Watch me."

She started toward the door.

Freddie stepped in front of her, his arms folded.

She took a side step.

So did he.

Quickly, she glanced around and saw that the back wall also had a door. She spun around and bolted toward it. Freddie ran after her.

She grabbed the doorknob just as Freddie's hands took hold of her waist. She turned the knob, but the door didn't open. Freddie tried to drag her away.

Putting both hands on the knob, she pulled harder. So did Freddie. Clutching the knob, she tugged at the door with all her might. Freddie wrapped his arms around her waist, trying to haul her away. Her feet lifted right off the floor. But she wasn't called stubborn for nothing.

Their footsteps echoed on the wooden stairs as Paavo and Yosh hurried up to the porno studio. A dark-haired man stood behind the counter talking to a blond man whose back was to them. Then the blond man turned around.

Paavo felt as if someone had plunged him into ice. For an instant, time stood still and he was fourteen years old again: afraid, grieving, filled with cold black hate.

It had been too many years, Paavo told himself. His eyes were playing tricks on him. Or his imagination was.

His memory had to have faded from the time he first searched for this man. No, not *this* man, but someone who resembled him. The flat gray eyes weren't really the same, were they? Nor was the big mole on the man's cheek. This couldn't be the man he'd searched for, for so long.

He was stockier than Paavo remembered, and his hair was a little thinner, a little shorter, a lot blonder, but that was all. The protruding lower lip, the heavy-lidded, darting eyes, the mole—they were the same.

"Axel Klaw," the man said, holding out his hand. "What can I do for you?"

Paavo tried to shake off the feeling, but it was as if

he were looking at the man through a microscope and all his features were enlarged and overwhelming. Paavo could barely stand to touch the offered hand. "Paavo Smith, Homicide, SFPD. This is Inspector Yoshiwara."

Klaw shook hands with both. "What seems to be the problem?"

Suddenly the past vanished, and blood rushed to Paavo's head, throbbing and pounding its way through him. Angie! She was here, with this man! Klaw stepped back from the icy force of the blue eyes focused on him.

"A young woman was seen entering these offices. We're here to pick her up," Paavo said. The chilled, unemotional voice seemed to come from someone else, not himself.

"Many young women come in here."

"She's little—"

"Most of my women are short. They aren't your typical models, you see."

"Dark hair—"

"More common than blond."

There were more questions, lots more questions that he wanted to ask, that he would ask. Someday. Soon.

"Her name's Angie."

"Doesn't ring a bell, Inspector."

The same smirk. Years ago, he hadn't been able to stop his sister from going off with this man. The coincidence was almost too much, yet he'd known every minute of his life that someday their paths would cross again. He just never bargained on Angie being in the middle when it did. It was like being caught in a nightmare.

"You damn well better get some bells ringing."
Each word was spoken with chilling exactness even
as Paavo took the front of Klaw's shirt and jerked his
face nearer.

"Hey, there, copper. I ain't done nothing. You've got
no right—"

"I got every right, Klaw. She came in here. I want
her *now*."

"Look, inspector, these broads, they all change
their names anyway. I mean, none of them who come
here tell the truth, so I don't pay attention to what
they say. If a young woman wants to work for me"—
he smiled—"*with* me, I got to be a most obliging fellow."

A muscle in Paavo's face twitched at Klaw's
words. "Her anonymity won't protect you, Klaw. You
get her now or you won't be able to jaywalk without
doing time. Is that clear? You want to be shut down?
It's the easiest thing in the world."

Just then they heard a loud crash. Screams and
shouts rang out, and then another crash. It sounded
like the filming of *Debbie Does the Terminator*.

Paavo and Klaw ran down the hall, reached the
doorway, and stopped. What had once been a movie
studio, all carefully partitioned off, looked like the set
of a biblical epic: Jericho after the walls came atum-
bling down. Partitions had fallen, lighting equipment
was strewn on the floor, and cameras knocked from
their stands lay broken. A bewildered jumble of voices filled the dusty, poorly lit room. Paavo and Klaw
glanced at each other briefly, each expecting the other
to offer information, and then surveyed the ruins.

Dazed actors scrambled to their feet and quickly

covered themselves with their hands, protecting their professional assets. Shrieking actresses sat bolt upright on the beds and couches they'd been performing on, holding sheets and clothing under their necks, either because of newfound modesty or to keep the dust and dirt off their well-oiled bodies. Cameramen and stagehands stood stupefied, as if wondering how to begin to put things back in order.

A bruising hulk of a man pushed a slab of plywood off himself and struggled to his feet. He brushed off his once-white sports jacket and reached up as if to be sure the thick gold chain still dangled from his neck.

"Freddie," Klaw thundered, "what the hell's going on here? How'd you do all this?"

"Me? I didn't do nothing! That dumb broad tried to go through a phony door, for chrissake. She wouldn't let go, and she pulled down the whole goddamn set. Then they all started falling."

Klaw turned purple. "Can't you do anything right?"

"Where is she?" Paavo demanded.

"What?" Freddie frowned at Paavo.

"I said where is she?"

Freddie turned and looked down at the plywood and scratched his head. "I don't know. I kinda lost track of her."

"Goddamn!" Paavo ran to the area where Freddie had been. "Angie!" he shouted, then started looking under plywood and partitions. He shoved some out of the way as he called Angie's name, needing to find her but almost afraid of what he might discover when he did. "Yosh!" Paavo yelled for his partner. "Get in here! Help me find her."

"Look at this mess," Klaw bellowed. "She's done a *Thelma and Louise* on me."

"They make films for us?" Freddie asked.

"Who?"

"Thelma and Louise."

"Shut up, jerk. Do something about this."

"Let me shoot her, boss," Freddie pleaded.

"You don't know where she is."

"I could find her."

Klaw told Freddie he couldn't find an intimate part of his own body.

"That's not so. You're hurtin' my feelings."

"What the hell do I care how you feel?"

"Paavo," Yosh called. "Stop. Look who I found."

There in the doorway, beside Yosh, stood Angie. Relief surged through him.

"She snuck out the back," Yosh said, "and would have been long gone except I told her you were in here looking for her."

Paavo climbed over the mess. "You okay?"

She nodded and stared at the warehouse. "Now I know how the domino theory works."

Paavo saw that despite her flippant words she was frightened. He touched her arm. It was ice cold. His throat tightened so he could scarcely speak. "Come on, Angie. Let's get out of here."

"These people are all crazy," she said.

The way she trembled as they passed Klaw made Paavo murderous.

"These broads." Klaw chuckled after them. "They all think they're gonna be Linda Lovelace, but then they get scared and freak out. Too bad. I thought this one showed real talent."

Paavo stopped at the top of the stairs and looked back. "Klaw, you're going to wish you'd never said that."

"Is she all right?" Yosh asked when they were on the sidewalk.

"She seems pretty woozy. I'll take her to the hospital," Paavo said.

"No, Paavo," Angie said. "It was scary when all that stuff started to fall, but luckily most of it landed on Freddie first. He made a good shield. I'll be all right."

"I want to be sure."

Angie began to chuckle, and then she laughed so hard the tears ran down her cheeks.

Paavo put his arm around her, holding her close, a worried frown on his face. "Calm down, Angie. You're all right now."

"I'm not hysterical," she said, when she could talk again. "At least, I don't think I am. It's just that when the partitions started going down, I saw—well, let's just say I didn't think anybody could do that." She chuckled. "Then I started running."

Paavo arched his eyebrows.

She leaned against Paavo's broad chest, enjoying the security he offered. "I'll tell you about it someday. But you'll think I was hallucinating."

Yosh whistled softly. "Remember, Paav, it's standard procedure to share what you learn with your partner."

"Let's call it privileged information," Paavo said. "I'll use Angie's car for now. In the meantime, why don't you start the paperwork for a search warrant on that place? I plan to go through it with a fine-tooth comb."

"No sweat, partner. Take care of her, and I'll call you soon as I get it. And don't forget you can tell me anything, privileged or not. I mean, I'm always eager to help."

20

Flashing his badge, Paavo bypassed the usual mountain of paperwork at Emergency Hospital and took Angie straight to a doctor. When the doctor finished his examination, he told Paavo she had a few bad bumps and bruises but she'd be okay. He saw she was pretty shaken and gave her a sedative to help her sleep.

"I'm taking you to my house," Paavo said when they were back in her car.

"I'll be all right," she whispered.

"I don't like the idea of you being alone after the doctor gave you that sedative."

"Maybe so," she said. "Paavo, Klaw knows my address. He saw it on my check. You don't think he'd . . ." She bit her bottom lip.

Paavo placed his hand over hers. "He won't bother you. He thinks you were someone who was too curious and too foolish for her own good, that's all."

"Thank God."

The fear in her voice hurt Paavo more than any physical blow could. He understood what was happening to her. Even though she'd gotten safely away from Klaw, her mind was assailing her with thoughts and images of what might have happened had she been trapped there. Men like Klaw and his henchmen were common in the ugly world Paavo knew, but Angie had never before had to deal with people who made a mockery of the values and regard for others that shaped her life. With them, it hadn't mattered who or what she was. They operated on base animal instinct, where the scent of fear was as powerful an incentive as power and money. She knew they would have liked nothing more than to scare her into surrendering to them, and the knowledge of that, even though it hadn't happened, was terrifying.

Paavo drove straight to his house. As he opened his front door, he was greeted by the thudding feet of Hercules, who then hurled himself against Paavo.

"This cat is so damned spoiled," Paavo muttered.

"Feed Hercules, Paavo," she said.

She refused to lie down on the bed. Despite the medicine the doctor gave her, the thought of closing her eyes and trying to sleep made her uneasy. The giddiness and euphoria she'd felt earlier over her clever escape from Klaw had evaporated, and now the memories of Klaw's lurid face and Freddie's strong hands were sharp and frightening.

Paavo settled her on his sofa, gave her a pillow, and covered her with an afghan and then hovered near to pat her shoulder or brush back a wayward curl from her forehead. He wondered what had led her to go back to Axel Klaw's studio but knew she'd tell him when she was ready. For now, he was content just to have her here.

He thought she'd fallen asleep when she said softly, almost calmly, "I looked through Karl Wielund's notebook."

"Notebook?"

"He used to keep notes of his recipes: what he cooked, when and why he changed the ingredients, the temperatures, all that. Mark took Karl's notes and brought them to LaTour's with him. In Karl's notebook, I found a number like the ones on the films of Sheila Danning you had."

"You remembered the numbers?"

"It wasn't too hard." Drowsily, she rubbed her eyes. "Anyway, I sort of gave the fellow at the counter, Dwayne, the impression I wanted to act in a film, and then I gave him the impression we ought to watch a movie together. He let me go into the storage room to find a film to watch. I found the outtakes for the film reel listed in Karl's notebook. The film was an old one, nearly twenty years old, but I still recognized the woman in it. It was Lacy LaTour."

"You're saying Henry's wife made porno flicks?"

"I saw more of Lacy in those photos than I ever want to see of her. They were sickening."

Hard though it was to imagine, he believed what Angie was telling him. Suddenly, it all tied together— Henry, Karl Wielund, and Henry's wife, connected through the photos found in Wielund's place. Paavo rubbed his chin. "So if Henry and Lacy are the link between Wielund, Wielund's landlord, Chick, Sheila Danning, and Axel Klaw, we only need to figure out who wanted to kill four of them and why."

Angie nodded wearily.

Paavo kissed her forehead. "Get some sleep, Angel."

"Don't leave me." She scooted downward so she was lying prone on the sofa, her head on the pillow. "How's that?" she asked, patting the edge of the sofa.

"It's fine." He gave a halfhearted smile at the small space and then stretched out beside her on top of the blanket. After a moment, he raised himself up on his elbow and looked at her. "Are you comfortable?"

"Oh, yes." She reached up to guide his head down to her chest. He gently placed a kiss in the hollow between her breasts and rested his head. She gently stroked his hair, and he felt himself relax. As much as she needed him now, so he too needed her. She was his peace, his refuge.

"Good," he murmured. "So am I. Now."

The sound of her breathing had deepened into sleep when Paavo heard a car stop in front of his house. He stepped to the side of the front window and looked out.

"Who is it?" she asked, suddenly awake, fearful.

"Your father," he said wryly.

"It can't be!" He could hear the dismay in her voice.

"It is. And he's got one of the police commissioners, Pat O'Reilly, with him."

"Police commissioner?" Bewildered, she pushed aside the blanket and stood up. The sedative had made her drowsy and foggy-headed. "Don't tell him about any of this, Paavo, please! Promise me."

Paavo gave her a sharp look and opened the front door. "Hello, Mr. Amalfi. Commissioner O'Reilly."

"Where is she?" Sal's look was withering. He

pushed the door wide, but halted abruptly as he stared at Angie's pale face, her disheveled state, the blanket on the sofa. "Angelina, what's happening to you?"

Angie looked at Paavo, her gaze imploring him to help.

"Everything's fine," said Paavo. He went to her side and touched her elbow, his gaze pointed.

She shook her head, refusing to tell her father the truth. His heart was bad, and he'd be too upset.

Sal's gaze fixed on his daughter. "I heard that today you went to a porno theater, or worse. Someplace where they make the films. Those people are the worst kind: drugs, diseases, guns. I can't believe you'd go somewhere like that. It's not like you, not my Angelina. I can only imagine you did it because you've been seeing this man. His influence is no good for you, no good at all."

She stepped closer to Paavo, her weight heavy against his supporting hand. "No," she said.

Sal glared at her. "No? Then why were you there?"

"It was nothing, Papà," she whispered, slowly shaking her head as she took a step toward Sal. Paavo released his hold on her.

Sal stepped closer to her, his hands twisting. "When the Commissioner heard where you were, he called me. I couldn't believe it. My baby, in such a place. I want you to come home with me this minute."

Stricken, Angie turned to O'Reilly.

"You're the daughter of one of my best friends," he said. "And you're going out with someone in the department. I feel a certain responsibility." O'Reilly glanced quickly at Paavo. "We'll discuss this tomorrow, Smith."

But Paavo had already figured it out. "You were checking me out, weren't you?" he asked Sal. "Because I was seeing Angie."

"What do I know about you, about your family? What does she know?"

Paavo ran his fingers through his hair, trying not to speak the harsh words that came to mind. Instead, he only muttered, "I can't believe this!"

"Paavo." Angie turned to him, her hand tentatively reaching for him.

"*Non importante,* Angelina." Sal picked her coat and handbag up off the chair. His face was florid. "*Andiamo!*"

Her father's flushed looks scared her. It was too soon after his surgery for him to become so upset. Did she have any choice but to go with him, to try to calm him? She glanced at Paavo.

Paavo saw the hesitancy in her eyes. He'd always told himself that if she had to choose between her family and him, she'd choose her family. He'd been right. The best thing for him to do would be to make it easy for her. He took her coat from Sal and put it on her, fastening the topmost button so she wouldn't get cold. "Go home with your father, little one," he said. "It's where you belong." His hand lingeringly, lovingly, tucked a curl behind her ear.

She seemed stunned and confused.

"Go ahead."

Sal took her arm and led her from Paavo's house. Obviously, Paavo had guessed right about what Angie wanted to do. She'd never listened to him so willingly before.

He shut the door behind them.

* * *

Paavo's frustration with the case, with not yet being granted a search warrant for Klaw's place, and with the whole business with Angie and her father went right over the top the next morning as he told Hollins how O'Reilly had been checking up on him. "Where does he get off?" he asked coldly.

"I don't know," Hollins replied. The lieutenant looked equally irate. No one, not even a police commissioner, could nose around about one of his best men without his okay.

Paavo paced back and forth in Hollins's office. "Doesn't O'Reilly have the brains to figure out that I was trying to get Angie *out* of that place?"

"I'll fill him in on the case. I doubt if he knows anything about what's going on. He's not a cop, he's a politician."

"Don't I know it!"

"Look, if you can get her to talk to O'Reilly, the heat'll be off for you."

"It's between him and me. I don't want her involved."

Hollins shook his head. "You got it bad, don't you? Why don't you just marry the girl?"

That stopped Paavo in his restless pacing. For a long silent moment he stared down at the floor. Considering how Angie left last night, there wasn't much chance of his seeing her again, let alone anything more, but he wasn't about to go into all that with Hollins. When he lifted his head, his expression was almost savage. "She'd be in danger every time I got a case she was interested in."

"Just keep her out of them."

Amusement eased some of the grimness from Paavo's face. "You don't know her very well, do you?"

Hollins chuckled. "Can't say I do."

"The trouble is," Paavo continued, "her poking her nose in my cases works. She's found the connection between the porn studios, Sheila Danning, Karl Wielund, and, now, Lacy LaTour."

"Who's Lacy?" Hollins asked.

"She's the wife of the restaurant owner, Henry LaTour."

"And?"

"She used to work in porno films. Axel Klaw has one of her films, and Karl Wielund knew about it."

From Vice, Paavo learned that Axel Klaw was associated with drug dealers and gamblers as well as porno operations, but Klaw was the Teflon King of Porn; nothing stuck to him, no matter how big the charge.

Klaw's record went back twenty years. At age twenty-five, he was already a drug pusher, too smart and ambitious to use his own product.

As Paavo turned the pages in Klaw's file, suddenly, there in front of him, was the story he'd wanted, yet dreaded, to see.

The record showed that a man named Alexander Clausen had been investigated in connection with the death by overdose of a nineteen-year-old woman named Jessica Smith. Some witnesses said they'd seen Jessie go into Clausen's apartment with him, but a number of others swore Clausen had been seen in other places throughout the night. The woman was dead, and no one ever proved who was or was not with her.

But the woman's little brother knew. Paavo had
seen his sister go with the man. And he remembered
how the man's hard, mean look had frightened him.
But Jessie had said he was fun.

Fun. God damn the man, Paavo thought. He stared
at a mug shot taken years ago of the young Axel Klaw.
I've spent a lot of years looking for you, Clausen. Now
you've fallen into my lap, I won't let you go again.

21

The sun was just peeking over the hills of the East Bay when Angie forced herself to get into her car, alone, and go for a drive around the city. She'd spent over a week at her parents' house. It was time to go back to living: back to her job at the radio, her history class, even her so-called apprenticeship at LaTour's.

A week ago, when she'd awakened in her old bedroom at her parents' home in Hillsborough, her father told her Paavo felt she was in his way and didn't want to have to deal with her as he tried to find Chick's murderer.

She'd been stunned. She remembered that Paavo had found her at Klaw's and had taken her to the hospital, where she'd been given a sedative. She rarely took medicine, and it hit her hard. After that, nothing but a faint memory of Paavo's warmth lingered before it all blurred together. Somewhere in the back of her mind, though, a vague memory of Paavo telling her to leave made her father's words ring true.

As the days passed, though, the memory of those last hours with Paavo came back to her, filling her more and more with the sense that she'd been safe. Yet her father told her Paavo didn't want her there, and Sal wouldn't lie to her. Still, he might have misinterpreted.

But if Paavo cared about her, wouldn't he have at least phoned to ask how she was? How could he not? She missed him so much she could hardly bear it.

Even though Paavo didn't call, didn't try to see her, she knew there was a reason, a very good Paavo-like reason. No matter what her father told her, Paavo wouldn't toss her aside. The warming realization came to her that she trusted him. She trusted that when he was ready he'd see her again.

She drove through Chinatown, around Union Square, and over to the burgeoning theater district on Mason. On Bush, she turned and made a stop at an alley called Burritt Street. A plaque there never failed to tickle her.

On approximately this spot
Miles Archer,
Partner of Sam Spade,
Was done in by
Brigid O'Shaughnessy.

The Maltese Falcon lives. She smiled, but then frowned and read it once more.

It wasn't until she was almost at the top of Russian Hill that she realized what it was about the plaque that had bothered her. All this time she'd been thinking about a *man* as the murderer of Chick and Karl. But maybe she needed to find out more about the women involved, especially Lacy LaTour, now that she knew about the porn connection. Lacy just might be the key to the murderer, or even be the murderer herself.

When she returned to her apartment, she found that her jaunt around the city had lifted her mood considerably.

She was going to wait patiently for Paavo and, in the meantime, figure out who killed Chick and Karl. And somehow, some way, some day, she'd get even with Axel Klaw besides.

Just as she had forced herself to return to her own apartment, so she forced herself to go back to Henry's radio show. It was mercifully routine.

Afterward, it was time to check in on LaTour's. Henry had thought she'd been sick with the flu, on the verge of pneumonia, and insisted she stay away until she was one hundred percent better.

She was greeted warmly at LaTour's, and Mark Dustman immediately put her to work helping make a large pot of bouillabaisse.

Angie waited until Dustman and his assistants were busy and then went into the office. She picked up the telephone receiver, dialed the time, and held it to her ear by tucking it against the crook of her neck. This way, although she looked as if she was making a telephone call, she could go through the books.

To her surprise, the restaurant was doing worse than she ever imagined. Each month ended with a negative balance. She ran her finger up and down the columns, looking at headings and amounts to see if anything looked out of line. Not that she could see. It was just a very expensive place to run.

She flipped back some pages to scan individual accounts of income and outgo. It was the beluga caviar that stopped her first. Three hundred pounds of it? Being sold at LaTour's? She didn't think so. Why on earth would Henry have bought so much of the stuff? Eighty-five pounds of saffron? Did Henry plan to season all the rice in Spain? Saffron was so costly it was sold by the quarter ounce! Lobsters. Henry didn't have lobsters on his menu. Périgord truffles. What was going on here?

When Henry came in, he peered into the pots and harrumphed that it all looked passable, while Lacy took a look at the amount of clams and mussels in the bouillabaisse and let Dustman have a barrage of her human calculator talk about the expense involved. The bottom line was, he needed to use one and a half cups of water to every cup he now used when making the soup, in order to nearly double their profit margin. He declared it would taste like watery swill. Lacy didn't care. She worked on the accounts, paying bills, posting income and outgo, and trying to squeeze a profit out of the business.

Angie stayed at the restaurant until the kitchen closed at 11 P.M., then helped the staff clean up. Throughout this time, as she watched Henry and Lacy, she racked her brain to come up with any rational explanation for the large quantities of expensive foods she'd seen on their books.

There was something fishy here, besides the caviar.

She really ought to let Paavo know what she'd found out. Although earlier today she'd decided to wait patiently for him to contact her, sometimes patience, like virtue, was not its own reward. She went into the office and reached for the telephone, then drew back her hand. The hurt she felt whenever she recalled her father's words, about Paavo not wanting her to "bother" him, hit her once more, despite her resolve that there was more to the story. She pulled out a chair and sat.

She thought about Paavo holding her and making her feel safe and secure, peaceful. Suddenly she remembered Paavo and her father arguing; someone else was there. Who? God, why couldn't she remember! Her father and Paavo; then her father growing more upset; then her realization she had to get him away from there and calm him.

She stood. Of course. She should have known! Well could she imagine Paavo thinking she'd chosen her father over him, that she left for no good reason except that Sal asked her to. No wonder he hadn't phoned or tried to contact her in any way.

She ran from the restaurant to her car.

"I can't believe this," Paavo said when he opened his front door and found her standing at the entry.

"Hi, there!" She hoped she sounded a lot more carefree and at ease than she felt.

"Hi, indeed." He stuck his head out the door and looked up the street, then down. "Is your father nearby? Or maybe the mayor is lurking in the bushes this time. Thank God your father's not friends with the president or I'd have Air Force One flying overhead."

She brushed past him and went into the house. "Forget the president. If I wanted to be really safe, I'd call Frank Sinatra."

She reached into a paper sack she carried. "Look. Coffee filters and a fresh pound of Italian roast from Graffeo's." Without another word she went into the kitchen and put on the Melitta.

He followed her. "What's this about?"

She gave him an innocent look. "I wanted to see you. What else? Now go sit down. I'll be right out."

His gaze held caution, but beyond that she saw, or hoped she saw, a flicker of pleasure that she was there.

While the coffee was dripping, she put chocolate-dipped *biscotti* on a plate on the coffee table. In a short while, she poured them each a mug of rich coffee, took it into the living room, and sat on one end of the sofa while Paavo sat on the other. She curled her legs under her and turned to face him, her elbow on the backrest.

Paavo studied her. "Is everything all right."

"I'm back at my apartment. I'm doing fine."

His sharp look told her he wasn't fooled.

"Anyway," she said, "I did want to tell you about something that might affect your case. I saw something most peculiar today at LaTour's restaurant. It probably doesn't mean anything, but you mentioned looking at Wielund's and Italian Seasons accounts, and I know you had no reason to go over Henry's, so I thought I'd check them out for you."

Blue eyes showed his interest in her words, even as his lips thinned until she was sure he wanted to scold her like a wayward child for taking another risk. Instead, he said, "You found something peculiar, you said?"

"That's right." She leaned conspiratorially closer and told him all about the strange food and spices she saw listed as purchases for LaTour's, and then she told him what was so strange about them.

Before she was through, Paavo was on his feet and pacing.

"If the money wasn't going to buy those foods, and from what you say, it wasn't, where was it going?" Paavo asked. "And since we've found that each month Karl Wielund made a big deposit into his bank account, we also have the question of where *that* money came from. The obvious answer is it went from LaTour's to Wielund's. But if so, why?"

"You think Karl was getting money from LaTour's?"

"We can't rule out blackmail," Paavo said.

Angie could scarcely believe it. "But what possible reason would Wielund have for blackmailing Henry, unless it had something to do with Lacy and the porno film. Was Henry paying Karl for help with his restaurant? After all, Henry has at least one recipe that I know was Karl's. Maybe there were others."

Her lack of conviction in her own words was reflected by Paavo's shaking head. "I can't believe chefs would kill over recipes, despite their competition. But Lacy's films are a different story. It wouldn't be the first time photos and films like that turned up later in life in the hands of a blackmailer."

"Remember how Lacy fainted when Karl's body

was found? Maybe she killed him and figured he'd be lost in the snow until the spring thaw, and she fainted from shock that he'd been found."

"Could be," Paavo said. "Then, too, the snow and the length of time from when Wielund was killed until the autopsy was performed might have thrown the estimate off. Maybe he wasn't killed while Henry was on the radio. Maybe it was after. Or even before. Henry could be our man."

"I still can't see Henry hurting anyone," Angie said. "But logically, it's got to be him."

"It all points his way, or to Lacy. But remember, whoever is behind this may well have killed three people, and maybe Sheila Danning as well. A woman couldn't have killed Danning, except as a man's accomplice. Whatever this means, I don't want you taking any more chances. Until we catch whoever's behind it, keep away from Henry LaTour."

"I never take chances."

"Not much." A chill went down his back at how much worse it could have been for her at Klaw's. His thoughts turned to the way he'd brought her to his home afterward, to hold her. Since his talk with Sal Amalfi at Chick's funeral, only once had he stayed with Angie through the night, and he was still haunted by the memory of how good it had been. He understood why alcoholics couldn't take even one drink. "Well, Angie, thanks for the coffee and cookies."

"Thanks?"

He stood.

So did she.

He steered her toward the door. "It's late and I

don't want to keep you any longer than necessary. I appreciate all you found out about this case. You did just great."

"Great?"

"I'll see you back to your apartment. I'll make sure you arrive safe and sound, then I'll be on my way."

"You don't have to do that."

"I want to." He opened the door.

She stiffened her shoulders, sent him a glare that should have skewered him on the spot, and, head high, walked out of the house. "I don't need a police escort," she said. "I'll be just fine. I know all about taking care of myself."

22

Angie fully intended to stay away from the LaTours, but the next day Lacy telephoned her, sobbing so hard and sounding so drunk she could hardly speak. "Angie, it's terrible. Henry's been arrested!"

"Lacy, have you been drinking?"

"Only to settle my nerves. I can't take it, Angie. Not another second. What will I do if Henry's in prison?"

"What was he arrested for?"

"Karl's murder! Oh, Angie, you've got to help me." She hiccuped loudly. "It was that detective, the one you brought to Karl's memorial service. I thought he was a friend! Now I don't know what to do. Maybe if you talked to him, told him Henry would never hurt Karl. Henry's a darling! You know that." She started crying loudly into the phone.

"Pull yourself together, Lacy. Drink some black coffee. I'm sure Paavo's just talking to him about something."

"But he was read his Miranda rights. At least, it sounded like Miranda rights."

"Did you call your lawyer?"

"No. Henry said he'd handle everything, that I shouldn't worry."

"He's right."

"But, what about the radio show? How can I handle Chef Henri's part? I don't know anything about cooking! I might ruin Henry's career!" Lacy cried with unabated hysteria.

"It's nothing to worry about."

"But it is! The thought of being on the radio scares me to death. And . . . and I had a little vermouth. Just a thimbleful, mind you. But since I never drink, it's gone straight to my head."

Godzilla's thimble, Angie thought.

Lacy rambled on. "What if I say something foolish or something that upsets Henry? What if the police keep him and I have to go, day after day, back to the radio station, trying to answer questions from callers, trying to be witty like my Henry, to keep his listeners?" An onslaught of sobs got in the way of her words.

"I've got an idea," Angie said.

"Oh?"

"I could do it for you. I know the answers to most of the questions, and I've never been tongue-tied. I can hardly remember ever being nervous, come to think of it." Visions of the expressions of the station executives after listening to her witty, knowledgeable, fast-paced, exciting radio show made her whole body tingle. "Sure, I'll go on for you. I'd love to do it."

"Oh, God, would you? You're not just being nice, are you?"

"Heck, no. This is an opportunity made in heaven."

"An opportunity?" Lacy sounded shocked.

Angie guessed she hadn't been her most diplomatic. "To be helpful," she added quickly.

"Ah! In that case—"

"Wait!" A vision of Paavo waggling his finger and warning her to stay away from the LaTours flashed in front of her. "Let me just make a couple of phone calls to be sure I have the time."

"The time? But you were planning to be there anyway with Henry, weren't you?"

"You never know," Angie said. "I'll call you right back."

With that, she hung up.

"Homicide Department, may I help you?" the nasal voice intoned.

"Inspector Paavo Smith, please."

"One moment."

It didn't take long for the woman to tell Angie that Paavo wasn't answering his phone. Angie asked to speak to Inspector Yoshiwara.

"Hey there, Angie." Yoshiwara's voice boomed. "How's it going? Seen any good movies lately?"

She winced. "That's sick. Look, I need to reach Paavo. Any idea where he is?"

"He's not here. Can I take a message for him? Or, maybe there's something I can help you with? Hey, the big P.S. told me about you finding out someone's been skimming the take at LaTour's. Good work!

You might be going into the private eye trade before you know it."

"I don't think so. Is he with Henry LaTour?"

Yosh hesitated a moment, then said, "You guessed it."

"Are they there?"

"I think they're talking at LaTour's restaurant."

"Was Henry arrested?"

"Not as far as I know."

It took Angie less than a second to decide. Lacy was drunk and Paavo was probably gathering the last bits of evidence to use against Henry. What danger could there be?

"Thanks, Yosh. Would you do me a favor and tell Paavo that I'm doing Henry's radio show? Lacy called. She's upset and has been drinking and is in no condition to go on the air. I volunteered to go on for her."

"The radio show, huh? Pretty brave, Angie, old girl."

"Or pretty foolish."

"Anyway, I'll let him know. Let's see, that's a twelve o'clock show, right? I'll try to listen to it. Paavo too, if he's free."

"Great. I'll give you a special hello."

After calling Lacy back to tell her everything was set, Angie went to KYME. She'd never noticed it before, but the call letters looked distinctly like "cwyme," as in the way Elmer Fudd would say "scene of the cwyme."

Angie arrived early so she'd have plenty of time to tell the station manager and his assistant that she'd be doing Henry's show today, and possibly several days in the future, due to a personal problem. But it was near lunchtime, and she'd learned they'd gone to McDonald's.

Well, she'd go ahead without their okay. Since *Lunch with Henri* was ranked seventy-eighth in the greater Bay Area, she figured no one really cared who ran it. Or *if* they ran it. The old Conelrad Alerts had had higher ratings.

Angie picked up her reference cookbooks and waited outside the studio booth for the show ahead of Henry's to end. A man whose name Angie could never remember held a lively talk show on fly-fishing. The fact that almost no fly-fishing was done in the Bay Area didn't seem to bother him, nor did the fact that he got even fewer callers than Henry. Maybe it wasn't Henry's fault his show did so poorly. Maybe the fly fisherman put the audience to sleep.

Since she wouldn't have any call screener, she realized she'd have to take the phone calls blind. She just hoped she didn't get the funny little man who called at least three times a week to ask if this were Marvella's French Laundry. After politely telling him no every time, Angie had finally replied that if he called one more time, she'd donate his clothes to the nearest homeless shelter. He'd remembered her threat for two days and then called again.

Ten minutes until showtime.

The station engineer, sitting at his console in a separate glassed-in area, paid no attention to her.

At five minutes before the hour, to her surprise, she saw Lacy go into the engineer's booth. The engineer nodded sagely as she spoke to him.

A short while later, Lacy joined Angie. "I'll screen your calls," she said.

The woman looked awful—almost as bad as she'd sounded earlier on the phone, in fact. Her hair was uncombed, her makeup smeared and caked, and she had put on a plaid blouse with a striped skirt, no nylons, and black flats. "Are you sure you feel up to being here, Lacy?" Angie asked.

"I want to be." She looked ready to cry.

Angie felt sorry for her and knew how important it was to take her mind off her man troubles. "Well, good then. I was sitting here thinking about all the kooks who call. I had one guy who phoned all the time and insisted he speak to Rush Limbaugh. I finally told him I was the chief feminazi and he never called back."

Just then, the fly fisherman left and Angie and Lacy went into the studio booth. Lacy tucked a loose strand of hair behind an ear. Her hands shook. "Let's move these partitions so you won't be distracted by the engineer or others who might walk by."

"It doesn't matter."

"Oh, yes. You want to do your best."

They moved the screens.

Angie sat in Henry's chair and watched as the clock's minute hand pointed straight up and then the second hand ticked off the remaining time until noon. She pressed the earphones close against her ears, but she couldn't hear *The Teddy Bears' Picnic.*

"There's no music," she whispered to Lacy.

Lacy turned toward the engineer's booth but she couldn't see him, because of the screens. She leaned toward Angie. "That's because it's Henry's music, not yours."

Angie looked stricken. She glanced at the clock. Time to start talking, *past* time to start, in fact. She sat up in her chair feeling badly rattled, as all the great opening lines she'd practiced flew right out of her mind.

"Hello, ladies and gentlemen. I know I don't exactly sound like Chef Henri, and that's because I'm not."

She glanced at Lacy, who was busy chewing a stubby fingernail. Angie licked her lips and went on.

"My name's Angelina Amalfi, sitting in for Chef Henri, who's having a very special lunch today. I've spoken to many of you in the past when you've called in to ask Chef Henri about food preparation."

For some reason, she glanced at the microphone. Just as they tell mountain climbers never to look down, seeing the microphone made the full impact of what she was doing hit her. There she sat, with every word she spoke going out over the airwaves all over the greater Bay Area, whether anyone was listening or not. Her mouth grew dry, perspiration beaded on her forehead, and her mind went blank.

"So . . . so now, instead of talking to you on the phone, I can sit here and talk to myself like Chef Henri does. I mean, talk into this mike, without any feedback. I don't mean talk to *myself,* of course. . . ."

Angie swallowed hard. She'd never, ever make fun of Henry again.

"Well, why don't we go to the phones?" She glanced at the monitor. Not a single call had come in. She wiped her forehead. "Let me give you those numbers, first. Today, why don't we talk about all the good things we can get right here in San Francisco? Being a port city and all. I mean, I've met people from the middle part of the country who've never eaten an artichoke. Can you imagine? Probably not even a kiwi. Now, on the East Coast there are a lot of different kinds of fruits and vegetables, but I don't know what they are." Oh, me, she sighed. Should she slash her wrists now or later?

The call monitor was lit up, but Lacy hadn't handed her the name of the caller or the topic. "Oh, a caller," Angie said. At least someone was there. She hit the open-line button. "Welcome to *Lunch with Henri*. This is Angie. How may I help you today?"

The light on the line went out.

"Hello?" Angie said once more and then looked again at the microphone. "I must have hit the wrong button, folks." She gave a halfhearted laugh. "Whoever it was, be sure to call back, and we'll put your call right to the front of the line! No waiting for you. No sirree."

The line remained empty.

"Angie." She looked up. Lacy stood before her, then reached over and shut off Angie's microphone. "No one's going to call."

"What are you doing?" Angie took off her headphones.

"I'm sorry. I should have stopped you earlier, I guess, but I was afraid you'd walk out. I couldn't let you walk out."

"I don't understand."

"I . . . I changed my mind about you doing Henry's show. I told the engineer to spend the hour playing golden oldies."

Angie stood. "What?"

"I had to see you alone—because of this." She took a gun out of her purse.

Angie backed up until she bumped into a partition. "Lacy, no!"

Paavo sat on one side of the desk in the small office at the back of LaTour's restaurant and faced Henry. "I appreciate your willingness to discuss these accounts with me," he said. Henry had stacked books of payables and receivables on the desk before them.

"No problem. Anything I can do to cooperate in finding the murderer of our fellow chefs is fine with me. Especially since, I hasten to remind you, Inspector, I too was threatened."

Paavo studied Henry as he spoke those words. The man looked and sounded surprisingly sincere. Of course, Paavo had also witnessed more than one murderer declare his innocence in equally compelling terms. "I remember, Mr. LaTour. Now, before hiring Mark Dustman, were you the head chef at your restaurant?"

"I still am, actually. But I spend much time on the sidelines, so to speak, doing my radio show and writing cookbooks."

"Who orders the food for the restaurant?"

"I do—er, did. Now, I leave it up to Mr. Dustman."

"Let's look at these books."

Henry put on his reading glasses and still had to hold his head back abnormally far in order to see the columns.

"As you can see," Paavo said, "each month since

November, your expenses have exceeded your income."

"Yes. It's the recession, you know."

"I'm sure. Let's check that." Paavo looked at the gross income figures for the past six months and saw they were surprisingly consistent. "If gross income is consistent, it must be that your expenses have increased."

Henry looked puzzled. "If anything, we've been doing all we could to economize. I've even taken to going to"—he shuddered—"places like Costco to get some standard supplies. Please, don't let word of that get out!"

"Generally you deal with a set group of food and restaurant wholesalers?"

"Yes. DMP Distributors, Rose's Kitchen; you know them, don't you? We go to markets for special items, not the routine."

Paavo didn't know them at all, but that was okay; at least he'd managed to turn Henry's attention to the food expenses. He was curious to see if Henry would notice the same kinds of things Angie did—if Angie was right. She knew food, but she'd never worked in a restaurant before this little stint at LaTour's—not that he knew of, anyway.

"See, here are the food expenses," Henry said. "I hadn't had time to make many changes in my menu since August, so these items will be remarkably consistent. I hardly had to think about them, in fact. I had standard orders for most deliveries." He began to flip through the pages. "Let's start with August. The bottom line is all we need. Here's September, about the same as August. Same for October. Just like I told you. And now, November—"

He stopped short.

"What is it?" Paavo asked.

"Just a minute," Henry said, light beads of perspiration glistening on his forehead. "There's something wrong here."

Paavo, too, looked at the numbers. "November's expenses seem to be about ten thousand dollars higher than October's. Can you explain it?" Paavo asked.

"I . . . I'm not sure. Normally, everything is so simple in a restaurant. You buy raw ingredients cheap, cook them, then sell them for a lot more money. That's it. Here, we have a list of the cost of the raw ingredients." Henry's fingers covered his mouth as he looked again at the November figures. After a while, he turned to December, then scanned what had been completed so far for January.

Paavo also peered at the numbers. "If it's so simple, can you tell me why November and December are both almost ten thousand dollars higher than previous months?"

"I have no idea." Henry was sweating profusely at this point.

"Do you keep these books, Mr. LaTour?"

"No. I don't have much of a head for figures, I'm afraid. My wife does the bookkeeping."

"Your wife?"

"Yes. She's a regular wizard at numbers. Can do a lot of math in her head even."

"Does she also do the banking?"

Henry wiped his forehead with his handkerchief. "Yes." He flipped to the back pages where Lacy listed out details of the various columns. "Saffron, truffles," he muttered, mopping his brow, "beluga—Oh, my!"

"Mr. LaTour?" Paavo said. The restaurateur looked ready to faint.

"I—I'm sorry, I just . . ." He swallowed, staring glassy-eyed at the books.

"Did you authorize the purchase of those foods?"

He shook his head, nearly on the verge of tears.

So Angie was right.

"What happened, Mr. LaTour," Paavo asked, "to make November, December, and January different from the prior months?"

"I have no idea."

"No?"

"None! Believe me. I don't understand it myself."

"You never checked these books?"

"No. Why should I? I trust my wife."

"Do you realize, Mr. LaTour, that the way these books are written, it appears that phony expenses of food were placed in the account books to siphon off ten thousand dollars each month?"

Henry looked from one page to the next. "It does appear that way."

"Does anyone besides Mrs. LaTour work on these books?"

"No one."

"No accountant?"

"None."

"Tax preparer?"

"Lacy does our taxes."

Paavo looked at him skeptically.

"She saves us lots of money."

"I'm sure she does."

Henry riffled the pages back and forth, leafing

madly through them. "I don't understand it. I just don't!" He looked frightened and confused. "I don't know what to tell you."

"Perhaps you can tell me where I can find Mrs. LaTour."

"You think she was taking this money?" Henry asked. "She wouldn't! What reason would she have?"

"I have reason to believe this money was going to Karl Wielund. It looks like he was blackmailing her. Now he's dead."

"You think Lacy was being blackmailed? That she killed Karl? It's not possible! For one thing, she never said a word to me about it."

Paavo didn't think he had to point out that murderers or people being blackmailed often didn't announce it, especially not to their spouses. "Perhaps it was because of you she did it?"

Henry seemed to shrivel. "No, Inspector Smith." He shook his head and suddenly looked very old. "As much as I wish it were true, I know in my heart I'm not the type of man to drive a woman to commit murder. Not even my own wife."

23

Angie looked from Lacy to the gun and back to Lacy again. Lacy's hands were shaking worse than glass in an earthquake. Angie tried to calm herself. Somehow she had to take control. "What's this all about?"

Lacy glanced down at the gun, letting the barrel drop so that it was pointed toward the floor, and shook her head. "He's trying to make me take the blame. It's all coming apart." She gave a harsh sob and tears filled her eyes.

"What is? Who do you mean? Henry?"

Lacy shook her head. "Axel promised me everything would be all right, but it isn't." Suddenly she shrieked at Angie. "Why couldn't you leave us alone?"

Angie's heart nearly stopped. "I didn't do anything, Lacy."

Lacy stared at her, and her expression changed from

anger to desperation. She placed the gun on the table where Angie had been sitting, as if even holding it had become too much of an effort for her. "Karl was *bad*," she said harshly. "He was a horrible person. I didn't care when he died. He deserved it!"

Angie inched forward a step. If she could just keep Lacy talking, perhaps she could grab the gun. "Why did he deserve to die?"

"He was blackmailing me!"

Angie's pulse beat harder. So she and Paavo had been right. Wielund *was* a blackmailer. "Was it because of the kind of films you made years ago? I don't think people would care much anymore." She tried to make her voice soothing. "You'll be all right, Lacy."

"You're wrong there, Angie." Lacy said. "People care; they always do. And Henry will. He won't . . . he won't want me anymore."

Angie could see the hysteria building in Lacy again. "That's not true."

"What do you know? The snobs, the in-crowd, take every chance they can to look down their noses at me. You belong. You don't know what it's like to have to claw your way to respectability, to find someone and something that's important in your life and then have to struggle to keep them."

Angie was horrified, both by Lacy's words and the way she looked and acted. "I'm sorry, Lacy," she said. "Let me try to help you. Please."

Lacy paced back and forth. "That damned Sheila Danning. I should have known she was trouble, damn it. Lousy, stupid little bitch!"

Danning? Angie glanced from the gun to the glass that looked out beyond the studio booth to the full radio station. No one was there. She inched closer. "I don't follow."

Lacy's tears began again. "Axel said I was an accomplice. That if he was fingered, I'd be too. But I was just trying to help Sheila. She needed money, just like I did. Over the years, sometimes I'd see Axel. He'd always give me money. He even gave some to help the restaurant—not that Henry knows. But we needed it. It wasn't so bad of me to take that money, was it, Angie?"

"Uh, no, of course not."

"Axel needed talent. I meet girls loaded with it. New to town, looking for a job as a waitress or whatever. Shit! Whoever said she was going to die, goddamn it to hell!"

Angie's skin began to crawl as she pieced together Lacy's tirade. "Was Sheila Danning making a movie for Klaw when she died?"

Lacy's eyes widened. "I said it was an accident!"

Angie's stomach knotted as she imagined—no, she *knew,* from all that she'd seen of those people—the kind of terror that must have filled Sheila Danning's last minutes. She looked at Lacy with disgust. "You know what happened to her, don't you, Lacy? You know how horrible it must have been."

Lacy covered her ears. "It's not true!"

"Did Sheila tell Karl Wielund about her job?" Angie asked, now only about five feet from the gun. "Did she tell Karl that you sent her to Axel Klaw, and about your films, so that when Sheila died Karl began to blackmail you?"

Lacy wrung her hands. "Yes. He was horrible. A brute!"

"And that's why you, or Henry, killed him." As Lacy just looked at her, dumbfounded, Angie lunged for the gun.

"No!" Lacy snatched the gun away just before Angie's fingers closed on it.

Henry had declared that Lacy wouldn't kill for him. Much as Paavo wanted to believe otherwise, Henry's words had the ring of truth. In fact, the more Paavo thought about Lacy, he wondered if she could, in fact, kill three people in cold blood. Somehow, he couldn't see it.

"Even if Lacy didn't kill Wielund, something did happen between them," Paavo said. "Look at these books. The money didn't just walk out of your restaurant and into his."

Henry rubbed his forehead and then nodded. "Yes. Something did. But I don't know what, or why. She started acting strange in November. I didn't understand. I still don't. She seemed so distracted, so removed. I thought . . . I thought maybe she didn't love me anymore."

"Why do you say that?"

He fidgeted with his tie. "I guess I was jealous. She kept on talking about Karl Wielund and how well his restaurant was doing. He was like an obsession with her. She even fainted when we heard he had died. Frankly, I was glad he was gone. I thought things would be all right between us after that, just Lacy and me, just like before. But then she hired Wielund's cook, Mark Dustman. We didn't need him. We still don't. The only good thing about him are all the recipes he brought with him from Karl's old restaurant."

Henry's words triggered something in Paavo's brain. "Dustman brought you the recipes?"

"Yes."

Paavo tapped his fingers on the desk, searching his memory. If only he'd paid better attention when Angie was talking about food! "Was one of the recipes some kind of veal—no, lamb, or something like that—in some kind of pie crust?"

Henry's mouth dropped open. "You mean the filet of lamb in puff pastry? How did you know that was one of Karl's? Dustman told us no one would know. He said we could—" Henry glanced at Paavo, suddenly realizing he'd said too much. His cheeks turned fiery red. "Dustman said we could pretend it was ours. And I'm ashamed to say I tried to."

Paavo leaned back in his chair, deep in thought. "Were you aware, Mr. LaTour, of your wife's connection with a man named Axel Klaw?"

"Who?"

"Were you aware that she was ever involved in pornography?"

Henry stood. "This has gone far enough, Inspector Smith! I've cooperated as much as I can, but for you to slur my wife's good name—"

"Sit down," Paavo ordered. "We'll worry about reputations later. Right now, we've got a dead waitress, Sheila Danning, who was killed last November, and who knew Wielund and Axel Klaw."

"November? What? I don't understand! This Klaw is nothing—"

"Your wife knew Klaw, and possibly Danning as

well. And it looks like Wielund was blackmailing her."

"Coincidence!"

Paavo leaned closer to Henry. "Chick Marcuccio knew you had Wielund's new recipe, and now he's also dead."

Henry paled and tried to scoot back farther from Paavo.

"Then," Paavo continued, "your wife hired Mark Dustman, who knew all these people." Mark Dustman, who had also lied about knowing Sheila Danning.

"Yes?"

Paavo rubbed his jaw. "Dustman had Wielund's notes and recipes. Nona Farraday wrote an article on Wielund that said he worked on new recipes *at home,* not at his restaurant."

"He did?"

Paavo stood and began pacing back and forth in the small office. "And Wielund's landlord, looking in the kitchen, said the place looked like it was missing something. Like it'd been cleaned up." Paavo stopped and faced Henry. "Wielund's notebook! The one with his recipes! The killer would have been the one with the time and opportunity to take it."

Henry also stood. "Dustman?"

"But Dustman had an alibi. He went to work, showed up in the kitchen, got everything started, then went into the office and handled Eileen Powell's work all day. It might be that no one actually saw him, only saw the light on in the office, assumed he was there working, and didn't dare disturb him. He could have killed Wielund and driven up to the Sierras in three hours in Wielund's car. After rolling the car with

Wieland's body off the cliff, he could have walked a short distance and then hitched a ride. There's an airport in Tahoe. To fly back takes less than an hour. He'd still have been back in time to put the finishing touches on the dinner menu. But why?"

The shrill ring of the phone startled them both. Henry picked it up and in a moment handed it to Paavo.

"Smith here."

"Sorry to bother you," Yosh said, "but there's something you need to know."

"What is it?"

"Angie called. She told me to tell you she'd be doing Henry's radio show today since he was with you. I thought I'd turn it on and listen to her. But something's wrong. Do you have a radio there?"

Paavo motioned to Henry to turn on the radio. The dial was located properly for KYME, but instead of Angie talking about cooking, warbling over the air was the mellifluous voice of Doris Day, singing "Que Sera, Sera."

24

"*Don't shoot, please,*" Angie cried, her arms outstretched imploringly. "Please, Lacy!"

"You've got to believe me, Angie! You're my only hope."

Angie's throat seemed to close. She didn't know what to say.

"This is the gun that killed Chick," Lacy said. "I heard him confront Mark Dustman in LaTour's kitchen about giving us Karl's recipe. Mark tried to deny it, but he couldn't explain how we could have gotten it, if not from him. Next thing I knew, Chick was dead."

"What are you saying?"

"Mark planted the gun on me. He said everyone would think I killed Wielund and then Chick. And you do think that, don't you? Mark was right!"

"No. I never did. I thought—" She stopped, suddenly realizing how foolish it was of her to ever suspect poor, bumbling Henry of such crimes. She bit her bottom lip. "Please, Lacy, put the gun down. Please."

"You couldn't possibly have suspected Henry, could you?"

She took in Lacy's earnest gaze. "Only after the threat came over the radio. It seemed too phony, too much of a setup to throw suspicion away from Henry and not at all in keeping with the rest of the killer's style."

Lacy shook her head, and her arms dropped to her sides. "That was me. I called. I did it to throw suspicion away from Henry and me. If anyone suspected us, if they looked into my past, they'd find out about my films, and Axel, and maybe even Sheila Danning. I couldn't let that happen."

Angie nodded, not saying a word.

"But then Mark told me you were going to tell your friend the cop that Henry or I did it," Lacy explained. "When your friend came and arrested Henry, I realized that all the other stuff—the films, and even introducing Sheila to Axel—were nothing compared to this, to murder! I had to see you, to explain. To tell you Henry and I are innocent."

"Mark Dustman!" Angie whispered.

Lacy's weary tear-streaked eyes met hers. "Yes."

"Oh, my God!" Angie stepped to Lacy's opposite side from where she held the gun, and grabbed her arm. "Let's get out of here! Paavo didn't arrest Henry; they're just talking. They've gone to LaTour's. Dustman usually shows up there a little after twelve. If he sees the two of them together, he might start to worry and go looking for you. If he realizes you're here, with me, where we could have talked this through—" She shivered.

The two hurried out of the studio and nearly stumbled over the station engineer, lying unconscious on the floor just outside his console. He was breathing, but just barely. The back of his head was a bloody mass.

"Dustman's here already," Angie whispered. "Get down." She tugged on Lacy's arm. They dropped to the floor, below the glass surrounding the console.

Lacy looked ready to faint from fear. "Let's get out of here."

"Wait. He's got to be hiding somewhere."

"I've got a gun," Lacy said, suddenly recalling the weapon she still held in her hand.

"That's probably why he didn't burst in on us. He wants to be able to take it away from you."

Lacy inched forward, peeked around the console, and looked back at Angie. "All clear. Let's run to the door and get out of here."

"I've got a better idea. Let's go in the engineer's console, lock the door, and call nine-one-one. It's too risky to run. He might be hiding anywhere."

"I'm not letting myself get trapped in there!" Lacy's whisper was harsh. "I'm getting out!" She stood up slowly, waving the gun from side to side. All remained quiet. She took a step, then another and another.

Angie didn't know what to do. If she stayed here, she was unprotected, but following Lacy also scared her to death. Holding her breath, expecting Mark to leap out at her at any moment, she crawled in the direction Lacy had gone.

Lacy had almost reached the door that led to the outside corridor when, from behind a metal file cabinet, Mark Dustman reached out and grabbed her hand.

He twisted her arm. The gun dropped, and he threw the terrified Lacy to the floor.

Angie darted past them toward the door. She hadn't even reached it when she was slammed against the wall. Her breath came out in a painful *whoosh*. A hard arm went around her waist; cold metal pressed against her temple. "I can shoot you here if I have to. It'd just be a little quieter in a sound-proof booth." Dustman chuckled.

"Why, Mark?" Angie cried.

"Shut up!" He dragged Angie closer to Lacy. "Get up."

Lacy cried. "I can't. I think you broke my arm."

He shoved the fallen woman with his foot. "Move it! You're going to shoot Angie and the engineer and then, in remorse, you're going to kill yourself. Now get the hell up!"

Lacy sobbed hysterically. In disgust, Dustman pushed Angie aside hard, knocking her into a supply cabinet, then reached down for Lacy, grabbing her hair to pull her to her feet. She screamed.

Paavo and Henry stepped off the elevator. A scream pierced the air, and Henry began to run.

"Stay back!" Paavo ordered.

Henry didn't listen but burst into the radio station. "Lacy!"

Paavo first saw Angie, leaning against a cabinet, her face terror-stricken, and then Mark Dustman. Dustman let go of Lacy's hair and spun around, his arm outstretched, in his hand a .38 caliber revolver.

Paavo grabbed the back of Henry's suit jacket and

yanked him back as hard as he could, into the corridor, just as a shot rang out. Henry cried out, falling and landing hard against Paavo's bad shoulder. A mind-numbing pain went through Paavo as he pulled out his gun. Dustman's frantic gaze met his.

Suddenly, Angie hurled herself hard against Dustman's back, shoving him with all her strength. Dustman stumbled forward as his gun went off, the bullet wild and wide of the mark. Instantly, Paavo was on top of him, wrestling him to the ground and taking his gun.

As he locked the handcuffs on Dustman, Paavo's eyes caught Angie's. His heart was still in his throat as he thought of the chance she'd taken, throwing herself at the gunman. He smiled. "Good job," he said.

"Thanks." Her voice quivered. Nervously rocking back and forth on her heels, she looked from Henry, who was sitting on the floor looking at a bullet wound in his leg, to Lacy, still crying, to the bloodied engineer, to Dustman lying there handcuffed, and back to Paavo. Then she fell to the ground in a dead faint.

25

Angie sat quietly on a metal chair and watched the proceedings. Yosh had been right behind Paavo and Henry, so he could help Paavo deal with the crime unit, the paramedics, the patrol officers who came to take Dustman in and book him, and Angie.

Paavo, always the consummate professional, had left her pretty much on her own once he saw she was all right. He had worked with the other officers, talked to Henry and the engineer, calmed Lacy, and made sure he read Dustman every right he had coming. No way was Paavo going to let this guy walk on some technicality.

At a point where the others quieted down a bit, Paavo walked over to Angie and held out his hand. She took it, and he led her into the corridor, backing her against a wall, his large frame shielding her from the curious stares of anyone who might wander into the hallway. His hands traced over her arms and shoulders. "You're so pale," he said.

"I'm okay," she answered softly. "I thought he was a friend, though. It's hard. . . ." She bowed her head, unable to say more.

His fingers lightly stroked her cheek as his thumb outlined her brow, her chin; then, tipping her head upward, he lowered his mouth to hers in a light kiss.

She wrapped her arms around him, burying her face in the crook of his neck. He held her close, until some warmth once again flowed through her veins and the shivering she hadn't even been aware of ceased. When she felt strong again, she straightened and pulled back from him, knowing he still had a lot of work to do.

He stepped back, seemingly ready to go inside, but then, surprising even himself, he pulled her into his arms and gave her a long heart-stopping kiss. She held him tight, kissing him back, loving him with all her heart.

A slight cough, then another, caused him to look up. Yosh stood in the corridor. "The paramedics are ready to take Henry, Lacy, and the engineer to the hospital. How about I go with them to get Lacy's and the engineer's statements?"

Paavo stepped away from Angie, trying unsuccessfully to appear nonchalant. "Sure. I'll deal with Dustman and get Angie's statement."

Yosh nodded. "Seem to be doing that already," he murmured, then he turned and headed back inside.

Paavo adjusted his tie and led Angie, who couldn't help but smile, back into the radio station.

As the officers hauled Dustman away, Angie told Paavo all that had happened and all that had been said.

She insisted on going down to Homicide with Paavo when his work was completed at the studio. The way her adrenaline was pumping, sitting quietly at home was the last thing she wanted to do. She might even think of something more to tell him.

Instead, she spent two hours sitting alone in the reception area. Finally she walked over to Yoshiwara's desk.

Yosh glanced at her. "I guess Paavo will be through interrogating Dustman sometime soon. I'll sure be interested in hearing why Dustman killed all those people."

"Me, too." Angie sighed. "I can only think of one reason, and it goes back to the first speech he made at Karl's funeral."

"Oh? What's that?"

"Well, Mark kept talking about the restaurant as if it had been *theirs*—his and Karl's. And he said he'd been the one who talked Karl into coming to San Francisco in the first place."

"So?"

"Well, Wielund's was on the verge of being number one in the city, a world-class restaurant. But everyone knows that to be a world-class restaurant, you absolutely must have a world-class chef. It's ironic, but quite often the cook who brings a restaurant up to a certain level of prominence isn't the one who continues to run it. Instead, as it nears the top, its owner looks for someone with a big reputation to give it a final boost. Karl knew this. So did Mark. I'd never actually heard that Karl was looking for a new chef, but with the money he was getting from Lacy, he would have been able to afford one of the best."

"Interesting."

"If Mark heard anything about Karl planning to throw him over for another chef, well—"

"Eileen Powell!" Yosh cried.

"What do you mean?"

"She'd gone to Paris. What better place to look for a new chef?" He raised his eyebrows in satisfaction.

"That's right." A thought struck Angie. "I wonder if Eileen didn't suspect something like this, and that's why she got away from all these people."

"It wouldn't surprise me," Yosh said. "But now I have a question for you. Whatever made you tackle Dustman like you did?"

A shudder went through her. She remembered seeing Dustman pull the trigger and hit Henry; she remembered Paavo's wince as Henry's head banged into his shoulder, and how Dustman shifted his gun toward Paavo. She fought the dryness in her mouth as she looked up at Yosh. "I've seen Paavo shot once," she said softly. "I wasn't about to chance seeing it again."

Yosh nodded approvingly. "Got it."

She ran her fingers over the side of her hair, pushing it back behind her ears. "I wonder why Paavo's taking so long?"

"I don't know. It can't be much longer. I expect he'll be back any minute."

"Okay."

"Why don't you go home, Angie? I can have him call you."

She thought of how strained their relationship had been lately, until he showed her, at the radio station, that he still cared. She didn't want him to lose that feeling. "I'll wait a little while longer."

She wandered over to Paavo's desk and sat in his chair.

"Sitting here, I can see what it's like working in Homicide. Maybe it'll help me understand him a little, right?"

Yosh smiled. "I think you understand him a lot better than you realize, Angie. Better than he realizes, too."

Angie looked at the papers on his desk. Most were carefully placed in manila folders. A glance at Yosh's desk told her that not all detectives did that. Yosh's desk looked like a blizzard had struck it. She should have known Paavo was a neatness fanatic, organized and orderly. Maybe that was why she drove him so crazy.

She thumbed through the carefully labeled and alphabetized folders on the stand-up rack at the side of his desk: DANNING, GREUBER, KLAW, MAR-CUCCIO, WIELUND. Klaw? The others were all murder victims. But Klaw was still alive. She pulled the folder out of the rack.

"That's confidential, Angie," Yosh said. "Not for the public. Sorry."

"Oh, of course." She pushed the folder aside, away from her, and folded her hands, waiting.

About ten minutes later, Yosh turned to her once more. "Would you like some coffee?"

"Love some."

He went out to the coffee machine. Quickly, she slid her fingers inside the folder, grabbed the top pages, and pulled them out. Riffling through them, she came across a history of Klaw's prior arrests. She slid the other sheets back into the folder and placed

the history—a rap sheet, she thought it was called—
on top of the folder. She folded her hands again.

Yosh came back into the squad room. Jumping up
from Paavo's desk, she hurried over and took the coffee he'd bought for her. Thanking him, she returned
to Paavo's desk. After a few sips of dirty dishwater
posing as coffee, and a few smiles at Yoshiwara, she
put the coffee down again, sidled a bit closer to the
rap sheet, and, not touching it, began to read.

Klaw had been given only one conviction—heroin
possession—with a suspended sentence if he'd enter a
methadone program. She glanced over the page until
her eye caught a name, then a date, twenty years earlier.

Axel Klaw, who at the time was still using his real
name of Alexander Clausen, had been questioned
concerning the death by heroin overdose of nineteen-
year-old Jessica Smith. Angie stopped reading and
shut her eyes briefly, her heart pounding. Then she
read on.

Clausen, age twenty-five, was suspected of being a
dealer, of introducing young people to drugs. But the
police couldn't find anyone willing to testify against
him. Clausen had been seen with Smith at local bars
throughout the evening. Smith's family, a stepfather
and young brother, swore she'd never used drugs
before. She was found by her brother in Clausen's
apartment. For lack of evidence, no charges were
brought against Clausen. A reference was made to
Jessica Smith's own file, where more detail of the
investigation into her death could be found.

Angie carefully slid the rap sheet back in the file,
then sat unmoving for a moment. Finally she picked
up the coffee, leaned back in her chair, and then spun

it around so that she could stare out the window, lost in thought.

"Well, well, why do we have the honor of *her* presence?"

Angie looked up to see Inspector Luis Calderon talking to Yoshiwara. Yosh cast a reassuring glance at Angie before answering. "She's waiting for Paavo. I think he's wrapping up some interviews."

Calderon grinned. "She's gonna have a long wait. I passed him driving down the street as I headed back here. He turned onto the Bay Bridge."

Angie frowned. The Bay Bridge led to Berkeley— and Axel Klaw. She jumped to her feet. "Yosh, will you come with me? I think I know where he's gone."

Astonished, Calderon yelled, "You can't let her drag you around, man. You got work to do. Paavo's a big boy. He can take care of himself."

"She's not dragging anyone anywhere, Luis. She did a damn fine job today for all of us. I think you owe her an apology. And I think you owe Paavo one as well."

Angie wasn't about to wait. The thought of Paavo going off alone to face Klaw made her nerve endings do handsprings. Grabbing her purse, she ran to the elevator and pushed the down button again and again. Before the elevator arrived, Yosh was at her side.

26

Paavo sat in Axel Klaw's office with Lieutenant Bert Janosky of the Berkeley Police Department. Klaw sat behind an enormous polished mahogany desk, a poster-size black-and-white photo of a woman's naked torso on the wall behind him. The walls of the office were painted black, and the upholstered furniture was red leather.

"Thank you for your cooperation, Mr. Klaw." Lieutenant Janosky stood. "Since you know nothing about Karl Wielund or Mark Dustman or the other men he killed, I don't think it'll be necessary for you to come to the station at this time."

Klaw beamed as he too stood. "My pleasure. I always cooperate with the police."

Janosky looked at Paavo, who remained seated. "Shall we go, Inspector Smith?"

"You go ahead. I'd like to talk to *Mister* Klaw about something."

"What's this?" Klaw demanded. "Haven't I cooperated enough?"

"This isn't your jurisdiction, Smith," Janosky warned.

Paavo smiled coldly. "Let's just say I might be here as a customer."

Janosky's mouth dropped open.

"Fine." Klaw held out his hand to the lieutenant. "Janosky, it's been a pleasure, as always."

They shook hands. "Remember, Klaw, keep your nose clean." As he stepped toward the door, he gave Paavo a last glance. "You too, Smith."

Paavo just nodded, and in a moment Janosky was gone.

Klaw eased himself back in his chair, his hands clasped behind his head as he regarded Paavo. "You wanted to talk. I'm waiting."

"I wanted to talk about Alex Clausen."

Klaw stiffened and smiled mirthlessly. "I don't."

"I want to talk about a string of murders Clausen was involved in. Starting with Jessica Smith and ending with Sheila Danning."

Klaw blinked; then recognition filled his eyes. "Smith. A common name. Most Smiths aren't even related."

"But some are."

Klaw studied Paavo. "So that's it. The little brother grows up to become a hotshot cop, to right the injustices of the world."

"That's it."

Klaw held his hands out, palms up. "I don't know anything about anything. I'm clean. You can check."

"And I've got Lacy LaTour, who I'm sure will be quite willing to say otherwise."

"I don't think so."

"She knew Sheila Danning. She knew where Sheila was and what she was doing the night she was murdered. That case is still alive and well—especially now that we know where to look. Somehow, Homicide thought Danning was a sweet young thing from Tacoma, struggling on a cocktail waitress's salary in the big city. How they ever got that idea, I don't know. I wonder if her so-called parents even *were* the real parents. Homicide went up one blind alley and down another with that case three months ago. But we're back on track now, and that track leads straight to you."

Klaw removed his hands from the desktop and placed them in his lap. "You're just bluffing, Smith. You don't have anything on me, and you won't get anything."

"You never know."

"You don't know Lacy—or me."

Something about the look in Klaw's eyes, the tightening of his jaw, warned Paavo. He pulled out his gun. "Don't try it, Klaw."

Klaw's eyebrows lifted, then a malevolent grin spread over his face. "How'd you know I had it?" Klaw slowly lifted the gun he'd been concealing under his desk. It was pointed at Paavo. "Drop it, Smith." His tone was icy. "Then leave. You shoot, and my boys will make sure you don't get out of here alive."

The door swung open. "Mr. Klaw." Dwayne from the front counter burst into the room. "These people insist—"

Paavo didn't turn to see who'd entered. He knew

the minute he took his eyes off Klaw he would be a dead man.

"Holy Christ!" The voice sounded like Yoshi-wara's.

Klaw's eyes met Paavo's, and he slowly put down his gun on the desk, then pushed it forward, out of easy reach. Cautiously, Paavo placed his own gun on the desk. Then Klaw turned to the people who had burst in, and Paavo, for the first time, glanced their way. Dwayne still held the doorknob, his mouth agape. Yosh had his hand on his holster, and behind him, Angie was trying to look around his bulk.

Klaw smiled at their audience. "We were just showing off our revolvers. No need to look so startled, folks. No danger."

Paavo stood, placed his gun in his holster, and walked toward the door. "You haven't seen the last of me, Klaw. I'll be talking to Lacy as soon as I can."

"By the way, Mr. Klaw." Dwayne looked from Paavo to Klaw, then at his watch. "About a half hour ago there was a most unfortunate happening." He paused to be sure he had everyone's full attention. "Mrs. LaTour had a heart attack in the hospital. Didn't even have time to call for help. Seems she just stopped breathing."

"What?" Yosh gasped. "Impossible." They had driven over in Angie's car, not Yosh's with his police radio.

Angie didn't take her eyes off Paavo's closed, set face. She had never seen his eyes so devoid of emotion.

Klaw chuckled. "If Dwayne says so, it must be true."

Dwayne folded his arms. "It's true. Believe me."

Klaw laughed long and hard.

"Enjoy this now, Klaw," Paavo said in a quiet voice that was more frightening than if he had shouted in fury. "Just remember the old saying about the one who laughs last." He left, not before seeing the fear behind Klaw's bravado, but even that gave him no satisfaction.

Angie stayed behind, staring at Klaw, not wanting to believe Lacy was dead. But the longer she stared, the more certain she became that it was true—and that it wasn't her heart that made her stop breathing. Lacy had chosen to work with this man; she'd died by him as well.

Angie's frown deepened. "You know what else, Klaw?"

He lifted one eyebrow.

"I plan to be your worst nightmare."

Klaw threw back his head and laughed harder than ever.

Angie had to run to keep up with Paavo as he marched toward his car. Yosh hurried along behind her. Paavo reached the car and unlocked it.

"Are you okay?" she asked, her hands on the door, as she gasped to catch her breath.

"Who me? I'm just great! How the hell do I look? And what business is it of yours anyway?" he bit out savagely.

She stepped back, stricken.

"Damn it, Angie, when the hell are you going to learn to keep out of police business? You've got no right to go running around to places like this, with me or Yosh or anyone else. Is that clear? Can you understand me?"

"Yes, but—"

"But nothing! You don't belong. Keep the hell away from me and my job!" Paavo got in his car, slammed the door shut, and drove off.

They stared after him until finally Angie went to her own car, Yosh close behind her, his face grave and concerned. She drove without speaking while Yosh prattled on about the case.

Angie wasn't able to think about it. She was still trying to get over the shock of seeing Paavo and Klaw pointing guns at each other. Ready to shoot. Ready to die. She'd thought her heart would stop. How could Paavo show such careless disregard for his own life? Damn him, why was he that way?

Angie dropped Yosh off at the Hall of Justice. No sense going upstairs. Paavo wouldn't want to see her now.

She drove back to her apartment.

Alone, seated on the Hepplewhite chair, she sipped hot tea. The "classic" pornographic movies she'd purchased sat atop her VCR. Picking them up, she took them into the kitchen and put them in a brown paper bag.

"Mrs. Calamatti, are you down there?" she called into the garbage chute.

No answer. Even Mrs. Calamatti had abandoned her. "Look out below!" she called and dropped the movies. That was the best place for them. She felt all right throwing them out because Mrs. Calamatti didn't own a VCR.

Angie curled up in front of her bay windows. In the night darkness, the beacon from Alcatraz rotated, illuminating the bay every five seconds. At least some things never changed.

But she had. Her radio job was gone, and Paavo had withdrawn even further from her life. At one time, she'd wished he'd give up being a cop. But that was childish, she realized. He'd never give it up, not even for her, and especially not when he was so close to getting the man responsible for his sister's death.

Paavo had always been there when she needed him, but other than that he was never there for *her*—never there to simply "be" together. He couldn't accept what she had to offer, and he couldn't, or wouldn't, let them have the togetherness she needed.

Angie leaned forward, holding her head, her elbows on her knees. She hadn't truly understood, before encountering Axel Klaw, just how ugly Paavo's world could be. While she recognized the greed that could corrupt a basically good man like Karl Wielund, the mistaken pride that would allow Lacy LaTour to be used by a man like Klaw and then blackmailed, and even the wrongheaded ambition of a man like Mark Dustman, she'd never before encountered, face to face, anyone with the complete lack of morals of the degenerate creature known as Axel Klaw.

And as much as Klaw held his gun emotionlessly on Paavo, so too had Paavo held his gun on Klaw. She covered her eyes, trying not to see the horror of that scene. But no matter how hard she tried, she couldn't get it out of her mind.

Her father wanted her and Paavo to separate. So

did her sisters. So did Calderon, and possibly Yoshiwara as well. Maybe all those people did know what
was best, what was right. Suddenly, she felt too tired
to fight them any longer, too tired to go on caring so
much. Paavo had told her once that he loved her.
Once, and then never again. She'd lived off that one
time for months. Now it was no longer enough.

The Alcatraz beacon shimmered and grew misty
through her tears.

27

Paavo had to admit to more than a little trepidation as he knocked on the door of Angie's apartment. For sure, she'd be angry after the way he'd treated her the day before in Berkeley. Being unable to arrest Axel Klaw put him in no mood to be civil with anyone, and he'd taken his frustration and anger out on her. He'd lost control, badly.

The Berkeley PD put Klaw under twenty-four-hour surveillance and the search warrant for Klaw's studio was finally approved, but the BPD would handle it. They'd look into Sheila Danning's murder as well. Hollins ordered Paavo to let them take the lead if they wanted it, since Klaw's studio was in their jurisdiction. He would. But he'd be looking over their shoulder.

He still wasn't sure how his gun duel would have played out had he and Klaw not been interrupted. A stupid stunt, yet holding that gun on Klaw had felt good. He almost hated to admit to himself just how good, especially since a part of him suspected that if they hadn't been stopped, they might easily have killed each other. Hell, they might still.

All the more reason, he thought, to apologize to Angie. That was the only reason he'd come here this evening, to apologize. It was only natural to shower and wear clean clothes, along with the cologne she'd bought him. He couldn't apologize properly if he looked scruffy. Same with the box of long-stemmed red roses he held. So what that he could have eaten for two weeks on what they cost him. He couldn't imagine giving her anything less.

Maybe it was stupid to be here. But the guilt he felt had only deepened when Yosh told him why she'd tackled Dustman and how she'd led Yosh to Berkeley. She'd been wonderful. And she deserved to be told. As well as to be told he was fifty kinds of idiot for hurting her—a hardheaded fool who didn't deserve her.

And to ask her to forgive him.

He knocked again, feeling more foolish with each passing minute he stood there.

A door opened across the hallway. A head peeped out. "She's not home," Stan Bonnette said, with immense satisfaction.

"Do you know when she'll be back?" Paavo asked, much as he hated to ask Stan anything about Angie.

"Maybe never."

Paavo turned cold. "What do you mean?"

"She packed a couple of suitcases this morning, gave me her key, and said she'd send some movers over to pack up the rest of her things."

"Where are the movers supposed to deliver her things?"

"She didn't tell me."

"What's the name of the moving company?"

"I don't know."

"What about her furniture, her cooking stuff?"

"Listen, Inspector, this isn't one of your cases. I'm just helping out my neighbor, okay?"

"Fine. Good neighbor Stan. That doesn't answer the question."

Stan sighed. "They'll stay here—I guess until she decides if she wants to come back or not."

"Did she drive?"

"She didn't leave me the key to her car. But then, she never did let me drive it."

"Any message for anyone? For me?"

Stan's lips curved into a smug smile. "Not a single word."

Paavo got off the elevator on the third floor, walked to apartment 301, and knocked on the door.

Mrs. Calamatti opened it. "Oh, hello. You're Angie's young man, aren't you? The one who thinks he's Roosevelt."

"I thought you might like these flowers, Mrs. Calamatti," he said.

Her eyes lit up with pleasure, and she opened her arms to receive the box of roses. "Why, thank you. What a lovely surprise!"

"You must promise me, though, never to go into a dumpster again."

"Never?"

He took out his badge and held it before her. "Never."

She sighed. "I see. Well, in that case, never."

"Good. Well, good-bye." He walked back toward the elevator.

"Oh, young man?"

He stopped and turned.

"Could you take a moment to help me, please? My son and daughter-in-law gave me a VCR nearly two years ago. I put it away in the closet and never hooked it up because I didn't have anything to watch. But now, could you hook it up for me?"

"Sure," he said. "I'd be glad to."

Once home, Paavo fed Hercules and then called the special directory assistance number the force used and found out Sal Amalfi's unlisted phone number in Hillsborough, a tiny exclusive enclave nestled among some hills on the San Francisco peninsula.

The maid answered his call.

"This is Inspector Paavo Smith," he said, "San Francisco Police Department. I'm calling to speak to Miss Angelina Amalfi."

"I'm sorry, but she isn't here."

Damn, he'd been sure she'd gone back to her parents' house. Now what? "Do you know where I can reach her?"

"No, sir. But she's expected back this evening."

He nearly jumped for joy. "This evening? Thank you."

He left the house, got into the car, and put the key in the ignition. Instead of turning the key, though, he folded his arms over the steering wheel, staring straight ahead.

Why was he planning to rush off to Hillsborough? She'd left without telling him, without leaving him any kind of message. After all his backing away, telling her it'd never work between the two of them, and her insisting that it would, he'd finally won. He'd told Aulis he was the one in control, and this proved it.

She was gone. It was over.

"All right, Miss Amalfi. Thank you!"

Back in the house, Paavo walked straight through the living room and into his large, thoroughly empty kitchen.

He opened the refrigerator. Yellowing Miracle Whip and Heinz 57 Ketchup with black gunk growing from the cap down into the bottle were the only things still recognizable. In the freezer was the bag of Italian roast that Angie had bought. She said it'd keep a long time in the freezer, since she knew he wasn't home much to use it.

He got out the coffee, then the filters, then the Melitta. It had a glass carafe and a plastic cone. He knew he was supposed to put a coffee filter in the cone, and the coffee in the filter, but then he had no idea how the coffee was supposed to be made. He remembered the old percolators—just put cold water in the pot, put the cone on top, and put the whole thing on the stove to cook. He stacked them up.

No, that didn't seem right.

With the new automatics, it seemed they just poured cold water in them. Maybe he should pour the cold water into the cone? No, that didn't seem right either.

He picked up both, twisting and turning them round and round, trying to find some kind of a switch or a dial or an instruction. Somewhere. Anywhere.

Nowhere.

Finally, he shoved everything back in the cupboard, took out a kettle, and boiled water for a cup of instant, just like always.

Angie's coffee was a lot better.

He sat in the living room. It was absolutely quiet. No Angie to ask him to light the fireplace, to talk to him, to quiz him about his cases or badger him by asking if he'd thought about this or that. Hell, he should be happy she wasn't here. Now he could have a little peace in his life once again. Forget all about her.

He probably never would forget, though, the first time he ever saw her, a pretty little thing trying to act sophisticated and tough even though her dishwasher had exploded and nearly flooded her apartment, or the first time he found out what it was like to kiss her. He'd never forget her overwhelming family and the love of music she gotten from them—everything from heavy operas to fat men singing songs in incoherent Italian.

He'd never forget the way she could brighten his day with a simple smile or tell crazy stories to make him laugh. She could be whimsical or wild, starry-eyed or madly passionate.

He'd never forget Angie.

Hadn't his friends encouraged him to find a woman like Rebecca, though? It'd never work out with someone who didn't understand police work, they'd said. Look at Calderon. Fifteen years with a woman, and then she'd walked out on him.

Fifteen years. He wondered what it'd be like to spend fifteen years with Angie. It wouldn't be dull, that was for sure. Open, joyful, and trusting; she was everything he wasn't.

Everything he needed.

If they'd had that much time together, they might even have had a kid or two. Despite himself, he found he liked kids. Maybe because he'd never had much of a childhood, he liked seeing kids have fun, liked seeing them enjoy life before all the garbage that comes with adulthood happened to them.

He looked again around his quiet home. Kids could make a place lively. Too lively at times.

His old partner, Matt, had a great kid, a four-year old named Micky. Paavo needed to go over for a visit. It'd been almost a week since he'd been there. He'd always liked spending time with Micky, and after Matt died he'd promised himself he'd be there as much as he could for the boy.

But to have his own kid . . . ?

This was nonsense. He drained the awful coffee he'd made and decided to go to bed. Why not have a long peaceful night's sleep?

But in bed, it was only worse. He lay there, staring at the darkened ceiling and feeling as if what little light there was in his life had gone out of it completely.

Paavo and Yosh sat in Chief Hollins's office.

"We just got a confession," Paavo said. "Dustman explained it to us. His attorney was there. They'll probably try for an insanity plea."

"What was the reason he killed?" Hollins asked.

"Actually," Yosh said, "Paavo's friend Angie hit the nail on the head. Wielund planned to start interviewing some high-class master chefs, and when Dustman found out he went off the deep end. They fought, but Wielund wouldn't relent. Dustman felt betrayed and killed him."

"Dustman became suspicious when he saw that Wielund had a lot of extra money each month," Paavo added. "He followed Wielund and eventually figured out it was Lacy LaTour who was being blackmailed. After Wielund's death, when the lawyers shut down the restaurant, Dustman decided to pick up where Wielund left off with Lacy and force her to give him the job as chef at LaTour's. More than money, he wanted prestige. He snuck back into Wielund's house to write down a few recipes from Wielund's notes, when he heard us show up with Greuber. Panicked, he took the whole notebook and hid in the garage. Greuber apparently decided to poke his nose around in the garage and ran right into Dustman."

"The funny part was," Yosh said, "Dustman never even knew *why* Wielund was able to blackmail Lacy."

"Strange case," Hollins said, holding a match to his cigar and taking a few long drags. "So now he's confessed and you've made an arrest in Lacy LaTour's murder, your work on this case is done. It's up to the DA to get convictions."

"Arresting Klaw's head sicko, Freddie, for holding a pillow over LaTour's face wasn't hard," Paavo said. "We've got prints and witnesses who can place him at the hospital. The hard part will be getting a jury not to believe whatever phony alibi Klaw sets up to get Freddie off."

"We've got an idea how to do that, Chief," Yosh said.

Paavo leaned forward. "With the information

LaTour gave about Danning's death, we've got the break in that case we needed. We're going to nail Klaw for the murders of Sheila Danning and Lacy LaTour."

Hollins nodded. "That's good, but we've got a little problem."

Paavo stiffened. "What do you mean?"

"I got a call from the chief of police over in Berkeley. He began by apologizing that one of his men had doubted the charges one of my men was making—that'd be you, Smith."

Paavo nodded, anxious about what was to come.

"The chief then went on to tell me that Klaw's porno studio had been cleaned out. Not even a fingerprint left to call our own. And Klaw made the slip from the team they'd had on him."

Paavo shut his eyes. This news only confirmed what he'd expected—that Klaw had connections, big ones, and the seedy little porno studio was nothing but a front. But he also expected Klaw to turn up again in time. Klaw had too much invested, too many connections in this area, to leave it completely. And I'll be waiting for him, Paavo vowed silently.

He opened his eyes to see the chief and his partner watching him intently.

"Have patience, Smith." Hollins pointed the cigar at him. "And be careful."

28

Back at his desk, as much as he hated the fact that Klaw had slipped underground for the moment, Paavo had an even more pressing problem to deal with. Using a little judicious telephone work, he tracked down the Bodega Bay realtor Angie had used. After a satisfactory talk, he left Homicide.

Instead of heading across the city toward home, he drove south, toward Hillsborough. He didn't allow himself even to think about what he was doing as he turned onto the brick driveway that made a half-circle in front of the sand-colored mansion that was the Amalfi home. He rang the doorbell and the maid opened the door.

"Paavo Smith. I'm here to see Miss Amalfi."

"Won't you come in, Mr. Smith?" The maid led him across the marble-floored entry to the library. "I'll see if Miss Amalfi is available."

Paavo had been to the house only once before, but he hadn't forgotten the vaulted ceilings, the tapestries, the heavy mahogany furniture that made the house look more like an expensive villa on the Mediterranean than a home in California. He crossed the library with its leather-upholstered furniture and book-lined walls to stand before French doors looking out onto manicured lawns that would have made a golf course gardener jealous.

A man's slightly accented voice said, "Inspector Smith."

Paavo turned to see Sal Amalfi enter the room. "Mr. Amalfi." He walked toward Sal and extended his hand. The older man gripped it in a strong, quick handshake.

"I want to talk to you—Paavo."

"Sure—Sal."

Sal's eyes narrowed ever so slightly. "I know there was some kind of trouble, but Angie won't tell me about it, and not even Commissioner O'Reilly will say."

"Maybe there's nothing to tell."

"There was something." Sal's eyes sharpened. "Now, though, she says she doesn't even want to think about it anymore."

Paavo realized Angie's father wanted him out of the house, didn't want him seeing or disturbing Angie. "All I want to do is apologize to her about the other day."

Sal lifted his chin. "I don't think she needs your apology. I think she needs time to forget."

Although he understood the fatherly concern, Paavo spoke with all the sincerity and conviction he possessed. "I know you want to do what's best for your daughter. And I know it's crazy for me to be here, to want to see her, and it'd probably be a lot easier if we never met again. But I believe, I think—no, I *feel*—that'd be no good for either one of us."

"What's that supposed to mean?"

"All I mean is, if I'm lucky, despite everything I've done, she'll agree to see me."

"So that you can apologize to her?"

At Sal's question, Paavo realized he wanted that, and much more. He also recognized that Sal had been purposely misunderstanding him, purposely pressing him to explain.

Paavo wasn't one to bare his feelings to anyone, not even the few people he'd ever loved. But he knew he had to let her father know just how special Angie was to him, that what he felt for her was real and deep. Yet when he looked at Sal and tried to explain, all he could say was, "I miss her."

Sal nodded thoughtfully, his expression penetrating, as if taking in the full measure of the tough close-mouthed policeman. "You care about her a lot, don't you?"

Paavo drew in a deep breath. "Yes. Very much."

Troubled concern warred with resignation as Sal studied Paavo. Finally, he gave a defeated sigh. "I've heard about you from Serefina as well as from Angelina. Serefina's got a keen eye, and she says you're okay. I have my doubts, as you know. I don't like you seeing Angie."

He walked over to a world globe and spun it, watching the blue ocean merge with colorful countries as the world spun round and round. He slid his hands into his trouser pockets and faced Paavo once more as the globe slowed down.

"I guess I can't fight all three of you. Angelina's miserable. It's like living with a rain cloud in the house. Do what you have to do. But be sure. And *go slow.*"

Paavo's spirits leaped. "I will."

"Good, because Angelina won't!" Sal shook his head. "I'll get her," he said, and left the room.

Despite how good he felt at having overcome the first hurdle, Paavo braced himself to face Angie. There'd probably be tears. He felt the inside pocket of his sports coat for the clean handkerchief he'd tucked away there this morning. The thought of seeing her cry was making him, a hardened police veteran, break out in a sweat.

He waited a full fifteen minutes before he heard the *click-click* of her high heels on the marble entry hall. She appeared in the doorway. He stood up slowly, holding his breath, hoping she wouldn't be too terribly upset.

She didn't look upset at all. Instead, she looked dazzling in a red silk dress with black trim and jet buttons. Her hair didn't have a strand out of place; it was elegantly swept back off her face, with more blond highlights than he remembered. Her makeup was flawless, her eyes clear and sparkling, and her lipstick and long, long fingernails a dazzling cherry that matched her dress.

"Hi, there. How nice to see you."

She smiled and crossed the room to him, her hand outstretched. He mechanically lifted his, and as their hands clasped, she leaned forward in a quick air kiss, pressing her cheek to his. The tantalizing scent of tea roses wafted up and did crazy things to his heartbeat. Then she dropped her hand and stepped back.

"Won't you sit down?" She gestured toward the sofa and chairs.

Speechless, he sat on a sofa. She took a chair, catty-corner to him.

"You look very nice," he said, once he'd found his voice. Nice, hell, she looked beautiful. Gorgeous, even.

"Thank you."

"I wanted to apologize for two days ago. I was so angry with Klaw, he was all I could think about."

Angie wondered if she'd heard right. Paavo apologizing to her? "I understand perfectly," she said nonchalantly.

"You do? When you left your apartment so abruptly, I thought I'd upset you."

She stood up, biting her tongue. Upset her? With such powers of observation, he should become a detective. She walked behind the chair, running her finger along the piping on the headrest. "I wasn't upset, I just needed a change."

"Do you need *much* of a change, Angie?"

Blue eyes held hers, and her breath caught. She loved looking into his eyes; she could get lost in them. He stood also, ready to move closer.

Abruptly, she turned her back on him, running her finger now along the spines of books in a case. "I came down here to find out," she said.

"Angie, I miss you. I think I'd like to see you again. Soon."

A strange buzzing sounded in her ears, in her head. She turned slowly. "You what?"

"I think I'd like to see you again."

She felt herself turn cold, then hot. She gripped a leather-bound volume as the anger that she'd so far managed to control began to bubble up in her. "You think?" She hefted the weight of the book. "You *think?*"

"Yes. What—"

She threw the book. He ducked and it sailed over his head, knocking over a clock on the mantel. "You mean you still don't *know?*" She threw another.

"Hey!" It hit him on the arm and bounced to the floor. He opened his mouth to protest, then sidestepped just in time for the next book to graze the side of his head. "Angie, stop!"

"I don't care what you *think,* Paavo Smith! Or what your so-called buddies think!" She threw again, but this one he caught in midair and tossed aside.

"Oh!" she shrieked.

He caught the next book, too, and started walking toward her.

"If you ever decide you *know* how you feel, Paavo Smith, then I just might *think* about changing my mind about you!"

He was close enough that all she could do was take a book and slam it against his chest. He grabbed her wrists, stopping her. "Feel better now?" he asked, grinning.

She was so angry she could have turned inside out. How she would have loved to wipe that smirk off his face. "Don't touch me!" She hated the way she loved it when he touched her.

He let go of her wrists.

"I've had it, Paavo," she said. "I don't want to see you anymore."

The finality of her words hung in the air. She saw him pale, and knew she did as well.

"I'm sorry," she said, her throat aching. "But I

can't stand loving you when you don't love me back. I don't want to feel this hurt anymore. Not ever."

"Angie." His eyes, his voice were hollow. "You don't understand—"

The low roar of a sports car approaching the house filled the room, and Paavo stopped talking as Angie's attention turned to the window. A new green Jaguar XJS came to a stop in the driveway behind Paavo's old Austin. "You must excuse me," she said, her bottom lip trembling as she smoothed her dress, "but Joey Marcuccio is here. My date."

Paavo stared at her. The book must have hit his head harder than he thought. Did she say she didn't want to see him and was going out with a man named Joey? She had always been the forgiving one, the generous one. "Who?"

She lifted her chin. "Chick's son. My friend Terry's brother. He's always been after me to go out with him. So has my family. I decided I would. Everyone's quite happy about it."

"Joey Marcuccio? The kid who used to rub pie in your face? I thought you didn't even like him. How can you go out with him?"

"That was when we were little." She heard the car engine shut off. "He'll be here any second. Come on." She looped her arm in Paavo's and led him out of the living room and down the hallway to the kitchen.

"What are you doing?"

She opened the back door and pushed him out into the garden. "As soon as Joey and I leave, you can slip out the side gate. 'Bye."

Before he could get over his shock, she slammed

the door shut. The loud *click* that followed sounded as final as her words back in the house. Paavo Smith found himself gaping at a closed door.

"Joey, how nice," Angie said as she opened the front door.

"Are you having some work done on the house?" he asked. "There's an old battered car in your driveway—"

"Ignore it." She took hold of his arm and pulled him into the library.

"Angie, what—" He pointed at the books strewn about the floor.

She scowled at him. "Is something wrong?"

"No, not at all," he mumbled.

She smiled, forcing herself to be gracious. It took about five minutes, though, to realize why she'd never gone out with him before, despite her fondness for his father and his sister.

He didn't resemble them in any way. Not even in looks. While Chick was tall and broad-shouldered, Joey was slight; and while his sister Terry was pleasantly plain, Joey saw himself as the second coming of Clark Gable. Above a long pencil-thin neck, he had slicked-back brown hair, a narrow nose, thin lips, and Serengeti horn-rimmed brown-tinted glasses.

He was also the most self-important person Angie had ever met. Not only did he have his brokerage business to brag about, but now he also owned half of Italian Seasons.

Angie really wasn't interested in hearing how difficult it was to manage not one but two dizzyingly successful endeavors. She wanted to tell him he should leave her and go back to work. Heaven forbid he miss the chance to make another nickel.

But she didn't. She was all dressed up, and if she went up to her room she knew she'd spend all evening fretting about Paavo and thinking of all the smart things she should have said or done instead of so stupidly throwing him out of the house. He was probably on the phone right now, calling Nona Farraday to help him get over his bruised ego. And Nona would do it, too.

"Ready? I've got reservations at Ernie's. Nothing but the best for my little Angie."

She cringed. She hated being called "little Angie." Besides, she knew Ernie's was pricy. For him to say so was nothing short of tacky.

"Sure." She tossed a jacket over her arm as Joey took her elbow.

As Joey was shutting the front door behind her, she noticed Paavo standing in front of his Austin. He looked mad enough to spit nails through a two-by-four. Their eyes met, and he started toward her.

Uh-oh, she thought. She'd have to hurry, as much as she could in high heels and a narrow skirt, to Joey's car.

"Who's that?" Joey asked, standing stock still and staring at the big man striding toward them. "I wonder if his car broke down."

She tugged at Joey's hand. "Ignore him. Let's go."

"Angie!" Paavo called. Joey pulled back his hand.

"Go away!" she shouted at Paavo, then wobbled, alone, down the front steps to the brick driveway.

As she pivoted toward Joey's car, Paavo took hold of her arm and spun her toward him. "I need to talk to you."

She jerked her arm free. "No, you don't."

"Excuse me," Joey said, bouncing around the two of them.

"I'm sorry, Angie." Paavo leaned toward her. "I *know* I don't want you going out with anyone else."

"It's a little too late for that, Inspector!"

Paavo looked stunned. Good, she thought, even as her heart contracted painfully at the hurt in his eyes.

"Let's go, Angie," Joey said, clutching her elbow and hurrying her to his car.

"Listen to me." Paavo followed. "I do care about you. I want to be with you."

Her nose went in the air as Joey opened the passenger door for her.

"Wait." Paavo grabbed the door. "I rented the house in Bodega Bay for the weekend. We can go up tomorrow night. Remember how much you liked it there?"

Joyful astonishment at his words flashed through her for a moment, but she forced the feeling aside. Without a word, she got in the Jaguar and slammed the door shut. Paavo just managed to pull his fingers away in time. Joey blanched, then ran around to the driver's side and got in.

"Angie, listen to me. Don't go with him. I love you," Paavo said softly.

A warm giddiness came over her. She would have heard those words if he'd only whispered them. So perhaps the one-and-only time he'd said them before wasn't a fluke. This time, though, she wanted to be sure.

Joey turned on the ignition. "You what?" she called over the noise of the engine.

"I love you."

"What?"

"I said I love you, goddamn it!"

She jumped out of the car and waved toward the house. "Did you hear that, mamma?"

"Si! Fa bene, Angelina!" Paavo glanced over to see a grinning Serefina shoo a worried-looking Sal back into the house and shut the door.

His gaze turned to Angie.

She took a step toward him. "Did you really rent the place in Bodega Bay for us?" she asked, her voice soft and wondering.

He stepped closer to her. "I did."

"Without asking what my plans were?" She repeated the words he'd said to her in what seemed a lifetime ago.

"It seemed like a good idea at the time," he admitted, admiring the creaminess of her skin, the long lashes that cast shadows on her cheeks whenever she gazed downward, the fullness of her lips.

Her brown eyes were glowing. "Why?"

He stared. "Why?"

She nodded.

He dropped his gaze. His big black Florsheims pointed at her small red designer high heels. Raising his eyes once more, he took in every special, loving inch of her. "Because I wanted to do something you might enjoy. Because I'm sorry for the way I treated you. Because it *isn't* wrong to care, or to love, or to show your feelings the way you do. In fact, it's wonderful. I never wanted to hurt you. And I *do* love you back, as you put it, even if I haven't really learned how to show it."

She placed her hands on his chest, feeling the steady pounding of his heart. Not only had this big tough strong man made the arrangements for them to be together but he'd shouted his feelings loud enough for all the world to hear. "Inspector," she said, "I think you're learning."

He wrapped his arms around her, pulled her close, and kissed her as if he never wanted to let her go.

"Ah, excuse me! Excuse me, Angelina!" Joey Marcuccio leaned across the white leather seats of his XJS and peered up at them through an open window. "Does this mean you don't want to go out with me tonight?"